A LITTLE GIRL IN NEED OF A DADDY, AND A HOLIDAY ROMANCE THAT MAKES THREE LONELY PEOPLE INTO A FAMILY

"Sometimes, if you believe, special things can happen at Christmas. Annie called them miracles. I'm going to believe really hard. If I do, maybe a miracle will happen."

Rush sighed, knowing better than to crush her childish faith. This holiday season, he needed his own miracle. But he'd long since stopped believing in such things. Anything special that happened would have to be up to him.

JANET DAILEY

It's A
Christmas Thing

ZEBRA BOOKS
KENSINGTON PUBLISHING CORP.
www.kensingtonbooks.com

ZEBRA BOOKS are published by

Kensington Publishing Corp.
119 West 40th Street
New York, NY 10018

All Kensington titles, imprints, and distributed lines are available at special quantity discounts for bulk purchases for sales promotion, premiums, fund-raising, educational, or institutional use.

Special book excerpts or customized printings can also be created to fit specific needs. For details, write or phone the office of the Kensington Sales Manager: Attn.: Sales Department. Kensington Publishing Corp., 119 West 40th Street, New York, NY 10018. Phone: 1-800-221-2647.

Zebra and the Z logo Reg. U.S. Pat. & TM Off.

First Kensington Books Hardcover Printing: June 2019
First Zebra Books Mass-Market Paperback Printing: October 2019
ISBN-13: 978-1-4201-4561-8
ISBN-10: 1-4201-4561-4

ISBN-13: 978-1-4201-4563-2 (eBook)
ISBN-10: 1-4201-4563-0 (eBook)

10 9 8 7 6 5 4 3 2 1

Printed in the United States of America

This book is dedicated to my friend and helper,
Elizabeth Lane.

Chapter 1

Branding Iron, Texas
Late October

Dr. J. T. Rushford yawned as he took the south highway out of Branding Iron. A light autumn rain peppered the windshield. He switched on the wipers and punched the radio up to full volume. Tammy Wynette's Mississippi twang blared out of the speakers. "Stand by Your Man" had never been Rush's favorite song, especially since his divorce last year. But what the hell, at least it might help keep him awake.

He'd been up since 2:00 AM, tending a colicky mare. Now it was almost 7:00. The mare was doing fine, but Rush felt like warmed-over roadkill. He could only hope to get a few hours of sleep before the next call.

Running a mobile veterinary service out of his black Hummer H1 Alpha had turned out to be a great business idea. But it had its drawbacks—no operating room or X-ray machine, and only a limited space in the Hummer for lab work. No hired help, and no downtime. He was answering calls on his cell phone at all hours.

He'd hoped to build a clinic on the Christmas Tree Ranch, which he ran with his partners, Travis Morgan and Conner Branch. But building a clinic took time and money. Between his practice and the need to shore up the ranch's budget, he was short on both.

Switching off the radio, he made a left turn onto the narrow lane that led to the ranch. As he neared the weather-beaten frame house, he glimpsed Travis and Conner outside doing chores—tending to the two huge Percheron horses they'd rescued and the four cows, each with a half-grown calf, that the partners had bought as an investment last spring.

They'd probably left coffee on the stove for him, maybe breakfast, too. But all Rush wanted this morning was to stumble into the house and crawl into bed.

He parked the Hummer next to the shed where the sleigh was kept under a canvas tarp. During the Christmas season it would be hitched behind the big draft horses, to be used for family sleigh rides and to carry Santa Claus in Branding Iron's annual Christmas parade.

But now, with Christmas still two months away, the partners were busy with another project.

It was Conner who'd come up with the idea of having a Halloween celebration, with pumpkins for sale, a marshmallow roast, hot apple cider, and rides on the old hay wagon that Travis had inherited with the ranch. The pumpkins, planted last spring, were ripe for harvest, the orange and black decorations going up, and the wagon being readied for hayrides.

Conner would drive the team. He was pushing for Rush to go along on the hayrides to play his guitar and sing while Travis took care of things at the house. Rush had agreed on the condition that he might need to leave for an animal emergency. He almost hoped he'd be called away. Singing, especially on Halloween, brought back too many bittersweet memories.

Claire, the little girl he'd left behind in Phoenix, had loved hearing him play and sing. He remembered how she used to laugh and dance, holding out her little skirt as she twirled like a mini-ballerina. Last year, when she was three, he'd taken her out trick-or-treating on Halloween. Dressed as a little black cat, she'd charmed the whole neighborhood. If he'd had a movie star on his arm, Rush couldn't have been prouder.

A week later, Sonya, his wife, had given him the news that had shattered his world.

The little girl he'd adored from the first moment he'd held her in the hospital was another man's child.

This year Claire would be four. He tried not to think about her too much. But he couldn't help wondering what kind of costume she'd be wearing and whether Andre—her father—would care enough to walk her around their affluent Phoenix neighborhood.

And with Christmas coming up . . . But he wasn't

even going to think about Christmas. Without Claire's childish excitement, Christmas would be just another day—another bad day.

Rush had climbed out of the vehicle and had almost reached the front steps when a furry black-and-white streak came hurtling around the house like a missile aimed at his legs.

"Bucket! You crazy mutt!" Rush did his best to fend off the dog's yipping, licking welcome. He was fond of the scruffy Border collie mix; but this morning he was too tired for games. Picking up a stick, he threw it as far as he could. As Bucket raced after it, Rush kicked off his dirty boots and, leaving them on the porch, made his escape into the house.

The tempting aroma of coffee drifted from the kitchen, but the last thing he needed was something to wake him up. He fished his phone out of his pocket and laid it on the counter. When his partners came inside, they would check his voice-mails and wake him if there was an emergency. That done, he dragged himself down the hall to his bedroom, undressed, rolled into bed, and sank into sleep.

The shaking, creaking bed woke him with a start. He opened his eyes to see Conner grinning down at him.

Rush mouthed a curse. He didn't know how long he'd been asleep, but it wasn't long enough. "What time is it?" he muttered.

"Coming up on nine o'clock." Conner, a former

champion bull rider, was wiry and quick, a man who never missed a chance to tease or play a joke. "I know you haven't been asleep long, but I thought you might be interested in hearing this voicemail."

He held the phone close to Rush's ear and tapped the message key. Rush's pulse kick-started him awake as he recognized the cultured female voice.

"Dr. Rushford, this is Tracy Emerson. I hope I haven't caught you at a bad time, but I need your help. This stray cat showed up on my back porch last night. I brought her inside and gave her some milk. She drank it like she was starved. But something about her doesn't seem right. I'm afraid she might be sick. I need to be in court at one thirty today, but if you can get here before then, I'll be home. Sorry, I've never had a cat, and I don't know what to do for her. Here's my phone number."

By now Rush was sitting up. He grabbed the notepad he kept on the nightstand and scribbled down the number. Conner's grin was almost splitting his face.

"Man, you've hit the jackpot! You've had a thing for that hot lady judge since last Christmas. And she finally gave you her phone number."

"Yeah." Rush swung his feet to the floor and forced his aching body to stand. "All it took was a sick cat."

Conner shook his head. "You look like hell and you smell like a stable. If you want to impress her, you're going to need a shower."

"Butt out, Conner," Rush said. "I'm not going on a date. This is just a professional call."

"Sure it is," Conner said with a knowing wink.

"Hey, what's going on?" Travis's rangy frame filled the doorway. A former highway patrolman, Travis had inherited a rundown ranch almost two years ago. Last year the three friends had begun selling the pine trees they'd discovered on the property, which they'd renamed Christmas Tree Ranch.

"Our boy here just got a voicemail from his dream woman." Conner was enjoying himself.

"You mean the judge?" Travis's expression brightened. "Wait till I tell Maggie!"

"Take it easy," Rush growled. "The woman's got a sick cat, that's all. Now get the blazes out of here and give me some peace while I call her back."

After shooing his partners out of the room, Rush closed the door, sat down on the bed, and took a moment to gather his thoughts. He'd met Municipal Court Judge Tracy Emerson last winter, when he'd gone to the city court to clear up a baseless littering charge against the ranch. When the bailiff had called the court to order and the judge had walked in to take her seat on the bench, Rush had sat up and taken notice.

Tracy Emerson was a tall, cool Grace Kelly blonde. Even in somber black robes, with her hair pulled into a no-nonsense twist and black-framed glasses perched on her elegant nose, the judge was a knockout.

Rush had known better than to look for a rebound so soon after his divorce, but by the time the trial was over, ending in reduced charges for the ranch, he'd been intrigued enough to do some checking. He'd noticed she wasn't wearing a wedding ring, but that didn't mean she was available.

Maggie Delaney, Branding Iron's mayor and Travis's steady girlfriend, knew everybody in town. When Rush had asked her, Maggie had given him the bad news. Tracy Emerson was recently widowed. Her husband, a successful lawyer, had died of a brain tumor eight months earlier. She was still dealing with her grief.

Rush had put his fantasies aside. Her Honor wasn't ready to date, and neither was he. But his partners had gotten wind of his interest in the lady. Travis and Conner had teased him unmercifully.

Now, ten months after that day in court, she'd given him an excuse to see her again. And if Rush's reaction to her phone call was any indication, he was, at least, open to possibilities.

Dared he hope she'd moved on past her mourning? Was there a chance this might turn out to be more than a professional call?

Don't be an idiot, Rush told himself. The woman had taken in a stray cat. She needed a vet to check the animal. And he was the only vet in Branding Iron.

He glanced at the number he'd written down, then realized that all he needed to do was return her voicemail. He waited while the phone rang once, then again on the other end. What should he call her? Ms. Emerson? *Mrs.* Emerson? Tracy?

Your Honor? Hell, maybe he should just hang up and call her back when he didn't feel like a high school sophomore asking for his first date.

"Hello. Thanks for calling me back, Dr. Rushford." Her voice had a breathless quality, as if she'd hurried to answer the phone.

"You say you've got a sick cat?" he asked.

"Yes." She hesitated a moment. "I'm not sure what's wrong with her. She looks . . . sort of swollen. And she keeps trying to hide. How soon could you come and look at her?"

"I can be there in about forty-five minutes. But I'll need your address."

"Oh—of course." She gave it to him. "Thanks. I'll be watching for you."

Rush took a quick shower, brushed his teeth, and put on fresh jeans, a plaid shirt, and the good boots that he avoided wearing in stables and corrals. When he walked out into the kitchen, Conner was frying eggs and Travis was mixing pancake batter.

"How about some breakfast? I know you're anxious to get to that good-looking judge's place," Conner teased, "but you don't want to go off hungry, do you?"

"Just keep a plate warm for me." Rush headed for the front door.

"Only if you promise to tell us everything when you get back," Travis said.

"I'm guessing there won't be much to tell."

"You never know." Conner gave him a roguish wink. "Good luck with the cat—and the lady."

Rush strode to the door. Bucket was waiting on

the porch, the stick at his feet. He picked it up in his jaws, his tail thumping expectantly. "No games this morning, you old rascal." Rush opened the door to let the dog into the house. "Go on in. Pester somebody else for a change."

Inside the Hummer, Rush checked the GPS. He recognized the address. The judge lived in the older, nicer part of Branding Iron, an enclave of tall sycamores and paved sidewalks, on the far side of town. Her place wouldn't be hard to find.

The morning was clear, the sunlight bright enough to make him squint. The fall leaves had begun to fade. A stray breeze sent them fluttering from the trees in showers of muted red, brown, and gold.

Except for rare glimpses in town, he hadn't seen Tracy Emerson since that day in court. He'd been a different person then, still in shock from the abrupt loss of his marriage, his practice, his home, and the little girl he'd believed to be his daughter. Seeing Tracy for the first time had given him a flash of hope—the chance of better times ahead. But that was all it had been—a flash.

Coming into town, he stopped for the first of Branding Iron's two traffic lights. The intersection, where the highways crossed, brought back the memory of last year's late-night storm, when he'd braked too hard on the icy road and slid into Travis's pickup truck. He'd been lost that night— lost in every possible way. But Travis had brought him home to the ranch and offered him a new life. It had become a good life, with friends, a roof over his head, and the chance to grow a new business.

Even being single was something he'd come to accept.

Rush had lived a womanless existence since coming to Branding Iron. Not so his partners. Travis and his spunky red-haired Maggie were all but engaged. Conner had women all over town, and he liked to keep them guessing.

Rush had shrugged off his own situation. He hadn't been ready to risk the pain of a new relationship. But one phone call had been enough to change his mind. Now he found himself looking forward to being with a beautiful woman.

But what was he thinking? This wasn't a date, or even a social visit. He was on his way to check on a business client's cat. That was all. But if he was entertaining a few fantasies, at least it would help take his mind off missing Halloween with the child he still loved.

The judge's house was smaller than those around it, a Craftsman-style bungalow with a stone front, leaded windows, and English ivy cascading over the broad front porch. A gray Mercedes sedan, old but in good condition, was parked in the driveway. This was just the kind of place where he'd imagined a woman like Tracy might live.

A woman like Tracy. Aside from the fact that she was attractive and well-educated, the truth was that he hardly knew her at all.

He found his medical bag, added a few sample cans of cat food to its contents, climbed out of the Hummer, and crossed the sheltered porch to the door. Reminding himself not to expect anything beyond a professional call, he pressed the door-bell.

There was a beat of silence. Then, muffled by the door, he heard a scrambling sound and a thud, like something heavy falling to the floor.

Rush was about to break his way into the house when the door opened.

The woman on the threshold was smaller than she'd appeared in the courtroom. She was dressed in ragged jeans and a baggy, faded sweatshirt. Her blond hair, escaping from its loose ponytail, hung in damp strings around a face that was bare of makeup. A small gash above her left eyebrow was oozing blood. There was no cat in sight. But a griz-zled tan dog, some kind of pit bull mix, was eyeing Rush as if it wanted to rip his throat out.

Maybe he had the wrong house. Or the wrong woman.

The man staring down at Tracy was drop-dead gorgeous—tall, with dark brown hair and dark eyes set in a George Clooney face. The logo on the Hummer parked out front, along with the medical bag in his hand, reminded her that he must be from the mobile vet service she'd called. But why did he look so familiar? Surely, if she'd met him before, she'd remember him.

"Are you all right?" he asked.

"Yes, I'm . . . fine." She steadied herself with a hand on the door frame. "Why should you ask?"

"Because you're bleeding." His gaze went to the

tender spot where her head had struck the drain-pipe under the sink. She touched it gingerly. Her fingers came away smeared with blood.

"I'm here about a sick cat," he said. "But you look like you could use some attention first—you are Judge Emerson, right?"

"Right. Tracy." How had he known she was a judge? There were some missing pieces to this puzzle. "Come on in," she said, opening the door wider.

"Will that be all right with him?" He glanced down at the dog, who'd placed his body between his mistress and the stranger in the doorway.

"Don't worry about Murphy. He looks tough, but he's really an old softy." She scratched the dog's ears. "It's all right, old boy. Go and lie down." Murphy thumped his tail and drooled on her bare foot before curling up in his bed by the fireplace.

Tracy stepped aside to let Dr. Gorgeous into the house. For a long time after Steve's death, she'd had no desire to look at a man in an admiring way. Even now, after eighteen months, the slightest glance jabbed her with guilt.

Especially today.

"Let's have a look at your head," the vet said. "Do you mind moving into the light?" Tracy recalled his name now, from the business card she'd picked up at the library. It was Dr. J. T. Rushford. But she still couldn't remember where she'd seen him before. Heaven save her, how could any woman forget that face?

Standing with her by the window, he examined the oozing lump on her forehead. "That's a nasty little gash but I don't think it's bad enough to need stitches. While I clean it, maybe you can tell me what happened. Not that it's any of my business, but something tells me it might be an interesting story."

"You wouldn't believe it." Her laugh sounded more like a whimper as he dabbed the wound with an antiseptic pad he'd taken from his bag.

"Try me."

"Well . . . This is going to sound so stupid." She took a deep breath. "Just before you returned my call, I'd discovered that the kitchen sink drain was clogged. I tried using a plunger. That didn't work, but I figured I still had time to fix the problem before you'd show up. I got a wrench and a bucket and crawled under the cabinet to take the trap apart."

"I'm impressed. You must be a handy lady." He found a Band-Aid in his bag and tore off the wrapper.

"It doesn't take a man to unscrew a pipe connection. And doing it myself beats paying a plumber."

"I hear you." He laid the Band-Aid over the gash above her eyebrow. Even the light pressure of his fingers made her wince. "Sorry," he said. "After I leave, you might want to put a cold pack on it—a bag of frozen vegetables works fine for that. Meanwhile, I can't wait to hear the rest of the story."

Tracy fingered the Band-Aid, feeling the swollen soreness beneath. "I was under the sink, on my back, with the bucket under the trap, when this mouse came out of nowhere and ran right across my chest."

"You're kidding!" He chuckled. "I'll bet that scared you."

"Not really. I'm not afraid of mice. But it did startle me. I let out a yelp, sat straight up, and banged my head on the pipe so hard that my ears rang. The bucket tipped over and went rolling across the floor—and then, when I heard the doorbell, I knocked over a stool while getting up. If you heard it fall, you probably thought the place was under attack."

"That did cross my mind. I was about to charge in and save you when you opened the door." His gaze narrowed. "Do you feel dizzy? Does your head still hurt?"

"Are you saying I could have a concussion?"

"It wouldn't hurt to check. Let me have a look at your eyes." His hand cupped her jaw, tilting her face toward him. As he leaned closer, Tracy felt her pulse kick into overdrive. Everything about the man was attractive.

"I thought you came to see the cat," she said. "Can't you get in trouble for practicing on humans without a license?"

"Only if you report me. Here, hold still and look up at me, right into my eyes."

Tracy forgot to breathe as his gaze locked with hers. His eyes were the color of dark chocolate with flecks of caramel in their depths. Her throat tightened. Shimmering threads of heat trickled downward through her body.

Maybe she did have a concussion. At least it might explain the subtle urges flowing through her—almost as if she *wanted* this stranger, a man she'd barely met, to bend closer and . . .

But this was all wrong. When Steve died, her heart had died with him. That she could respond to another man—any man—was unthinkable, especially today, on the date of their sixth wedding anniversary.

She had hazel eyes—blue and green and gold, all the colors in one. Her lashes were dark, with a sheen of unshed tears. And her soft, vulnerable mouth was as tempting as . . .

What was he thinking? Lay an unprofessional hand on the woman, and his career could be over. At the very least he'd get his face deservedly slapped.

Rush forced himself to lower his hands and step away from her. "Your pupils look fine," he said. "No dilation. But if you get headaches or feel confused, don't hesitate to call your doctor."

She gave him a shaky laugh. "Thanks. I'm sure I'll be fine."

"Well, then the next question is, where's your cat?" Rush scanned the living room, which was tasteful and cozy, with overstuffed furniture, colorful cushions, and a wall of shelves filled with books and memorabilia. His gaze lingered on the mantel, where an eight-by-ten framed photo showed a younger Tracy with her husband and their dog on a beach, looking as if nothing could ever go wrong in their happy lives.

The dog, older now, his muzzle gone white, lifted his head and wagged his tail, as if aware that Rush was looking at him.

"Good boy," Rush said. The dog put his head down and closed his eyes. Still no sign of the cat.

"She isn't really my cat," Tracy said. "As I told you on the phone, she just showed up on my doorstep, but I could tell she needed help."

"And you had a soft heart. Where does she like to hide?"

"She likes closets. But her favorite place seems to be under my bed."

"Lead the way. I'll let you do the checking."

Bag in hand, he followed her down the hall and waited in the doorway while she looked for the cat under her bed—an old-fashioned four-poster covered with a bright patchwork quilt that looked as if somebody's grandma had pieced it with a loving hand. On a nightstand next to the bed was another framed photo, this one a headshot of her husband—chiseled features, blue eyes, and a TV newscaster's smile. The man would be a hard act to follow, Rush mused—especially since it appeared that Tracy was still very much married to her late husband.

If he had any sense, he would treat the cat, walk away, and forget her.

Tracy dropped to her hands and knees, raised the bed ruffle, and peered under the bed. "I see her," she said. "But I can't reach her, and she isn't coming to me."

"Try this." Rush took a small can of salmon-flavored cat food out of his bag, peeled back the lid, and held it out to Tracy. "Put this where she can smell it."

Tracy took the opened can and placed it a few inches from the bed. "Come and get it, kitty," she coaxed. "Come on. I know you're hungry."

Slowly and timidly, a small calico cat with matted fur crept out from under the bed, headed for the cat food, and began gulping it down in ravenous bites. Tracy knelt beside her, watching. "What do you think?" she asked.

"She wouldn't be eating like that if she was sick," Rush said. "I won't know for sure until I've examined her, but I can tell you one thing just by looking at her."

"What's that?" Tracy asked, gazing up at him.

"Look at that round belly on her. Unless I miss my guess, your cat's going to become a mother."

Chapter 2

"**S**he's *pregnant?*" Tracy stared at the handsome vet.

"It certainly looks that way. I won't know for sure till I've examined her. But first, let's give her a minute to finish eating. Aside from that belly, she's skin and bones. I'd say she's been on her own a while, and that she's had a pretty rough time of it."

"Poor little mama." Tracy stroked the cat's bumpy spine with a fingertip. "When I opened the door, she came right in. She lapped up the milk I gave her like she was starving."

"That's something I meant to tell you," Rush said. "Milk isn't the best thing for her. Most adult cats are lactose intolerant. She'll be better off with water and cat food, like these sample cans I'm going to leave with you—that is, if you plan to keep her."

"Keep her?" Tracy hadn't thought that far ahead. She'd never planned to take in another pet, let alone a cat. But how could she put the poor thing and her little family-to-be out in the cold?

"There's a shelter in Cottonwood Springs. You could take her there if you don't want her."

Tracy kept stroking the cat. "That sounds so heartless—dumping her off to have her babies in a cage—if they even let her live that long. I've never wanted a cat, but—oh!" A low rumble quivered through the bony little body. "Oh, listen! She's purring!"

A smile tugged at the vet's mouth. He pulled on the disposable latex gloves he'd taken from his bag. "Something tells me you've got yourself a cat," he said.

"For now, I guess." Tracy shook her head. "I never planned this. But at least I can give her a warm, safe place to have her babies."

"Well then, let me check her out and make sure she's healthy. Then we can talk about what you'll need for her. Will she be all right with the dog?"

Tracy rubbed the cat under the chin, feeling the purr vibrate beneath her fingertips. "Murphy's never been a cat-chaser. These days, he barely has the energy to hobble outside and do his business."

"If you'd like, I can give him a quick checkup while I'm here—no charge."

"Thanks. That's very generous of you, Dr. Rushford."

"Everybody calls me Rush. I hope you will, too."

"And the J. T. part of your name? What does that stand for?"

"That," he said, frowning, "is a family secret. Now let's have a look at the cat."

Rush picked up the cat with his gloved hands. The little calico tried to struggle, but she was too weak to offer much resistance as he checked her body, her gums, and her rectal temperature. Perched on the edge of the bed, Tracy watched him with a worried gaze. Rush could tell she'd already become attached to the bedraggled creature. When the cat started purring, her eyes had been as full of wonder as a little girl's.

He remembered seeing her on the bench in her black robe, stern, dignified, and completely in charge. This tender, vulnerable woman was the last thing he'd expected to find when he'd driven up to her house this morning. Something told him he was already in trouble. But he'd be a fool to fall for a widow who was still mourning her husband.

Today's visit would be strictly professional.

"The cat's pregnant for sure," he said. "I'd say she's probably due in the next few days. Otherwise, aside from being undernourished and dehydrated, she seems okay. I'm going to give her some worm medicine—it's fenbendazole, a kind that won't hurt her kittens. She'll need vaccinations, too, but those can wait."

"What do I need to get for her?" Tracy asked as Rush dropped the medicine into the squirming cat's mouth.

"She'll need a box in a quiet place, with something soft inside, like an old blanket or towel. She'll also need a water bowl and a dish for wet food, like the kind I'll leave you. And she'll need a litter box—with any luck, she'll know how to use it. Shop Mart should have everything you need."

"I can set her up in the laundry room." Tracy glanced at her watch. "I'm due in court at one thirty. It's barely eleven o'clock now. That should give me plenty of time for a run to Shop Mart."

Rush released the cat on the floor. She slunk back under the bed. "Now that she's eaten, she'll be ready for a long nap," he said. "You shouldn't have to worry about her for a while."

"What about the kittens?" Tracy looked anxious. "What do I do when she . . . what do you call it? Goes into labor?"

"Relax. Cats are good mothers. She'll know what to do. You won't even need to be there, unless you want to."

"What if something goes wrong?"

"It shouldn't. But if anything worries you, you've got my number. Don't hesitate to call me, even if it's in the middle of the night."

She laughed. "You may regret making that offer."

Try me, lady, anytime. Rush knew better than to voice that thought. He stripped off his gloves and pulled on a fresh pair. "Now what do you say we check your dog?"

The aging pit bull mix was asleep in the living room, where they'd left him. At the sound of voices, he opened his eyes and thumped his tail.

"Hello, Murphy." Kneeling, Rush stroked the dog to get him comfortable before the exam. "How old is he?"

"I don't know for sure," Tracy said. "Steve had him before we met. Murphy was the ring bearer at our wedding. But even then, he wasn't a young dog. I'd guess he's at least fifteen or sixteen."

Rush gazed into the old dog's eyes. "He's got cataracts. From the look of them, I'd say he's almost blind. Does he bump into things?"

"Sometimes. But the house is familiar. Most of the time, he manages to sniff his way around. But if anything unexpected gets in his way . . ." She shook her head, a lock of blond hair falling loose from the clip that held it at the crown of her head. "Is there anything you can do? What about cataract surgery, like they do on humans?"

Tears were welling in her eyes. *Damn, this isn't going to be easy.*

"It's been done on animals. But Murphy's an old man, close to ninety in human years. Even if he were to survive the surgery, he'd be miserable afterward. As long as he can find his way around the house, that's about the best you can expect."

"Oh." The word was a whispered sigh.

Rush gently pried open the dog's mouth. There were just a few teeth. At least one of them looked infected. No way to pull it without anesthesia, and Murphy was too old to sedate safely. "Can you get him up and walking?" Rush asked.

Tracy backed off a few steps. "Come here, Murphy," she coaxed. Murphy hauled himself to his feet and hobbled toward his mistress while Rush studied his labored gait.

"That's far enough, old boy." Rush's hands explored the old dog's arthritic joints and bony body. There was no sign of a lump that might suggest a tumor. That, at least, was good news. "How's his appetite?"

"Fine. He doesn't eat a lot, but he always eats something." Tracy sounded defensive, as if she might be bracing herself to deny bad news.

"His arthritis is pretty bad—something you'd expect in a dog his age. I can tell he's in pain. I'm going to write you a prescription for a joint supplement called Cosequin. It won't cure him, but it should make it easier for him to get around. I've got some samples at home. I can drop them off later for you to try before you spend the money."

"Thank you." She looked so hopeful that Rush was tempted to leave things like that. But if he didn't tell her the whole truth, he wouldn't be doing his job.

"The medicine should help him feel better," he said. "But he's an old dog. Life isn't much fun for him anymore. Sooner or later, you're going to have to face the—"

"No!" Tracy's voice quivered. "I won't stand for having him put down! Don't even talk to me about it."

"Tracy, you can't stop time—"

"Don't you understand?" The tears in her eyes spilled over.

"Murphy was my husband's dog. Steve loved

him, and so do I. He's all I have left of our time together. When he's gone—all those memories—"

"I understand." From where he stood, Rush could
see the photo on the mantel—the all-American couple on the beach with their dog. Tracy was an ap-
pealing woman. But Rush had gotten the message
loud and clear. She was strictly off-limits.

"Don't worry, I won't bring it up again," he said.
"At least not until you're ready."

"Thank you." She swallowed hard, wiping away
tears with the back of her hand.

Rush handed her the prescription he'd written.
"I can drop off the Cosequin samples when I come
back to town this afternoon. Would that work for
you?"

"I'll be at the courthouse until five o'clock. You
can leave them there, with the receptionist. There's
no need for you to come by the house."

"Fine." Rush glanced at Murphy, who'd hobbled
back to his bed again. "Any more questions before
I leave?"

"Just one. How much do I owe you?"

"Since you took in the cat as a Good Samaritan,
we'll call it no charge."

"Really?" Her stunning hazel eyes widened. "But
you came, you took the time. You even gave the cat
some worm medicine. There must be some way I
can repay you."

Was that an invitation to ask her out?

For an instant Rush was tempted. But no, this
was a professional visit. And she'd made it clear
that her heart belonged to her late husband. Rush
wouldn't have minded the challenge of a human

rival but competing with a ghost was out of his league.

Still, he could hardly leave the lady to fix a plugged drain on her own.

"If you want to repay me, you can let me fix your sink before I go," he said.

"No need. I can do it myself. I have the tools, and I've seen it done. Besides, unless you're moonlighting, you're a vet, not a plumber."

"Maybe so. But with that bump on your head, I'm not taking responsibility for letting you crawl under the sink again. Go sit down. This won't take a minute."

Still wearing his latex gloves, he walked into the kitchen, retrieved the bucket and wrench, and worked his way, on his back, into the shadowy darkness under the sink.

"Watch out for the mouse." Tracy pulled a kitchen chair close to the sink and sat down.

"I'm guessing you gave that mouse a good scare," he said. "He probably won't come out again until things quiet down. And once your cat gets wind of him, he'll be a goner."

"She's not my cat. I'm just giving her shelter while she has her babies. And I still don't know how I'm going to manage the kittens."

"Kittens can be fun," Rush said. "With Christmas coming in a couple of months, you should have no trouble finding homes for them. But after they're weaned, you'll need to get the mother spayed, so she won't have any more. There are too many homeless cats in the world."

"*If* I keep her."

"Or even if you don't." Rush positioned the bucket under the trap, used the wrench to loosen the connections, removed the trap, and dumped the messy-looking contents into the bucket. "That should do it," he said. "When I've hooked it up again, you can turn on the water."

"Thanks," Tracy said. "I could've done it, but it would have taken me a lot longer. We inherited this house from Steve's mother. When we moved in, I wanted to install a garbage disposal. I found out I couldn't use one here because the septic tank is as old as the house and we have to be careful what goes into it."

"I know what you mean." Rush held the empty trap in place and tightened the connections. "The septic tank we have at the ranch is the same way."

"The ranch?" Her eyebrows arched slightly.

"My partners and I run the Christmas Tree Ranch south of town."

"Oh!" She laughed, a surprising sound. "Now I remember where I've seen you. Last year in court— you showed up to dispute that littering citation against the ranch."

"That's right. And you were nice enough to reduce the charges."

"Niceness had nothing to do with it. I may be just a small-town judge, but I take my duties seriously. I did what I felt was fair."

"So, my charm had nothing to do with it?" Rush slid out from under the sink and sat up.

"Absolutely nothing."

"And afterward, you didn't even remember

me?" He stood, stripped off his gloves, and glanced around for someplace to dispose of them.

"Not until now." Tracy pointed to the trash receptacle at the end of the counter. "Thanks for checking the cat and dog, and for fixing my sink. Don't worry about the tools and the bucket. I can clean up."

"You'd be better off resting."

"I'll be fine. I'm feeling steadier already. And you must have better things to do with your time than play handyman. Go on. Get out of here before I start feeling guilty."

Rush tossed his gloves in the trash and picked up his bag, which he'd left on the counter. Last year, when he'd faced Tracy in court, he could've sworn he'd felt a spark of connection between them. But he'd been mistaken. Today, the beautiful judge had barely remembered him.

It was time to cut his losses and cross the lady off his imaginary list—even though hers was the only name on it.

"You're sure I can't pay you for your trouble?" she asked.

"I'm sure. I was glad to help out." Rush picked up his bag, which he'd left on the counter. "If you need anything, call me anytime. I mean it."

Crossing the front room, he stepped around Murphy, who was snoring in his sleep. In the open doorway, he paused and looked back toward the kitchen. Tracy was bent over, gathering up the tools.

"I'll drop off those Cosequin samples," he said.

She stood, her hair tumbling over the bandage he'd put on her forehead. A ray of sunlight, shining through the kitchen window, seemed to light her from within. Even in her baggy sweatshirt and ragged jeans, she was a goddess.

"Thanks, but there's no need," she said. "I can fill the prescription at Shop Mart today."

"It's no trouble. I have to come into town anyway, for an appointment." Rush stepped out onto the porch and closed the door behind him. So much for his unrequited crush. His partners would tease him about striking out with the judge. For now, he would just have to grin and bear it. For the future, all he could do was call this a lesson learned and move on.

Clutching Steve's old tools, Tracy stood at the front window and watched Rush walk out to the street. His long strides stirred the fallen leaves that covered the sidewalk. Caught by the breeze, they swirled around him in a shower of reds and golds.

Even from behind, the vet was pure eye candy. He was also gentle and kind, and she could tell he liked her. If she'd given him any encouragement, he might have asked her out. But even if he had, she would have turned him down. She wasn't ready yet. Maybe she never would be.

The memory of that day, eighteen months ago, when she'd sat by Steve's bed and watched him slip away, was as raw as if it had happened last week. And the fact that today would've been their wedding anniversary only deepened the pain.

Turning away from the window, she glanced down at her bare finger. At Steve's funeral, as she'd leaned over the casket to kiss him good-bye, she had impulsively taken off her gold wedding band and slipped it onto his little finger. Afterward, when it was too late, she'd regretted the loss. The ring had been a connection to the man she'd loved and the life they'd shared. Now it was gone forever.

Tracy paused for a moment to gaze at the photo on the mantel, taken by a friend on a Galveston beach, not long after their wedding. She and Steve had met in law school. They'd fallen in love on their first date but waited until after graduation to marry. Steve had graduated at the top of his class, Tracy with honors that same year.

They'd planned to work in Austin or the Dallas–Fort Worth area, but when Steve's widowed mother had needed care and offered them clear title to the family home, they'd returned to Branding Iron, where Steve had grown up. Steve had joined a law firm in nearby Cottonwood Springs. Tracy had filled a vacancy in Branding Iron's city court, ruling mostly on traffic tickets, petty crimes, domestics, small claims, and property disputes. It wasn't the glamorous, big-city job she'd dreamed of, but being with Steve had made it all right. Now that he'd been gone for more than a year, Tracy had begun to imagine more challenging jobs in more interesting places. Maybe it was time to sell the house and move on.

But long-range plans would have to wait. Right now, she needed to rush to Shop Mart, fill the prescription for the dog, and get a small truckload of supplies for the mom-to-be cat. It would be like helping out a little pregnant teenager, Tracy told herself. See to her needs, and when she's ready, send her on her way.

She finished cleaning up the kitchen mess and changed into clean jeans, a light blue hoodie, and sneakers. She could put on her court clothes later, when it was time to go to work.

The big-box store was crowded with people buying treats, costumes, and decorations for Halloween, which was just two days off. The aisles were festooned with orange and black crepe paper streamers. Fake skeletons, ghosts, witches, and spiderwebs dangled overhead.

Tracy, whose house didn't have so much as a pumpkin on the porch, grabbed an empty cart and tossed in a couple bags of miniature candy bars for the neighborhood kids. What did it matter? Three days from now, the Halloween decorations would come down and the Christmas displays would go up, along with that awful fake cinnamon smell and those cheesy Christmas carols blasting over the P.A.

Christmas.

Last Christmas, her first since Steve's death, had been the most miserable holiday of her life. With the blinds closed, she'd sat alone in the darkened living room, hugging Murphy and watching the classic-movies channel on TV. There'd been no Christmas tree, no gifts, and no phone calls. She'd turned off her phone to make sure of that. This year wasn't likely to be much better. Her only wish was to get through the holiday without sinking into a blue funk.

Christmas! Scrooge was right. *Bah! Humbug!*

Pushing the thought from her mind, Tracy wheeled her cart to the pharmacy counter, dropped off the Cosequin prescription, and headed for the pet aisle. There she picked up a set of bowls, some canned food that was similar to the samples Rush had given her, and a plastic litter pan with a cover. The two sections came in a cardboard box that would do nicely for the cat's bed.

She was looking at bags of litter, wondering whether to go cheap or pamper her pet with a deluxe product, when she heard a voice behind her.

"Tracy, what are you doing in the cat aisle? Have you got a new pet, or did you just take a wrong turn?"

Tracy turned to find Maggie Delaney, Branding Iron's statuesque, redheaded mayor, standing next to her. Tracy hadn't made many friends in Branding Iron. Her early life here had revolved around Steve. And after Steve's death, grief had built a wall around her. But she knew Maggie from work. The two women were casual friends—the only kind of friends Tracy had.

"What do you know about kitty litter?" Tracy asked.

"Not much. The little darlings poop in it, and their human slaves have to scoop it out every day."

"You must have cats."

"No," Maggie said, "I'm more of a dog person myself. Didn't you once mention that you have a dog?"

"Yes," Tracy said. "Murphy's an old sweetheart. But this little pregnant cat showed up on my doorstep, and when the vet came by—"

"The vet?" Maggie grinned. "You mean Dr. Rushford? Tall, dark, and drop-dead gorgeous?"

"Evidently, he's the only vet in town." Tracy paused, suddenly puzzled. "What's the matter? Why are you looking at me like that?"

Maggie's grin broadened. "Because the man's had a crush on you for almost as long as I've known him."

Hot color flooded Tracy's cheeks. "You're joking! How on earth would you know that?"

"Because his partner, Travis, is my boyfriend. Rush asked him if I could get your phone number. But when he found out you'd recently lost your husband, he decided to wait." Maggie's voice dropped to a conspiratorial whisper. "So, did he ask you out?"

Still blushing, Tracy shook her head. "No, he was all business. But he did fix my clogged sink, and he refused to let me pay him."

Maggie laughed out loud, causing an older woman with a loaded cart to frown in their direction. "All business, my aunt Sadie's bloomers! Rush is quiet. He doesn't reveal much about himself. But I'd say that's a sure sign he's interested. I'll tell you what." She leaned closer to Tracy. "The partners are having a three-night Halloween celebration at the ranch next week—marshmallow roasting, pumpkin carving, hayrides, the works. It's mostly to drum up business for the Christmas season, but it'll be lots of fun. I promised Travis I'd show up to help out. Why don't you come with me? If you want, you could even bring cookies or something to thank Rush for his help."

Tracy felt a door slam shut inside her—a door driven by grief, uncertainty, and guilt. "Thanks for the invitation," she said. "It does sound like fun, but—I'm sorry—something inside me is still saying no."

"I understand." Maggie gave her a sympathetic smile. "And here's hoping that one of these days something inside of you will start saying yes. Call me if you change your mind."

After parting from Maggie, Tracy picked out a bag of cat litter, along with a scoop, and headed back to the pharmacy counter to pick up the prescription for Murphy. As she tucked the small white bag into her purse, she remembered Rush's thinly veiled suggestion that soon she would have to deal with the end of her old friend's life. Even the thought brought tears to her eyes. Rush was right, of course. Dogs didn't live forever. All too soon, they grew old and feeble until it became an act of kindness to put them out of their misery. Still . . .

This Christmas could be her last with the old dog Steve had loved. She would find ways to make it special. But she couldn't think about it now, or she'd be a blubbering mess by the time she got to work.

She paid for her purchases at the checkout stand and loaded them into the back of her car. Maybe she should have accepted Maggie's invitation. Rush had been kind and helpful, and she was truly grateful. Perhaps . . . But no, showing up at the ranch would send the wrong message. She would have to show her gratitude some other way.

She glanced at the dashboard clock. If she hurried home now, she'd have time to mix up a batch of brownies and get them in the oven before she changed her clothes for work. She could leave them with the receptionist, to be given to Rush when he dropped off the Cosequin samples. If he didn't come by—well, that would be all right, too. The court staff could use a treat.

At home, she took a few minutes in the laundry room to line the cardboard box with an old sweater for a cat bed. In one corner she set up the litter box and put out food and water. There was no sign of the cat, but when Tracy checked under her bed, the little calico peered back at her with eyes like two golden moons. Maybe later, when the house was quiet, she'd smell the food and come out, Tracy told herself. Right now, it was time to whip up some brownies for the handsome vet she didn't plan to see again.

Rush had promised Noah Halverson, the farmer who owned the sick mare, that he'd come by and check on the animal that afternoon. Since the Halverson place was on the far side of Branding Iron, it wouldn't be out of his way to drop by the court and leave the samples for Tracy's old dog.

Branding Iron's courthouse was part of a complex that included the mayor's office, the sheriff's office, the police department and jail, and the li-

brary. When Rush pulled up outside the wing that
housed the court, he saw Tracy's Mercedes parked
in one of the slots reserved for judges. She'd probably be on the bench now, but since he hadn't
planned to speak with her, that was all right. He
would just leave the samples with the receptionist,
as she'd suggested.

Taking the sample packets in a ziplock bag, he
walked into the reception area. The middle-aged
woman at the desk gave him a knowing smile. "You
must be Dr. Rushford. The judge told me you
might be coming by."

"That's right. I just wanted to drop off these
medicine samples for her dog." He laid the packet
on the desk, next to a nameplate that said MAU-
REEN GRIMSHAW. "You must be Maureen," he said.
"Would you mind giving this to her? I don't want
to bother her when she's working."

"I'll make sure she gets it." Rush could swear the
woman winked at him. "And by the way, she asked
me to give you something from her." Maureen
thrust a shoebox-sized plastic carton toward him.
Through the transparent sides, the contents looked
like sheer chocolate decadence. "She said she'd
made them to thank you. But if you don't mind my
saying so . . ." She leaned closer across the desk.
"That lady doesn't make brownies for just anybody. Something tells me she thinks you're pretty
special."

"I'll keep that in mind. Tell her thanks." Rush
took the box and turned away. Looking past the
desk and down the hall, he could see that the door
to the courtroom was partway open. For a moment

he was tempted to walk down the hall, slip inside, and sit in the back, filling his gaze with the judge as she ruled on traffic tickets, shoplifting, and other petty issues.

But ogling Tracy in her courtroom would be a guaranteed way to give her the creeps. He would take the brownies home, share them with his partners, and help them get the ranch ready for tonight. With the Christmas season approaching fast, he'd have plenty to do in the weeks ahead. He could only hope the work would be enough to keep his mind off the little girl who was gone from his life and the woman who didn't want anything to do with him.

Chapter 3

After a long, grinding afternoon, settling five traffic tickets, two trespassing charges, one restraining order, one dog bite, and a long-running dispute over the ownership of a pregnant cow's unborn calf, Tracy swallowed a couple of ibuprofen tablets, hung her robe in her chamber, gathered up her purse and jacket, and prepared to leave for the day.

As she passed the front desk, Maureen, the receptionist, hailed her. "Hey, don't forget these!" She waved a ziplock bag containing what looked like small packets of medicine.

"Oh, yes." She turned back toward the desk. "I hope you thanked the good doctor for me."

"I did, and I gave him the brownies." She sent Tracy a mischievous grin. "Good heavens, you didn't tell me what a gorgeous hunk he was. By the time he walked out the door, I was drooling. I take it he's single."

"As far as I know, for whatever that's worth."

"Well, if you're smart, you won't let that one get away. If I were twenty years younger, girl, I'd get myself gussied up and give you a run for your money."

Tracy forced herself to laugh. "You've got the wrong idea, Maureen. Dr. Rushford and I are barely friends. He checked my animals and didn't charge me for coming by. I made the brownies to thank him, but also because I didn't want to be obligated."

"Uh-huh. Sure." Maureen winked. "Something tells me the man wants to be more than a friend to you. I may be overstepping, but you've been alone for well over a year. I know that, as a judge, you've got your reputation to think of. But nobody's going to click their tongue if you find somebody new. In fact, folks will be happy for you."

Tracy tried to ignore the tightening sensation in her jaw. Was it panic, or was she just tired? "I know you mean well, Maureen. But I'm just not ready. Maybe I never will be."

"Well, you might want to think it over, honey, before that nice vet gets away." Maureen glanced at the wall clock. "Have a good weekend. I'll see you on Monday."

Tracy drove home, grateful that the work week had ended. Over the past year, her life had settled into a safe, comfortable routine—work all week, shop and clean on Saturday, unwind with a good book or a long walk on Sunday, then back to more of the same. She didn't have to think or plan. She could be emotionally numb and still function in her drab little world. As long as nothing changed, she could cope. She would be all right.

But how long could things remain the same?

She parked in the driveway and entered her house through the kitchen door. Murphy was there to greet her, wagging his tail and gazing up at her with love in his clouded eyes. She walked him out to do his business in the side yard. When he was done, she brought him back in, refilled his food and water bowls, and then went to check on the cat.

Tracy found the laundry room door open—her own fault for forgetting to close it. There was no sign of the little calico. Her food dish was empty, but with the door open, Murphy could have sniffed his way to the tasty wet food and gobbled it up. If he'd done that, he'd probably scared the cat away.

The litter box had been used, so at least the calico knew where it was and what to do. But she must not have felt safe in the laundry room.

She was probably hiding in her favorite place.

In the bedroom, Tracy knelt on the rug and peered under the bed. In the far corner she could just see the outline of a furry head and two pointed ears. "Come on out, kitty," she coaxed. "It's all right. You're safe."

The cat didn't move.

Crawling under the bed to get her was out of the question. The space under the bed would be a tight squeeze for Tracy, and even if she managed to grab the cat, she'd probably get some nasty scratches.

"Fine, just stay there," Tracy said to the cat. "When you decide to come out, I'll feed you and give you a nice brushing. But when that happens will be up to you."

Standing, she kicked off her shoes and changed into her sweats. When she left the room to make herself some supper, the cat was still under the bed. Never mind, Tracy told herself. The little calico would come out when she was ready.

By the time she'd made herself a cheese omelet and watched her favorite TV crime drama, she was getting sleepy. After washing her face, brushing her teeth, and checking under the bed for the cat, she crawled between the sheets and closed her eyes.

It was 2:14 in the morning when Rush's phone woke him. With a muttered curse, he reached for it on the nightstand. His fumbling hand knocked the phone to the floor. Swearing, he sat up and groped under the edge of the bed, where it had bounced. Whoever was calling at this ungodly hour had better have a damned good reason.

The phone was still ringing when he picked it up and looked at the caller ID.

It was Tracy.

In an instant, he was wide awake. "Tracy—" He paused to clear his throat. "Is something wrong?"

When she spoke, her voice was slightly breathless. "Sorry, I hate waking you, but I'm worried. When I got home from work last night, some food was gone, and the litter box had been used, but the cat was under the bed and wouldn't come out. She's still there and I keep hearing these little squeaking noises. I think she might be having her babies. What should I do? Should I try and move her to her box?"

"That's not a good idea. Just leave her alone for now. She should be fine."

"You're sure?"

"Do you want me to come?" Rush felt like a fish rising to the bait. What was he thinking? Hadn't he resolved to keep his distance from the woman?

"Oh, could you? I'd pay you whatever you charge for an emergency call."

"I'll settle for another batch of those brownies."

"Oh, no—at this hour, I couldn't ask you to come without paying you for your time."

"Double batch. Double chocolate. I'm on my way." Rush was grinning as he hung up the phone. This was crazy. But he could think of no better reason to get up in the wee small hours than Judge Tracy Emerson.

Tracy was just worried about the cat, he reminded himself as he pulled on his clothes, brushed his teeth, and finger-raked his hair back from his face. All she needed was to know that the little mother and her kittens were all right. He would give her that reassurance and leave.

With his bag, he walked quietly down the hall to the front door. His partners might have heard the phone, but they were accustomed to his late-night emergencies. Bucket, nestled in his blanket near the stove, raised his head, thumped his tail, and went back to sleep.

A chilly wind struck his face as he came outside to the Hummer. Leaves were blowing off the tall cottonwoods that lined the road to the ranch. By morning the hundred-year-old trees would be bare, the leaves carpeting the ground with brown and gold.

A storm wouldn't bode well for the second night of the ranch's Halloween celebration. But last night, at least, had been a success, with plenty of families showing up for the hayrides and fun. Maggie had come to help and to be with Travis. In a quiet moment, she'd taken Rush aside.

"I tried to talk Tracy into coming with me," she'd told him. "I think she was tempted. But in the end, she said she wasn't ready."

"Thanks for trying to play matchmaker," Rush had said. "But that doesn't surprise me. After talking to her, I'm not sure she'll ever be ready."

Maggie had given him a smile. "Well, don't give up on her just yet," she'd said. "Tracy's a lovely person. She deserves some happiness, and so do you."

The words came back to Travis as he drove into town and wound through the back streets to Tracy's house. Maggie had meant well. But Rush wasn't sure he believed her. Some women only loved once in their lives. Tracy, he sensed, was one of those women.

She'd left her porch light on. After parking partway up the block to avoid any chance of gossip, he took his bag, walked back to her house, and climbed the front steps.

Tracy was waiting at the front door. Dressed in sweats, her hair tousled, her face bare of makeup, she still managed to look delicious. Rush bit back the temptation to tell her so. This visit, he reminded himself, was strictly professional.

"Thanks for coming," she said, ushering him inside and closing the door. "I've put some coffee on. It'll be ready in a few minutes. I don't want you falling asleep on your way home."

"Good idea." Rush paused next to Murphy's bed and reached down to scratch the elderly dog's ears. "How's the cat?"

"Still under the bed. I have a flashlight, but it needs batteries. Anyway, I'm not sure about shining a light in her eyes. It might scare her."

"Let's take a look. Lead the way."

Carrying the small flashlight from his medical bag, he followed her down the hall to the bedroom. He'd seen the room earlier, but he still couldn't help noticing Steve's photo next to the bed. It served as a constant reminder that this lady was off-limits.

"I was hoping the cat would stay in the box I fixed for her." Tracy knelt on the floor and lifted the edge of the quilt. "But she seems to have a mind of her own."

"Most cats do." Rush knelt beside her, steeling himself against her nearness. No doubt, Tracy's intent in calling him had been totally innocent. But being close to a beautiful, vulnerable woman he couldn't help wanting was putting all the wrong thoughts into his head.

Damn! He gave himself a mental slap and switched on the flashlight. He was here to check on the cat and her kittens. That was all.

The bed was too low for Rush to look underneath without lowering himself onto his belly. Stretching out on the rug, he directed the beam toward the underside of the bed, letting the reflected light fall on the cat and her new family. Turning his head, he gave Tracy a grin. "Come on down and take a look," he said.

She eased onto her elbows, her shoulder resting lightly against his as she peered beneath the bed. "Oh . . ." She breathed the word. "They're so tiny. And she's got four of them—one orange, one black, one gray tabby, and one white. Look—she's licking them with her tongue. Do you think she'll have more?"

"If she had more coming, she'd be restless. But she seems to have settled down. My best guess is that she's done."

"Should I move them into the box?"

"Not just yet. In a few days, when they're stronger and the mother is more accustomed to you, you can try it. For now, the best thing to do is leave them alone."

"But . . . they're under my bed." She'd turned to face him. "I mean, what if they go on the carpet? What about the smell?"

"Don't worry. The mother will keep them clean until they're old enough to eat solid food. And you mentioned that she'd already discovered the litter box for herself."

"I've got a lot to learn about cats." She gave Rush a tired smile.

"Don't worry, just let the mother do her job," Rush said. "Have you thought of a name for her?"

"A name?"

"If you're going to keep her, she'll need one."

She flashed him a stern look, reminding him that she was, after all, a judge. "But I haven't made up my mind to keep her. I said I'd take her in, but giving her a name, that's a commitment. Don't push me."

"Fine. You'll know when you're ready to decide."

"*If* I'm ready. And speaking of ready, I think the coffee's finished brewing." She scooted away from the bed and scrambled to her feet. "If you want a cup, you'll find me in the kitchen."

"I'll be a few minutes." Rush took his time to study the little calico and her kittens under the bed. Did the mother look alert and comfortable? Was she taking care of her babies as she should? Were the kittens all moving and responsive?

Only after he'd satisfied himself that all was well did Rush turn off the flashlight, ease himself back from under the bed, and get to his feet. He could smell the coffee. But he wasn't quite sure of the reception that waited for him in the kitchen. Tracy's prickly response to his suggestion that she name the cat had caught him by surprise.

Should he apologize? No, Rush decided. They were both tired—too tired to get into an emotional discussion. He would drink his coffee, promise to check on the cats later, and leave while there was still time to get some sleep.

Tracy was waiting for him in the kitchen. She filled a mug from the glass carafe on the coffee maker. "Cream and sugar?" she asked.

"I'll take it black, thanks." Rush accepted the mug and took a seat at the table. The coffee was strong enough to jar him wide awake for the drive home. "From what I could see, the kittens and the mother cat all look fine. Make sure she has plenty of food and water, and she'll do the rest. Don't be surprised if she moves the kittens. Mother cats will do that if they don't feel safe where they are."

"Can I touch them, or even pick them up?"

"It might be best to wait a few days. Give the mother a chance to know you and trust you, so she won't be upset when you handle her babies."

"Wow." She stirred half-and-half into her coffee. "I didn't realize cats were so complicated. They're almost like people."

"So, you never had a cat?"

"I never had any pets growing up. My family lived in an apartment, no pets allowed. After my parents and sister died, my grandmother took me in. She was a good woman, but she couldn't abide animals in the house. It wasn't until Murphy—"

"Wait—you lost your family when you were young?"

"Yes." Her voice was drained of emotion. "They were in a car accident when I was nine. If I hadn't been at a sleepover, I would've been with them." She paused, glancing down at her coffee mug. "There've been times when I wished I had been."

"I'm sorry." It was a lame response, Rush thought, but nothing better came to mind. He was seeing Tracy Emerson in a new light, as a woman defined by loss. Her family, her husband . . . Lord, no wonder the idea of putting down her old dog brought her to tears. And no wonder she seemed reluctant to take on a new relationship, or even to adopt a homeless cat.

Her smile was artificially bright. "What about you? Do you have a family somewhere?"

Rush swallowed the tightness in his throat. "Not anymore. I'm divorced. My ex-wife and—" He paused, deciding to save the whole story for another time, if that time ever came. "My ex-wife and her daughter live in Phoenix. She married an old boyfriend after we split up." And that was that. He would spare Tracy the ugly details—the shattering revelation, the DNA test, and the final good-bye that had ripped the heart right out of him.

Standing, Rush carried his empty mug to the sink. "I'll be glad to come back and check the kittens as they grow," he said. "No charge—except maybe more of those sinful brownies."

"I also make pretty mean chocolate chip cookies and wicked cinnamon rolls, if you'd like some variety. But honestly, I'd be happy to pay you in cash."

"Heck, I can get money anywhere. Home-baked treats are in a class by themselves." Rush picked up his medical bag. "How's Murphy? Did you give him the Cosequin?"

She walked with him to the door. "I got the first couple of doses down him. I suppose it'll be a while before we know whether it's helping."

"Well, call me if you have any concerns." Rush opened the front door to a blast of wind. "One thing more. If you want to avoid neighborhood gossip, you might want to have me come by during business hours. As a judge, you've got a reputation to consider."

"Yes, of course." Color bloomed in her face as she gazed up at him. Rush battled the insane urge to kiss her. He could almost imagine how sweet and tender those lips would feel against his.

But kissing Tracy would be the worst possible idea. Even if he didn't get his face slapped, a move like that would destroy her fragile trust like a shotgun blasting through a cobweb.

He left her and walked up the street, through the blowing leaves, to his vehicle. Maybe Tracy would never be ready for a relationship. But at least he could be her friend. After all, friendship was something they could both use.

But could he settle for friendship with the beautiful judge?

That question had yet to be answered.

Standing at the window in the dark living room, Tracy watched Rush stride up the street. She was still watching when the Hummer's lights came on, and the big vehicle made a U-turn and vanished around the corner.

She should never have called him. And she wouldn't call him again. The sensual stirrings she'd felt when he'd stretched out next to her to look under the bed had been so intense that she'd almost reached out and brushed his cheek with her fingertip.

Dr. J. T. Rushford had never made an ungentlemanly move toward her. Tracy's instincts told her she could trust him. But could she trust herself—especially when the cold hollow in the depths of her soul ached to be warmed?

No, she wasn't ready. The experience of loving Steve and losing him was still raw inside her. To move forward, to feel again, to risk again—even the thought terrified her. Being alone was safe. And even loneliness hurt less than loss.

She would make the brownies as she'd promised. But she wouldn't contact Rush again. If she had a question about the cats or Murphy's medication, she could look for answers online.

She was making the safe choice, Tracy told herself. Rush deserved a woman who had something to give. She wasn't that woman. She was doing him—and herself—a favor.

For Rush and his partners, the end of October marked the start of serious Christmas preparations. Not that they hadn't been working all along. Over the spring and summer, in addition to growing two crops of hay and caring for the cows and calves they'd bought, the partners had been tending the acre of Christmas trees that grew on a remote part of the ranch—shaping and trimming the branches, checking them for insect damage, and making sure that every tree had water from the nearby spring. They'd even planted new trees to replace the ones they'd cut and sold last year.

Since it was Rush's veterinary practice that provided a steady cash flow to the ranch, most of the other work had fallen to Travis and Conner. But with the Christmas holidays coming up, it was all hands on deck. Between his practice and needing to help with the trees, the yard, the supplies and equipment, the sleigh, and the massive Percheron horses that filled in for reindeer, Rush was kept busy every waking moment.

He'd never stopped thinking about Tracy, but as the busy days flew by, she hadn't called him. True to her word, she'd delivered on her promise of more brownies, but she'd given them to Maggie to deliver to the ranch. Now, after two weeks, it was almost as if she'd dropped out of his life.

Rush tried to tell himself it didn't matter. But it did. What if something had gone wrong? What if she'd needed his help and was too proud to ask?

On a bleak Saturday morning in mid-November, Rush found himself in town. A cancelled appointment had left him with time on his hands and several options. He could go to the barber for a needed haircut. He could have some coffee and pie at Buckaroo's on Main Street. He could go home . . . or he could drive by Tracy's and make sure she was all right. He wouldn't necessarily have to knock on her door, especially if she had company. But if her car was there and nothing looked amiss at the house . . .

By the time Rush made up his mind, he'd already driven halfway there. Only now did he realize how much he'd missed her, and how much he looked forward to seeing her again.

As he turned onto her street and saw the empty driveway, his spirits sank. She wouldn't be in court on the weekend, but maybe she'd gone shopping, or maybe she'd decided to catch up on her research while the courthouse was quiet. In any case, he'd missed her; and the disappointment was like a cold, heavy lump in the pit of his stomach.

He was driving to the corner to turn around when he caught sight of her vintage Mercedes in his rearview mirror. She was just pulling into her driveway. By the time he'd changed directions and parked across the street, she was climbing out of her car, her arms loaded with grocery bags.

"Hold on! I'll give you a hand!" He sprinted across the street and took the two heaviest bags. She looked surprised, and not in a happy way. "Maybe I should have called first," he said.

"So, why didn't you?" She mounted the steps and opened the front door. Murphy was there to greet her. The old dog thumped his tail and ambled back to his bed.

"I hadn't planned to come by." Rush carried the heavy grocery bags into the kitchen and set them on the counter. "It's been a busy time at the ranch, but I was in town with some time on my hands, and I got to wondering how the kittens were doing."

And you. He stopped himself from adding the words. He couldn't be sure where he stood with Tracy, but he knew better than to push her toward any kind of relationship.

She set her bags on the kitchen table. "Come on," she said with a hint of a smile. "I'll show you."

She led him to the laundry, a small, sunny room off the kitchen. The high-sided cardboard box she'd set up had a chair next to it, to help the mother cat jump in and out while keeping the kittens safely inside.

"I managed to move them in here after a few days," Tracy said. "Take a look."

Rush looked down into the box. The calico mother, well-fed and calm, was curled on an old blue sweater, nursing her babies. By now the kittens were two weeks old. Their eyes were open, and their little bodies were filling out. As many times as he'd seen kittens, Rush never got tired of watching them.

"They're looking great," Rush said. "You've learned a lot about cats since the last time I saw you."

"I had a good teacher. You were right about mother cats. She knew exactly what to do."

"So, have you given her a name yet?"

"Not a real one. I just call her Mama." Tracy reached down into the box and stroked the cat's head. "When will the kittens be ready for new homes?"

"After they're weaned and eating solid food. By then they'll be about two months old, just in time for Christmas. Your timing couldn't be better."

"Little Christmas presents." There was warmth in Tracy's voice and in her smile. If only she would smile at him like that, Rush mused.

"They'll need their distemper and rabies shots before they go," he said. "I'll throw those in as a favor. The mother's going to need shots, too. I'm guessing she was somebody's pet once, but there's no way to know whether they had her immunized. I'd do it now, but I'd rather not disturb her."

"I can't let you do all that for nothing," Tracy protested.

"Can I do it for brownies?" *Or to take you out to dinner?*

"Brownies it is, unless you'd rather have something else."

"Your call. I'm easy." He followed her back into the living room. Murphy opened his eyes, then went back to sleep. "How's he doing on the Cosequin?" Rush asked.

"A little better, I think. But since he spends most of his time sleeping, it's hard to tell."

"Well, let's have a look. Can you get him up?"

"I'll try." Tracy stepped back into the kitchen and took a dog treat from a jar on the counter. Crouching a few feet away from the old dog, she held out the treat and coaxed him to get up and go to her. Murphy roused himself and hobbled to his mistress for his reward. At least he seemed no worse than the last time. But there was no cure for old age.

"Good boy!" Tracy hugged the dog and kissed him between his ears. It tore at Rush's heart, seeing how much she loved the pathetic old creature and knowing what she faced.

"I can't see much improvement yet, but keep giving him the Cosequin. At least it might keep him from getting worse."

There were tears in her eyes when she looked up at him. It was all Rush could do to keep from taking her in his arms. It was time to walk away, before he made a fool of himself.

"I'll check back in a couple of weeks," he said,

moving toward the door. "Meanwhile, if you need anything, give me a call."

"We'll be fine," she said. "I and my entire little menagerie."

"And don't worry about the brownies," he said. "I know you have a life."

"We'll see." She opened the front door. "Thanks for stopping by, Rush. Have a happy holiday."

"You too." It was as good an exit line as any, Rush thought as he walked out and closed the door behind him. The holiday wasn't fated to be a happy one. But at least it would be busy—maybe busy enough to keep his mind off the missing pieces in his life.

Chapter 4

In late November the weather turned frigid. The first storm of the season iced the roads and blanketed the land with snow. Morning fog froze on trees and bushes, creating a fairyland of lacy white.

At Christmas Tree Ranch, the work continued from dawn until after dark. The partners grabbed food and sleep as they could, readying the trees and the ranch for the Thanksgiving weekend opening.

Even in busy times like these, the care of the animals had to come first. Chip and Patch, the two massive Percherons, were sheltered in the barn, the cows and calves under an open-fronted shed in their pasture. All of them needed food and water, and the horse stalls needed daily cleaning. Only Bucket seemed to enjoy the wintry weather. He romped and bounded through the snow as if he'd been waiting all year for it to arrive.

The biggest and most urgent task was to cut the trees and haul them to the Christmas tree lot at

Hank's Hardware in town. Hank Miller, the owner, was Travis's father. Last year, after settling a bitter rivalry, the partners had taken Hank into their business. He would be needing more than a hundred trees to open the lot on the day after Thanksgiving. After that, the ranch would keep him supplied with more as needed. At a fifty-fifty split of the profits, it was a good deal for everyone; and the townspeople would get fresh trees instead of having to settle for trees trucked hundreds of miles across the country.

There would be trees for sale at the ranch, too, as well as free hot cocoa, marshmallow roasting, candy canes, and sleigh rides. Families who wanted to pay extra could ride out to where the trees grew to pick and cut their own.

By Thanksgiving, with all except the last-minute preparations done, the partners were worn out and ready for a break. This year Maggie had cooked a turkey dinner at her house and invited all three of them, along with Hank and his girlfriend, Francine, who ran the Branding Iron Bed and Breakfast.

Earlier, Maggie had mentioned to Rush that she'd planned to invite Tracy, as well. Now, as Rush walked through Maggie's front door and basked in the aromas of turkey, hot rolls, and pumpkin pies, his pulse skipped with anticipation. He hadn't seen Tracy or talked with her since the day he'd stopped by her house. He'd done his best to convince himself that she wasn't interested. But as he glanced around the living room, a spark of hope ignited, flared . . . and died.

She wasn't here.

Standing in the entrance to the kitchen, Maggie caught Rush's eye and gave a subtle shake of her head. Not only was Tracy not here; evidently, she wasn't coming.

There had been seven places set at the table. Before the six friends took their seats, Maggie discreetly removed the seventh place setting. So, Tracy's decision must have been made at the last minute. Rush imagined her home alone with her old dog and her little family of cats. That she would turn down a delicious Thanksgiving dinner rather than face him across the table was the last straw. It was time to forget about the woman—permanently.

After Hank's brief grace, as the food was being passed, Rush's gaze moved around the table. Hank and Francine, both well into middle age, had nearly married when they were younger. But they'd gone their separate ways, only to rediscover each other a few years ago. Now they'd settled into a warm, supportive relationship. Travis and Maggie had been dating almost a year and still couldn't seem to take their eyes off each other. And Conner seemed perfectly happy with his rotating girlfriends and his carefree bachelor existence.

Only Rush had a gaping hole in his life.

Enough with the hand-wringing! Rush scolded himself. He had good friends, meaningful work, and a promising future. It might not be the whole package, but it was more than many people had. For now, he would have to be content and call it good.

*   *   *

The call came five days later.

Rush was pulling his boots off his frigid feet after a grueling eighteen-hour day when his cell phone rang. By the time his chilled hands had worked the phone out of his vest pocket, the caller had rung off. Let them wait, Rush thought. Right now, all he wanted was a hot shower and a good night's sleep.

But maybe the call was important.

With a sigh, he pulled the phone out of his vest pocket and checked the caller ID.

His pulse lurched when he saw the name.

Cecil Crawford was the caretaker in the house where Rush's ex-wife, Sonya, lived. His wife, Annie, served as housekeeper, cook, and part-time nanny. Rush knew the middle-aged couple well. They'd been with the family for years. Rush had left an emergency number with them. But he hadn't expected it to be used—not unless something was terribly wrong.

Rush's hand shook as he returned the call. Cecil picked up at once. "Rush." He sounded perfectly calm. "It's good to hear your voice."

"What is it, Cecil?" Rush was too worried for pleasantries. "Is Claire all right?"

"She's fine. Annie just put her to bed. Incidentally, we're not calling her Claire anymore. Andre said the name reminded him of his first wife. We're calling her Clara—it's been legally changed."

"Wasn't that confusing for her?" Rush asked.

"Only for the first week or two. Now she's fine with it. But she still misses you."

"There's not much I can do about that, is there?"

"Actually, yes," Cecil said. "We've got a bit of an emergency and were hoping you might be able to help."

"I don't see how—"

"Hear me out," Cecil said. "Sonya and Andre left after Thanksgiving on a five-week holiday cruise to the South Pacific. They left Clara here with us."

"They went on a cruise and left her over *Christmas?*" Rush swore silently. Sonya had never been the world's most attentive mother. But to go away and leave a child to spend Christmas with the hired help—what had his ex-wife been thinking?

"Clara seems all right with it," Cecil said. "She's used to being with us, and they left her some presents to open. We were planning to make sure she had a tree and cookies to put out for Santa. But something's come up, and we don't know what to do." He paused.

"How can I help?" Even as he asked the question, Rush felt stirrings of doubt. Any involvement with Claire—now, Clara, he reminded himself— could be a mistake. She'd barely had time to adjust to his absence and the new father who'd taken his place. Seeing her, then having to separate again, would hurt her in a way no child should be hurt.

"Here's the thing," Cecil said. "We just got word that Annie's father, who's in his eighties, has had a severe stroke. He's in the hospital, in Oklahoma City. Annie's mother is beside herself. We need to get there fast and stay, maybe for a long time. But what do we do with Clara?"

"Can't you reach her parents?"

"Even if we could, they're somewhere in the middle of the ocean. It could take them several days to get home. We might not have that much time." Cecil hesitated, as if weighing the wisdom of saying more. "The truth is, they've been having problems. They wanted some time alone to work on their marriage. They asked me not to disturb them unless there was a serious emergency."

"This *is* an emergency," Rush said.

"But it's not their emergency. It's ours. Could you take her for a few weeks? There's nobody else we trust. We can't have her with us in the hospital. And we can't go off and leave her with strangers."

Rush held back his answer. For the past year he'd ached to spend time with his little girl again; but he'd known that staying away was for the best. How could he say yes?

How could he say no?

"Please." Rush could hear the desperation in the good man's voice.

"All right," he said. "But I can't come to Phoenix. My partners need me here."

"I understand. We just need to get her to you. Are you still in Texas?"

"Yes, in a little town called Branding Iron. But there's no major airport close by."

"We need to fly to Oklahoma City. If we bring Clara with us on the plane, could you pick her up there?"

Rush took a moment to estimate the distance and time. It wasn't that far—a few hours each way by road. "That shouldn't be a problem," he said. "Call me when you've got your flight."

Rush ended the call and turned around to find Conner standing in the doorway of his room. Travis stood behind him.

"I hope you're going to tell us what's going on," Conner said.

Rush stood, weariness and worry dragging like a weight on his shoulders. "I guess it's time," he said. "Come on in the kitchen. It's a long story."

They gathered around the kitchen table. Travis took three Bud Lights out of the fridge and passed them around. Conner popped the tab on his and took a long swig. "We're waiting," he said.

Travis took a seat and opened his beer. "We haven't pried into your past because we figured it was none of our business, Rush. But we've got our own stories, and we don't judge others. Whatever you've got going on, know that we've got your back."

"Thanks, that's good to know," Rush said. And it was. These two were the best friends a man could have. He took a deep breath and began.

"I met Sonya, my ex, when I was just starting my practice. She was still in college and a real stunner, the whole package. Dark hair, big, green eyes— she'd been homecoming queen the year before, and first runner-up to Miss Arizona. To top it off, she had a rich daddy who gave her anything she wanted."

"I'm guessing she had plenty of guys to choose from," Conner said.

"More than plenty. The frontrunner was a fellow named Andre Duval. A race car driver, if you

can believe it. He was a real mover with the ladies.
I was a distant second, if that."

"I get the picture," Conner said. "You were the
boring, steady, nice guy that every parent wants
their daughter to marry."

"Thanks. That's just about right." Rush re-
sponded to Conner's grin with a mock scowl. "I
wasn't her first choice, but when she and Andre
had a fight and broke up, I was the one she turned
to. We got engaged—me with big dreams and a
load of student debt, Sonya with a fortune about
to drop into her lap. Soon after we got married,
her father died of congestive heart failure. We
moved into his big house—now hers—complete
with two family servants. In accordance with her
father's will, everything was in her name, not
mine. But she did pay off my student loan debt
and gave me the money to build a veterinary clinic
adjacent to the house."

Travis looked cynical. "I think I saw a TV series
based on that plot," he said.

The irony wasn't lost on Rush. "That's about
what it was like. Things went sour pretty fast. I
worked hard, trying to build my practice, but
Sonya owned everything, including me. And she
never let me forget it.

"We might not have lasted as long as we did, but
when she got pregnant, I made an extra effort to
hold the marriage together. At the hospital, when
I held that baby girl in my arms, I knew everything
we'd been through to get her here was worth it.
She became my reason for living. I couldn't get

enough of being her dad. She was mine, and no one, not even her mother, could take that away from me—or so I thought."

"I don't suppose you have a picture to show us, do you?" Travis asked.

"Not anymore." In an effort to forget Claire, Rush had destroyed his last photo of the little girl. But he couldn't erase the picture in his mind.

"Claire wasn't quite three years old when Sonya called me into the study. Her lawyer was there. He did most of the talking. Before Sonya got pregnant, she'd hooked up with Andre again. Recently, without telling me, she'd had DNA tests done. Claire wasn't mine. She was Andre's child."

Travis and Conner were silent. What was there to say about such a betrayal?

"Andre was back in Sonya's life, and she wanted a divorce," Rush said. "Since Claire wasn't my biological child, and I had never adopted her, I had no parental rights. I tried to start a legal fight, but I was up against a whole battery of expensive lawyers. I didn't have a prayer. There was nothing I could do except leave."

"And now?" Travis asked.

"From what I heard of your conversation, somebody needs a babysitter," Conner said.

"That's right." Rush stood and put his unopened beer back in the fridge. "I've agreed to pick her up in Oklahoma City and keep her here over the holidays, until her parents get back from their cruise. I guess I should've asked your permission before I said yes."

"No need," Travis said. "Hey, we like kids, and it's only for a few weeks. We'll make it work, won't we, Conner?"

"Sure," Conner said. "We'll show that young lady the time of her life."

"Thanks, both of you." Rush was grateful for his partners' support. But what was he going to do with a four-year-old girl—a girl who slept in a pink ruffled canopy bed at home, with a nanny to fix her meals exactly the way she liked them and keep her looking like a little princess? What if Claire . . . Clara hated the ranch?

Where was she going to sleep? He would have to buy or borrow a bed. And there was no spare room for her. Either he would have to set up her bed in a corner of his room, or move out and bunk on the sofa while she was here. She was going to need regular meals and somebody to watch her and keep her safe. And what about Christmas? Cecil had mentioned presents, but she wouldn't be able to bring them on the plane. He would need to buy her something to open. She would want a tree, of course. They had plenty of trees here, but no decorations.

Just thinking about what needed to be done was giving him a headache—to say nothing of the emotional trauma involved in having Clara back, then having to let her go again, maybe this time forever.

He was still questioning his own judgment when his phone rang. The caller was Cecil. They had their plane tickets and would be arriving in Oklahoma City the following afternoon. Rush promised to meet them at the airport. To get there in time, he would need to leave first thing tomorrow morning.

Travis and Conner had overheard the conversation. "Don't worry," Conner said. "We'll get things ready for her here. She'll be fine. It'll be an adventure."

An adventure? Maybe, Rush thought. Or maybe having Clara here would turn out to be a total disaster. All he could do was plunge ahead with the plan, be there for the child he loved, and hope for the best.

When Cecil and Annie arrived at the airport with Clara, Rush was waiting to meet them. He paced restlessly as the flight's arrival was announced and the first passengers began moving down the escalator into the baggage claim area. He willed himself to stay back and wait. No sign of them yet. But the plane had been a big one, he reminded himself; and, having bought their tickets the night before, they'd likely have been seated in the rear.

What would she be like?

A child could change a lot in a year. Rush knew that Clara would be taller, less of a baby, and even more independent than he remembered. She'd talked early and, even at three, had been able to carry on a fluent conversation. By now, she could be talking like a miniature adult. Those things Rush knew to expect. Other things—the important things—were fearful uncertainties.

How would she remember him? As the father who'd loved her, or as the person who'd walked out of her life and left her with a stranger? Had Sonya and Andre poisoned her against him? Had they lied to her? Or had they simply let him fade from her memory?

His thoughts fled as the three of them came down the moving stairs. Cecil and Annie looked much the way he remembered, but perhaps more careworn. Clara, dressed in a blue quilted coat, had lost her baby plumpness and sprouted long legs. Her features were more defined, her eyes large and dark, her long hair brushed into a ponytail. In her arms, she clutched her favorite stuffed toy, a fluffy white cat she'd named Snowflake. Rush remembered it well. He had given it to her for her third birthday.

At least she'd kept it and brought it with her.

As they reached the bottom of the stairs, Rush stepped forward and Clara spotted him. Breaking away from her protectors, she raced toward him and flung herself into his arms.

"Daddy!" she cried, clinging to his jacket as he swung her around.

Rush felt his heart shatter.

Looking beyond her, he saw Cecil and Annie coming toward him. There was nothing but sympathy in their eyes—they knew why Rush had left. And they knew that there was no way he could keep Clara beyond this bittersweet holiday season.

Cecil broke the silence. "Thanks for helping us out," he said. "She's been asking every fifteen minutes when we were going to get here."

Rush found his voice. "Come on, let's get your luggage. Then I'll drop you off wherever you need to go."

They picked up the bags from the carousel and headed outside to the car. Rush had stopped at a big-box store along the way to buy a booster seat for Clara. Annie buckled her in and took a seat beside her in the back. Cecil sat in the front seat beside Rush to give him directions.

"You can drop Annie off at the hospital," he said. "I'll go to the house, leave our suitcases there, and drive the family station wagon back to the hospital."

"How's your father-in-law doing?" Rush asked him. "Any news?"

"I called this morning. He's stable, but he'll have a long road ahead of him. Physical therapy, speech therapy . . . He's a tough old man. I hope he's up to it. I don't know how long we'll need to stay here, or even if we'll be able to go back to our jobs."

"Keep me posted," Rush said. "I'll need to know when Sonya and Andre will be back and how you plan to get Clara home."

Cecil shrugged. "I can't answer any of that now. I'm just grateful to you for taking her. It must not have been an easy decision."

"It wasn't painless, but it wasn't hard," Rush said. "There's no way I would've turned you down."

"Then we'll take this one day at a time," Cecil said. "I know you'll do what's best for her."

"I'll try," Rush said. But how could he be sure? When the time came to send her back home, he knew that he could stand the pain because he understood it. But what about Clara? She'd cried the first time he left, too young to understand the reason why. Would she understand this time? Was she old enough to accept that Andre was her father and Rush was not? Or would the coming separation hurt her all over again?

They left Annie at the hospital and drove Cecil several miles to a small house in a quiet neighborhood, where he unloaded the luggage from the back of the Hummer and promised to keep in touch. Then Rush drove away with Clara in the backseat.

"Can I come up front and sit with you, Daddy?" The word struck Rush like a knife through the heart.

"Nope," Rush said. "You have to stay in the back."

"Why?"

"Because it isn't safe up here, and because it's the law."

"Why?"

"Because if I had to stop fast, you could get hurt up here. Are you hungry? We could get something to eat."

"Can we have hamburgers? And fries? And chocolate shakes?"

Rush had to laugh. "Yes to all three. Just let me find a place."

He drove down a promising street and found a familiar chain restaurant. "How's this?" He parked and came around the vehicle to help her out of her booster seat.

"Fine. Can I take Snowflake with me?" She hugged the toy cat with both arms.

"I think Snowflake would be happier in the car," Rush said. "Look how pretty and white he is. What if you dropped him on the floor or spilled ketchup on him?"

"I don't like ketchup."

"Well, he could still get dirty. Or you could put him down and forget to take him back to the car."

"I wouldn't do that."

"Leave him and come on, Clara." He was still getting used to her new name. "Snowflake can keep the booster seat warm for you."

"Oh, okay." She climbed out of the booster seat and put the cat where she'd been sitting. "Let's go," she said.

Rush took her hand and let her lead him into the restaurant.

Damn it, but he'd missed her.

In their booth, she took off her coat and let it fall behind her on the seat. Underneath she was wearing a short pink dress that was knit like a sweater, with flowered leggings. Sonya had always dressed her in fussy, girly clothes. She looked adorable in them, but she was going to need something more durable for the ranch.

What if she hated it there? She wasn't used to cold weather, large animals, mud and snow, or sharing a run-down house, including the bathroom, with three big, gruff men. Keeping this little girl for the holidays could turn out to be a big mistake.

"What would you like on your hamburger?" he asked Clara as the waitress came to take their order.

"Just meat and a bun. You know that, Daddy."

"Yes, I do." He gave the rest of the order, wondering whether he should explain that he wasn't really her daddy. Skip it for now, he decided. Clara was too young to have a clue about the birds and the bees. But hearing her say the word was like a gut punch.

"Annie says you live on a ranch," Clara said while they waited for their meals. "Will there be cowboys?"

"My two friends are cowboys," Rush said. "We live together in an old house. It isn't fancy like your house in Phoenix, but we have a good time there, sort of like camping out. You'll have fun." *I hope.*

"Do you have horses? Can I ride one?"

"We have two huge horses named Chip and Patch. But we don't ride them. They're too big for that. We use them to pull the hay wagon in the summer and the sleigh in the winter."

"You've got a sleigh?" Her eyes grew large. "Like Santa Claus?"

"Exactly like Santa Claus." He gave her a smile across the table. "But we don't have reindeer. That's why we have Chip and Patch to pull the sleigh. Just before Christmas the town has a big parade, with Santa riding in our sleigh. You'll get to see it." Was he promising too much? What if this visit didn't work out?

"We have somebody else who rides in the parade," Rush said. "Our dog, Bucket, wears a hat and a little Santa suit and sits on the bench right next to Santa Claus. You'll meet Bucket when we get to the ranch."

And he'll probably jump all over you with his muddy paws. Rush kept that thought to himself.

"Will it be the real Santa in the parade?"

"You can decide for yourself when you see him." Travis's father, Hank, had taken over as Branding Iron's Santa last year. But Rush wasn't about to reveal that to Clara, who was still a believer.

The waitress brought their burgers, fries, and shakes. Both of them were hungry. They settled into silence as they devoured their food. Clara ate like a little lady, taking dainty bites and drinking her shake without slurping, the way most kids would. Clearly, someone, probably Annie, had taught her proper table manners. Rush couldn't imagine Sonya having the patience.

He couldn't help wondering how Clara had adjusted to Andre. Did she call him Daddy, too? But there was no point in wondering, Rush reminded himself. All that mattered was knowing she was happy and well cared for.

"Why did you go away, Daddy?" The question came out of nowhere, slamming into him with the force of a fist.

"Because your mom wanted to marry Andre."

"But why didn't you come back and see me?"

That was a tough one. Rush groped for the right words, not wanting to put the blame on her mother. "Because I knew I'd be sad when I had to leave you again. I was afraid you might be sad, too."

"But I would have been happy that you came." Her words were too wise for her years. She broke his heart.

He put money on the table to cover their bill and the tip. "If you've finished eating, let's get on the road. It would be nice to get to the ranch before your bedtime."

"Okay. I'm done." She slipped into her coat by herself and took his hand as they walked out to the parking lot. Snowflake was waiting on the booster seat. She picked up the toy, snuggling it close.

"I'll bet you could learn to buckle yourself in," Rush said. "Let me hold Snowflake while you try."

He gave her instructions, showing her where the straps crossed and how the buckles fastened. When she made a mistake, he corrected her gently. Rush had always loved teaching her things. Clara was a quick and eager learner, but it took her a good ten minutes to master the complicated harness. When she finally did it right, he clapped and cheered for her. "That's my big girl," he said. "Now you'll always know how to do it."

She grinned and held out her arms for Snowflake. "Let's go, Daddy," she said. "I want to see your ranch."

Rush closed the door, climbed into the driver's side, and started the Hummer's powerful engine. "Don't expect anything fancy, like your place," he said. "My ranch is a working ranch. The house and barn are old. My partners and I are fixing them up as best we can, but that takes time and money."

"Oh." She was quiet for a moment. "Can I play with the animals on your ranch?"

"The cows and horses are too big to play with," Rush said. "They could hurt you, even if they didn't mean to. But you can play with Bucket."

"Is he a puppy?"

"No, he's a grown-up dog. We don't even know how old he is."

"Why don't you know? Doesn't he have a birthday?"

"Dogs don't have birthdays."

"Some dogs do. I saw one on TV. He even had a cake."

"Okay. But Bucket doesn't have one."

"We could give him one."

"Maybe." Rush decided to change the subject. "Do you have any pets at home?"

"I can't have a pet. Andre's allergic."

"That's too bad." Rush remembered how she'd loved the small pets that had come to his clinic.

"Will Bucket be happy to see me?"

"He will. He's a friendly dog. But he's not a little dog. He's more like middle-sized. He gets dirty, so you won't want to hold him. But he loves to chase sticks, and he's really smart. He even helps us herd the cows and horses."

"Do you have snow . . . ?" She spoke through a yawn.

"Sometimes."

"Can we have music on the radio?"

"Sure." Rush found an easy listening station that

played Christmas music. The strains of "The Little Drummer Boy" drifted from the speakers. He kept the volume low.

The next time he glanced in the rearview mirror, Clara was asleep.

Chapter 5

It was almost twilight when Rush turned off the highway south of Branding Iron and drove down the narrow lane toward home. The last rays of sunset gleamed on the snow as they drove through the ranch gate. By now, Clara was wide awake. She bounced and squirmed in her booster seat, looking out the window and peppering Rush with questions.

"Are we here?"

"Where are the horses? Where's Bucket?"

"Can we play in the snow?"

"Where will I sleep?"

Tired as he was, Rush answered each question as patiently as he could. But the last one had him stumped. Before leaving, he'd had no chance to get her a bed. Unless his partners had taken care of the problem, he would spend the night on the sofa, while Clara slept in his bed. "We'll see," was all he said.

As he pulled the Hummer up to the house, the

porch light came on. He climbed wearily to the
snowy ground, retrieved her suitcase from the back
of the vehicle, and came around to open the door
and help the little girl out of her booster seat. She
clung to his coat with one hand, clasping Snowflake
with the other.

"Oh!" She gazed at the snow, seeing it up close
for the first time. "It looks so soft and fluffy. Can I
touch it, Daddy?"

"Hang on." Setting the suitcase on the porch,
Rush scooped a handful of snow off the railing
and held it for her. She let go of his coat and
poked it with a small, pink finger.

"It's cold!" She giggled, pulling her finger away,
then poking it again. "Does it taste good?"

"It tastes cold and wet, like ice, and it might not
be good for you." Rush tossed the snow away, put
Clara down, and picked up her suitcase. "Come
on, let's go inside and meet my friends."

"Are they nice men?"

"Very nice. Come on."

She shrank shyly against Rush's legs, holding
Snowflake close as he opened the door and ushered her inside. Travis and Conner were waiting in
the kitchen. They greeted her with friendly smiles.
"Howdy, Miss Clara." Conner was all Texas charm,
melting away her shyness. "Welcome to the ranch.
I'm Conner. Did you have a nice trip?"

"Uh-huh. But it was long." Clara looked him up
and down. "Are you a real cowboy?"

Conner grinned. "I'm as real as they come.
Travis here is still learning but he's coming along.
Would you like to be a cowgirl?"

"Uh-huh. But not tonight. I'm kind of tired. Where's my room?"

"We've got a little surprise for you," Conner said. "Do you like camping?"

She glanced up at Rush, then back at Conner. "I don't know. I've seen people camping on TV. It looks fun. But I've never done it. Will we camp in the snow?"

"We don't have to," Conner said. "Take a look at this! Your very own cozy camp!"

Travis, who'd been blocking her view of the darkened living room, stepped aside and turned on the light to reveal a blue nylon dome tent pitched in a corner. Rush had never seen the tent before. Conner must have brought it in his trailer when he'd moved to the ranch last year.

Clara hesitated, still uncertain. Glancing at his partners' faces, Rush could tell how much they'd wanted his little girl to like their surprise.

"Come on, let's look inside." Rush took her suitcase, held her hand, and led her to the tent. It wasn't tall enough for an adult to stand full height, but for a child, there was plenty of room. Inside was a sleeping bag with a pillow, laid on a cushiony air mattress. Next to the makeshift bed was a flashlight and a water bottle, with enough space left on the floor for an open suitcase.

"We wanted you to have your own space," Travis said. "But the house doesn't have a spare room. So, we thought the tent might work. You can zip the flap shut when you want to close it. Check it out."

When Clara hesitated, Rush laid her suitcase on

the floor of the tent and nudged her inside. She looked around, then sat on the sleeping bag and bounced up and down on the air mattress. Her small face transformed into a grin. "I like it!" she said. "It's like my own little house!"

Rush could see relief in the faces of his partners. Making her feel at home had mattered to them.

"So, take off your coat and stay a while," Conner said. "Would you like some hot cocoa and cinnamon toast before bedtime?"

"Yes, please." Clara's manners were impeccable. She was a little princess who'd landed among rough-living cowboys, like Snow White wandering into the cottage of the dwarves.

She handed Snowflake to Travis, shed her coat, and laid it next to her suitcase. She had just stepped out of the tent when the sound of furious scratching and barking came from the far end of the hall. Clara's dark eyes widened. "Is that Bucket?"

"Yup, and he's really anxious to meet you," Travis said. "I locked him in my room because I didn't want him to knock you over. Hang on, I'll get him." He strode down the hall and came back with the wriggling, wagging dog in his arms. Bucket had been bathed and brushed until his black-and-white coat gleamed. Rush hadn't seen him so clean since last year's Christmas parade.

Travis tried to hold on to the dog, but Bucket was too much for him. Squirming with eagerness, he worked loose from Travis's clasp, jumped to the floor, and came bounding to greet the newcomer.

Here comes disaster, Rush thought. But he couldn't

reach Clara in time to snatch her away. Bucket barreled into her, wagging, licking, and making happy little whimpers.

Alarm flashed across Clara's face. Then, recovering from her fear, she laughed. Reaching out, she hugged the dog, giggling as he licked her face.

It was strange, Rush thought. Bucket didn't know Clara. There was no reason he should be so happy to see her. He was an older dog—maybe he had loved a child in his unknown past. Or maybe he'd recognized a kindred spirit—small, openhearted, and eager to play.

"Can Bucket stay in my tent with me?" Clara asked.

"Not a good idea," Travis said. "Tonight, Bucket's had a bath. But if you let him sleep by you, he'll think he can do it anytime. You won't want him in your tent when he's been rolling in the mud. I've moved his bed to my room so he won't bother you in the night."

"One thing more," Rush said, holding up the toy cat. "You'll need to keep Snowflake in a safe place, or Bucket will want to play with him. Snowflake wasn't made to be a dog toy."

"I'll tuck him in the sleeping bag. He'll be there when I go to bed." She took the toy. With Rush keeping Bucket outside the tent, she stuffed it into the sleeping bag.

Conner was in the kitchen making hot chocolate and toast. "It'll be ready in a couple of minutes," he said.

"I want to put my jammies on first." Inside the tent, Clara was opening her suitcase.

"Do you need any help?" Rush remembered how he'd helped her get ready for bed when she was younger.

"I'm a big girl now, Daddy. I can get ready by myself." She zipped the tent flap and emerged a few minutes later, clad in pink Disney princess pajamas and tiny pink slippers with cat faces and whiskers on the toes. Rush noticed that she'd put her pajama top on backward and her slippers were on the wrong feet, but knew better than to point it out. The little girl he still thought of as his was proud of her independence—something she was bound to need growing up with a mother like Sonya.

"Let's keep your tent zipped so Bucket will learn to stay out," Rush suggested.

"That's a good idea, Daddy." She found the outside zipper tab and managed to close the flap by herself.

"Who's ready for hot cocoa and toast?" Conner called from the kitchen.

"Me!" Clara scampered to the table and let Conner boost her onto the chair he'd raised with a box on the seat. So far, so good, Rush thought as he watched her wipe her hands on the washcloth Conner had given her. His partners were the best friends he could have, welcoming his little girl like this. And Clara seemed happy to be here.

He would do everything in his power to leave her with joyful memories of this Christmas holiday—memories that might be the last she would ever have of him.

* * *

The next morning Rush was up at first light to help with morning chores. After making sure Travis had let Bucket outside, he unzipped the blue tent where Clara had gone to sleep. In the faint glow of dawn, he could see her cocooned in the sleeping bag, one arm cradling her fuzzy toy cat. She looked so sweet in slumber that he was tempted to leave her alone. But it wouldn't do to have her wake up all alone in a strange house.

Stepping carefully into the tent, he leaned over her, touched her shoulder, and murmured her name. She stirred and opened her eyes. Her smile, when she saw him, was like the sun coming up.

"Hi, Daddy," she said. "Is it morning?"

"Almost. I woke you up because I need to go outside and help with the work. My friends will be working, too, so you'll be in here by yourself for a little while. Is that all right?"

"Uh-huh."

"You won't be scared alone?"

"I'm a big girl, Daddy. I won't be scared. Where's Bucket?"

"He's outside, helping. Go back to sleep. I'll wake you when I come back inside."

"What if I need to get up?"

"Do you know how to find the bathroom?"

"Uh-huh. I went last night."

"Fine. If you get up, don't open anything in the kitchen or go into any of the bedrooms. In case you're hungry, I left some cookies and milk on the table. We'll have breakfast when the chores are done. After that, if you behave, I'll take you out to see the horses. Okay?"

She gave him a sleepy smile. "Can we play in the snow today?"

"If it's not too cold. We'll see." Had she packed anything suitable for the weather? Coming from Phoenix, she probably didn't have anything warmer than her lightweight coat and the little sneakers she'd worn. He would need to see that she had warm, sturdy clothes. He would also need to set up a routine for her, with a regular schedule and a set of rules to keep her out of trouble. The responsibilities he'd taken on were just beginning to sink in.

"It's early yet," he said. "Travis built a fire in the stove before he went out, but the house is still cold. You'll be warmer if you stay in bed a while. Okay?"

"Okay." Snuggling the toy cat, she closed her eyes. With luck, she'd sleep until he finished the chores and came back inside. Then what? Too bad he didn't have a book on a thousand ways to entertain a four-year-old. Maybe his partners would have some suggestions.

By the time Rush had finished his share of the morning chores, washed his hands, and returned to the house, Clara was sitting at the table, watching Travis spoon pancake batter onto the cast-iron griddle.

"Hi, Daddy!" She gave him a smile. Her ponytail was lopsided, with missed strands of hair hanging around her face. She was dressed in a fuzzy blue sweater with a ballerina-style net tutu over the flowered leggings she'd worn last night. Her sneakers, which were fastened with strips of Velcro, were on the wrong feet.

"Look, I got dressed all by myself," she said. "And I fixed my own hair."

Rush had to smile. "You sure did. I'm proud of you."

Her smile broadened, making him wonder if her "real" father ever praised her. He hadn't known Andre well, but Sonya's lover had impressed him as a self-absorbed ass.

"Here you go." Travis flipped two pancakes onto her plate. "Careful, they're hot."

"Can I butter them for you?" Rush asked. "If I remember right, you like your pancakes with plenty of syrup."

"I still do." She let Rush melt butter on the hot pancakes and drown them in maple syrup. When he began cutting them into bite-sized pieces, as he'd done for her in the past, she smiled and let him. At least she hadn't insisted on doing everything by herself.

After they helped clear the table and loaded the dishwasher, Rush kept his promise to show Clara the horses. The day was sunny, but the morning air was bitter cold. Realizing that her thin blue coat wouldn't protect her, Rush bundled the little girl into a blanket and carried her outside in his arms.

Bucket came bounding out of the barn to meet them, wagging his tail and standing on his hind legs for attention. Clara reached down to pet him, giggling as he licked her fingers. "He likes me!"

"He likes your fingers," Rush teased. "They probably taste like syrup."

"Why did you name him Bucket?"

"We didn't name him. That's just the name he came with."

"It's a silly name."

"I know. But he's a smart dog. He can make the horses and cows go right where they're supposed to. Ask Travis to tell you about the time Bucket chased a skunk under the back porch and got sprayed. That's a good story."

Clara giggled. "What happened to the skunk?"

"It ran away. Travis gave Bucket a good washing, but he smelled like a skunk for weeks."

Clara giggled. "I want to see the horses," she said.

With Bucket tagging behind them, Rush carried her into the barn and held her up to the gates of the box stalls to see Chip and Patch and stroke their necks with her small hands. She'd been around horses when Rush had his veterinary practice in Phoenix, but she was amazed at the size of the two huge draft animals. "They're so big! Do they really pull Santa's sleigh?" she asked.

"In the parade, they do."

"But they can't pull the sleigh on Christmas Eve 'cause they're too big to fly. That's why Santa needs reindeer. Right, Daddy?"

"Smart thinking." Rush wasn't about to shoot down her childish belief. She would figure things out for herself when she was older.

"Can we play in the snow now?" she asked as he carried her back toward the house.

"Maybe later." Much as he wanted to spend time

with Clara, Rush had appointments to keep—a follow-up on a pregnant mare, a litter of puppies that needed vaccinations, and a milk cow with an abscessed leg. And that was only for starters. He had yet to reply to the messages that had come in while he was away. He couldn't let his work slide when people needed him. And he couldn't ask his partners to watch her during this busy season.

"How would you like to ride around with me while I do my work?" he asked her. "You'll get to see some animals."

She sighed. After all, she'd spent most of yesterday in the Hummer. But Rush could tell she wanted to please him. "Okay. But I really want to play in the snow."

"You'll need warm clothes to play in the snow. For now, let's go inside." Rush carried her into the house, set her on the couch, unwrapped the blanket, and took her coat. In her fuzzy sweater and tutu skirt, with her ragged ponytail askew, she was an adorable waif. But how could he show up at his clients' homes with a little ragamuffin who looked like a candidate for the child welfare office?

"We'll need to change your clothes and do your hair before we go," he said. "Let's see what you've got in your suitcase." He followed her into her tent and sat on the sleeping bag while she opened her suitcase. Finding her something to wear shouldn't be a problem, Rush told himself. Surely Annie would have packed some sensible clothes for her.

One by one, she lifted out the contents of the suitcase—a pink Sleeping Beauty princess gown, complete with a little tiara; the black-cat costume she'd worn last year on Halloween; a red Ariel wig and a mermaid tail; a pair of child-size high-heeled sandals with elastic straps; a polka-dot swimsuit; a Minnie Mouse nightgown, and several toy-sized outfits for Snowflake. No socks. No underwear. No pants or coveralls. No toothbrush or hairbrush. Rush's heart sank.

"Did you pack your suitcase all by yourself, Clara?" he asked her.

"Uh-huh. Annie was crying 'cause her dad is sick, so I told her I could do it." She grinned, her gaze seeking his approval. "And I did. See, I brought all my favorite things. Can I wear my princess dress to go in the car with you?"

Rush surrendered with a shrug. Why not, as long as she was happy? "Sure," he said. "But if you're going to go outside and play in the snow you'll need some new clothes."

Clara clapped her hands. "We can go shopping! I love shopping. When can we go?"

Now what? Rush knew nothing about shopping for a little girl. How would he know what to choose? And how was he going to help her try things on in the women's dressing room?

"When can we go shopping, Daddy?" Clara repeated her question, more urgently this time.

Rush did his best to stall. "I'll have to figure that out. I've never shopped for girl things. I might need to get some help."

"Why don't you call Maggie?" Travis had come into the house just in time to overhear their conversation. "I told her about your getting Clara for the holidays. She said to let her know if you need anything. Clothes shopping for a little girl should be right up her alley."

"But has she got time?" Rush asked. "Being mayor isn't a job you can just walk away from, especially with the Christmas celebration coming up."

"You'll never know unless you ask. I'll give her a call." Travis whipped out his cell phone and walked into the kitchen with it.

"Tell her I'll give her my credit card," Rush called after him.

"No problem." The rest of Travis's words were muffled as he made the call. A few minutes later, he came back into the living room.

"Maggie says she's got meetings scheduled for most of the day. But she wants to help. She'll make some calls and get back to you."

"I really don't want to put her out—" Rush began, but Travis cut him off.

"You're not putting her out. She really wants to help. And when she makes up her mind to get something done, it'll get done. So just wait for it. You know Maggie."

With the court in recess for the holidays, Tracy was enjoying some time off. She still had paperwork to do and briefs to read, but she could do those things at home. This morning she'd slept late, awakened to feed Murphy and the still-nameless mama cat, and tuned in to a morning exercise program on TV.

When the session ended, she was sweating. She turned off the TV and stood in the middle of the floor, catching her breath and surveying her spotless house. She'd spent the past two days cleaning, and it showed—everything dusted, scrubbed, and in its place. But there wasn't a Christmas decoration in sight. The lights and ornaments she'd collected in the early years of her marriage, when Christmas was still magical, remained boxed in the attic, never to be used again. She couldn't bear to put them up, but she couldn't get rid of them, either. They held too many bittersweet memories.

She'd given up on Christmas for good, Tracy told herself. Last Christmas, her first without Steve, had been a nightmare of grief. This year would be easier. But nothing had changed. She was still alone, and still numb inside.

Maybe next year she could book a trip and get out of Branding Iron for the holiday season. Hawaii might be nice. Or even someplace like Costa Rica. But this year she had Murphy, who couldn't be left alone, and she still had to decide what to do with the calico cat and her growing kittens. Rush had offered to come by and check on her animals. But she hadn't heard from him. Maybe he'd given up on her and moved on. Fine. It wasn't as if she'd encouraged the handsome vet.

Right now, it was time to get herself together for the day. Maybe she could make batches of cookies, deliver them to her neighbors, and drop them off at the courthouse for her coworkers. Or maybe she'd call the volunteer agency in Cottonwood Springs and see if they could use her help. Anything to boost her sagging spirits.

She had just stepped out of the shower when the phone rang. The call was from the mayor's office. Tracy picked up to hear Maggie's cheerful voice.

"Hi, Tracy. How are you enjoying your time off?"

"Actually, I'm finding it a challenge to keep busy," Tracy said.

Maggie chuckled. "In that case, I can help you out. I need a favor—a personal favor." She paused, as if waiting for a reply that didn't come. "Hear me out before you answer. I'm really hoping you'll say yes."

"All right, I'm listening." Tracy liked the woman, who was the closest thing she had to a girlfriend. But Maggie could be pushy when she needed to get something done—which made her an excellent mayor.

"When was the last time you talked to Rush?" Maggie asked.

Tracy willed herself to ignore the skip of her pulse. She'd dismissed Rush as a lost cause. But the old stirrings were still there. "Not for a while. Maybe a couple of weeks."

"How much has he told you about his divorce?"

"He mentioned it once—that his ex had married her old flame, and that they had a daughter. Nothing more than that."

"The little girl's actually his stepdaughter," Maggie said. "It's a long, sad story. But to cut to the chase, because of a family emergency, he has her for the holidays. She's four. I haven't met her, but Travis says she's a little doll. Rush adores her."

"And the favor?" Whatever it was, Tracy had a feeling her heart would be put at risk. Red flags went up.

"Again, it's a long story," Maggie said. "Evidently, she packed her own suitcase, mostly with princess costumes. She doesn't have anything practical to wear on the ranch. She needs somebody to take her girl-shopping, with Rush's credit card, and buy her some clothes."

"Rush asked you to do it?"

"No, Travis did. He told me the story. I would've been happy to help, but I'll be in meetings most of the day. So I was hoping . . ."

"That I would do it." Tracy wasn't fooled. Maggie had been trying to get her and Rush together. This time she'd come up with a legitimate reason.

Maggie seemed to sense her hesitation. "If there's any reason you don't want to . . ."

"No, of course, I'll do it. Let me know what arrangement would work best." How could she say no? She'd already told Maggie that she wasn't busy. And she owed Rush a favor for helping with her animals. Things might be a little awkward at first, but what could be more fun than clothes shopping with a cute little girl?

Especially if she could forget that she might never have another chance.

"Thanks, you're an angel," Maggie said. "Let me call the ranch and get back to you."

A few minutes later, Maggie called again. By then Tracy had dressed in jeans and a sweater and combed the tangles out of her freshly washed hair.

"All set," Maggie said. "Rush just got an emergency call. He'll have to leave Clara with Travis. If you don't mind driving out to the ranch to pick her up, his credit card will be there for you. Once he's finished with his calls, he'll stop by your place and get her. Will that work for you?"

"That should be fine." Tracy had met Travis and knew the way to the ranch. But she couldn't help but wonder if Rush was avoiding her. Or was it Maggie's ill-disguised matchmaking he was avoiding? At least he'd be coming by her house later on. But Tracy never knew what to expect from him. He was a difficult man to read—but then, she was no open book herself.

After promising to pick up the little girl in forty-five minutes, Tracy finished doing her hair and makeup, checked on Mama Cat and her lively brood in their box, and paused in the living room to pet Murphy and give him his meds.

Her gaze lingered on the framed photo, taken on a Galveston beach with a younger, more active Murphy. Fit and smiling in their swimsuits, she and Steve looked like a poster for the perfect young American family—with a dog in place of a child.

A shadow darkened Tracy's thoughts as she remembered what the photo hadn't shown—the doctor visits, the temperature charts, the fertility drugs, and the disappointments, month after month. When Steve had been diagnosed with an inoperable brain tumor, the need for some part of him to go on had become urgent. But their time had run out—time made bitter by the reality that the fault wasn't with him; it was with her.

Chapter 6

Driving south on the highway, Tracy kept an eye out for the sign that said CHRISTMAS TREE RANCH. She'd heard people talk about the ranch and the beautiful, fresh Christmas trees that could be bought here and at Hank's Hardware. But she'd never visited the place. Last year, when they'd opened for business, she'd had no interest in buying a tree. She wouldn't be buying one this year, either, but that didn't mean she wasn't curious.

Face it, I'm curious about anything connected with Dr. J. T. Rushford.

After turning off the highway by the sign, she drove down the narrow lane and pulled through the open gate. The house, a dilapidated one-story frame with a broad front porch, certainly lacked a woman's touch. But someone had hung light strings along the roofline and wrapped them around the supports that held up the overhanging eave. Cut trees leaned against racks in the front yard. Tracy inhaled their fresh fragrance as she climbed out of the car. From somewhere beyond the rolling pastures and snow-covered hills came the whine of a chainsaw biting into wood.

Several vehicles were parked in the side yard. Tracy didn't see Rush's Hummer, but she'd already been told that he'd had an emergency call. Never mind, Rush wasn't the reason she'd agreed to come here.

Travis came out onto the porch to greet her. She'd met him a few months ago when he'd come by the city building to take Maggie to lunch. Maggie had hit the jackpot with the tall, soft-spoken ranch owner. The two of them seemed to be made for each other.

"Hi, Tracy," he said. "Have you come to pick up the princess?"

"If she's ready."

"Oh, she's ready, all right. She's been over the moon about meeting you and shopping for new clothes. Come on in and meet her."

Tracy mounted the porch and walked through the door he opened for her. The little girl who stood in the living room was dressed as Disney's Sleeping Beauty in a pink princess gown, with high-heeled plastic sandals on her feet and a rhinestone tiara on her pretty head. With dark hair and big, dark eyes, she looked as if she'd stepped out of a fairy tale.

She wasn't exactly dressed for a trip to Shop Mart, but as long as she was happy and got what she needed, Tracy was willing to play the game.

Spreading invisible skirts, Tracy dropped a curtsy. "Your Highness," she murmured.

The little girl giggled. "That's not my name. My name is Clara."

Tracy rose, a bit awkwardly, from her curtsy. "I'm Tracy, Clara. I've come to take you shopping. Are you ready to go?"

"Uh-huh. I just need my coat. It's in my tent." Turning, she headed for a blue nylon dome tent that was pitched in the living room. "Do you like my tent? I'm camping out."

"What a good idea," Tracy said. "You won't even get cold at night, or be kept awake by coyotes."

Clara unzipped the tent and stepped inside. While she was rummaging for her coat, Travis handed Tracy a credit card. "Rush says the sky's the limit," he said. "But she'll need a warmer coat and some boots and gloves, as well as the basics like jeans, underwear, and socks."

"Leave it to me," Tracy said. "I'll get her everything she needs, and we'll have a good time."

"Oh, one more thing." Travis picked up a booster seat that had been left on a chair. "Rush wanted to make sure you had this in your car. If you don't mind waiting a minute, I'll go out and install it in your backseat."

He picked up the seat and strode out to her car. Maggie had mentioned that he was a former highway patrolman. It made sense that he'd be safety-conscious. But he'd seemed genuinely concerned about getting Clara the right clothes, too. He and Maggie would make wonderful parents, Tracy thought. With luck, they'd get married and have a big, happy family.

Rush, too, seemed to have the makings of a

good father. Tracy had seen for herself that he was gentle, kind, and responsible. Maggie had passed on Travis's comment that he adored his little step-daughter, even though she wasn't his biological child. Maggie had hinted that there was more to the story. But unless Rush chose to tell her, that was none of her business, Tracy reminded herself.

Surely, Rush would want children of his own someday. That would put her out of the running from the get-go. Besides, she and Rush barely knew each other. Today she was repaying a favor. That was all.

Clara emerged from the tent wearing her blue, quilted coat, which looked slightly lopsided because of the way she'd buttoned it. Turning, she zipped the tent flap shut. "If I leave it open, Bucket could come in all wet and dirty and roll around on my bed," she explained. "Okay, I'm ready to go shopping now."

Tracy looked her up and down, from her shiny tiara and misbuttoned coat to her long princess skirt and plastic high-heeled sandals. She looked like an adorable misfit, but everything was manageable except the shoes. Those shoes would have to go.

"Don't you have any warmer shoes, Clara?" she asked. "You'll freeze your toes in those sandals."

"I've got sneakers," she said. "But these are my princess shoes. Princesses don't wear sneakers."

Little fashionista. Hiding a smile, Tracy tried to look stern.

"It's snowy outside. And the floors inside the

store are slippery. You could fall down and get hurt in your princess shoes. If you wear them, you won't be able to walk around. I'll have to carry you like a baby."

Those last few words seemed to hit home. Clara sighed. "Okay. I'll wear my sneakers. But can we take my princess shoes with us?"

"Sure." Tracy waited while Clara unzipped the tent flap, climbed inside, and emerged minutes later with her high heels in one hand and her little sneakers on the wrong feet. As she closed the tent flap again, Tracy slipped the credit card into her purse and glanced outside to make sure Travis had finished installing the booster seat.

"Are you ready to go?" she asked Clara.

The little girl clapped her hands. "Ready! It's time to shop till we drop!"

Clara insisted that she knew how to fasten herself into the booster seat. Tracy watched as she struggled with the straps and buckles. After several tries, she finally got it right.

"Good for you!" Tracy exclaimed. "You kept trying, and you didn't give up."

"I told you I could do it," Clara said. "My daddy showed me how. I just had to remember."

As Tracy climbed into the car, a four-wheeler ATV rolled into sight along a snow-packed wagon road that came from the far side of the ranch. It was pulling a two-wheeled trailer loaded with fresh Christmas trees. The driver gave her a friendly wave. Clara waved back. "That's Conner," she said. "He's a real cowboy. He even rode bulls in the rodeo. And that dog sitting by him is Bucket."

Tracy returned the wave as she backed the car out of the driveway. She hadn't met Conner Branch, but she'd certainly heard of him. Two of the women she worked with had dated him. Both had fallen hard for the man, but Conner had moved on, leaving behind a trail of broken hearts. According to one lady who'd given up on him, Conner was simply having too much fun to settle down.

As far as Tracy could tell, Travis was a one-woman man, Conner was a player, and Rush . . . Rush seemed to be a loner, with an air of brooding sadness about him. Maybe this adorable little girl had something to do with the reason why.

By the time Tracy had turned onto the highway, Clara was peppering her with questions.

"Do you know my daddy? His name is Rush."

"Not very well. We're just friends," Tracy said.

"Do you like him?"

"He's a very nice man."

"My mom says that Andre is my real daddy—she even had a doctor take a test. He stuck a stick inside my cheek. I guess he did the same thing to Andre, 'cause my mom said that the sticks came out the same. That meant that Andre was my father, and Rush had to go away."

Tracy's hands tightened around the steering wheel as the truth sank in. Rush's ex-wife hadn't just married her old flame. It appeared that they'd had an affair, and that he'd fathered her child—a child that Rush had believed was his own until faced with the proof of the DNA test.

What a monstrous betrayal.

"That must have been very sad for you," she said to Clara.

"It was." Clara sounded older than her years. "I cried a lot. But now I've figured it out."

"What did you figure out?"

"Andre is my father. But he isn't my daddy."

"Why is that, Clara?" Tracy could guess the answer to her question, but she wanted to hear it.

"Andre doesn't play with me. He doesn't read me stories in funny voices. He doesn't tuck me in at night or make me pancakes for supper. Daddies do those things."

"Did Rush do those things?"

"Uh-huh. He's the best daddy in the world. But he can't come to our house 'cause Mom is married to Andre now."

"But you could come here, right?"

"I'm not supposed to. I just got to come here 'cause Mom and Andre went away on a big boat."

"A cruise, you mean?"

"Uh-huh."

"Your parents went off and left you for Christmas?" That poor little girl. Her parents didn't deserve her.

"Uh-huh. They left me with Cecil and Annie. But then Annie's father got sick, so I got to go to my daddy—my *real* daddy."

Tracy hadn't understood everything Clara had told her, but what she could piece together told a heartbreaking story—a loving father and a trusting little girl ripped apart when a terrible secret had come to light. She could sympathize, but there was no way to change what had happened.

It came as a relief to see the entrance sign for Shop Mart just ahead on the right. When Maggie had asked Tracy to take Rush's little girl shopping, caution had warned her to keep her distance. But now that she understood the connection between Rush and the child who still loved him, she found herself being pulled from safety like a swimmer in a riptide.

Shop Mart, the only big-box store in the county, was a magnet for Christmas shoppers. The lot was so full that Tracy had to park in the last row, in the far corner. "Let's go," she said, slinging her purse on her shoulder and lifting Clara out of her seat. Half-melted slush coated the asphalt, splattering her as a car drove past. Tracy enfolded the little girl in the front of her coat, trying to shield her.

"I'll have to carry you into the store," she said. "It's too cold and wet out here for your princess gown."

Clara clung to her. "Is this winter?" she asked. "We don't have winter in Phoenix. It's warm all the time."

"This is a Texas winter," Tracy said. "Sometimes it's cold and snowy like this. Sometimes it rains. Sometimes it's warm and dry, even in December. Texas weather is full of surprises."

"Does Santa Claus come when it's warm?"

"Does he come to Phoenix?"

"I guess he just figures that out. Santa is pretty

smart." Clara gazed past the sea of cars to where people were swarming into the store entrance. "Santa comes to our Mall in Phoenix. Kids sit on his lap and tell him what they want for Christmas. Will Santa come to this store?"

"Not this store," Tracy said. "He doesn't come to Branding Iron until the Christmas parade."

"Then how will he know what kids want?"

Tracy scrambled for an answer. "They write letters and mail them at the post office."

"Can I write a letter? I'll need help 'cause I can't write much. Just my name. Annie taught me that."

"Sure," Tracy said. "After we buy clothes, you're going to my house to wait for your dad. I'll help you then."

They passed through the automatic doors and into the crowded store. "Stay close to me," Tracy said, putting Clara down. "It's crowded in here. I wouldn't want us to get separated."

"Take this." Clara unfastened her coat and thrust it up at Tracy. "I want people to see my princess dress."

"Fine." Tracy tucked the coat under her arm, anchored Clara's tiara, and looked around for an empty shopping cart. There was just one in the line. Clasping Clara's hand, she lunged and grabbed it just ahead of a large woman who glowered at her and moved away. Tracy could feel a headache coming on. Buying clothes would be fun. But fighting her way through mobs of Christmas shoppers would be exhausting.

"I know what, let's put you in here." She lifted

Clara into the cart and dropped the coat in after her. "That's better. Now I won't lose you. You'll look like a princess riding in her coach."

"Can I stand up?"

"You'll be safer sitting down. If somebody bumps into us, you could fall. Okay?"

"Okay." She sat on her coat, carefully spreading her skirt and adjusting her tiara. Tracy took a moment to spot the overhead sign that said CHILDREN'S WEAR. Pushing through the crowd, she headed in that direction.

She soon found out why her shopping cart had been the last one left. One damaged wheel made a squealing sound with each rotation, followed by a plop. *Squeal, plop. Squeal, plop.*

People turned their heads toward the sound. Clara smiled and gave them a perfect royal princess wave. Many of them smiled back at her, or even clapped.

Most of them were strangers. Glancing around, Tracy realized how few people she actually knew, even after more than five years in Branding Iron. While Steve had been alive, especially in that final year, her whole existence had revolved around her marriage and her job. After his death, their mutual friends, most of them in Cottonwood Springs, had drifted away, leaving her marooned by grief and loneliness. The townspeople who'd passed through her court saw her as a judge, not a friend. Even the men and women she worked with went back to their own lives at the end of the day—lives that didn't include her.

Tracy knew better than to feel sorry for herself.

If she was alone, it was because she'd failed to reach out to people like Maggie, who could be her friends. Making changes would be up to her. But where and how to begin—that was the question she had yet to face.

A familiar figure caught her eye and waved. Tall, handsome Ben Marsden was the county sheriff. His wife, Jessica, ran the local bed and breakfast with her mother, Francine, as a partner. Francine, she knew, was the girlfriend of Hank, who ran the hardware store and played Santa in the annual Christmas parade—and Hank was the father of Travis, who was one of Rush's partners.

Everyone in Branding Iron seemed to be connected. The place was a true community, a warm refuge for those who called it home. But Tracy had never felt like anything but an outsider—which was nobody's fault but her own.

The sheriff made his way through the crowd to her cart. His face broke into a smile as he caught sight of Clara. "Well, look at you," he said. "If I'd known that a real princess was coming to town, I'd have dressed up. Do I bow or shake hands?"

Clara giggled and held out a hand, which was almost lost in Ben's big fist. "My name is Clara," she said.

"Princess Clara to you," Tracy added.

"Howdy, Princess Clara, my name's Ben." He released her hand with a reassuring smile. "I have my own little princess at home. Her name's Violet. She's two, and I've come to buy her some pajamas. What color do you think she'd like?"

"Pink," Clara said. "Pink is for girls. But maybe

you should get her some violet pajamas 'cause that's her name."

"Good advice." He turned to Tracy with a questioning look. "Is she yours?"

"Hardly." Tracy shook her head. "Clara is Dr. Rushford's daughter. She's visiting her dad for the holidays, and she packed her own suitcase."

Ben grinned. "I can see what she brought."

"Rush is working today, so I got volunteered by Maggie to take Clara shopping and buy her some cowgirl clothes."

He looked down at Clara. "So, you're going to be a cowgirl princess."

"Uh-huh. Then I can play outside in the snow."

"Well, have fun." He turned to go, then glanced back at Tracy with a knowing look. "Rush, huh?"

Tracy didn't answer but she couldn't hide the flush of color that rose in her face. Denial, she knew, would only make matters worse. Had she already started a wave of gossip, showing up in town with Rush's little girl?

Ben chuckled as he walked away. Blast it, why did everybody have to be a matchmaker?

Struggling to ignore the persistent *squeal, plop* of the cart wheel, she pushed ahead to the racks of children's clothing.

"Let's shop till we drop." Clara repeated the phrase that she'd probably learned from her mother.

Tracy lifted the little girl out of the cart. "All right, Princess Clara. Lead the way."

* * *

Choosing a warm, hooded parka, snow boots, a matching knit cap and mittens, two pairs of jeans and two pairs of stretch pants, four warm shirts, a fleece vest, and a week's worth of socks and underwear took Clara and Tracy more than two hours. Shopping with Clara was fun, but the little girl had definite tastes and a strong will. Everything had to be the right color and the right style. And everything needed to be tried on and critically viewed in front of a mirror.

By the time they headed for the long checkout lines, with Clara in her princess costume once more, Tracy was teetering on the brink of exhaustion. As they passed the bakery department, the mouth-watering aromas of cinnamon and fresh-baked dough drifted from behind the counter.

"I'm hungry," Clara said. "Please, can I have a cookie?"

"That sounds like a great idea, especially since you said please." Tracy pushed the cart up to the counter.

"What can I do for you?" The young blond woman behind the counter gave them a sunny smile. Katy Parker, who had Down syndrome, was the daughter of Connie and Silas Parker, who owned Branding Iron's only garage. A favorite in the town, she'd been working in the bakery for the past year.

Her eyes sparkled as she caught sight of Clara in her princess costume. "My goodness, it's a real, live princess!" she said. "What do princesses like to eat?"

"Just one cookie," Tracy said. "She can choose. No need for a bag."

Clara surveyed the array of Christmas cookies, taking her time while Tracy fished for change in her purse. At last the little girl pointed to a row of iced gingerbread men. "I'd like one of those, please."

Katy used a square of tissue to pick up the cookie and pass it across the counter to Clara. "I made this myself. Special for little princesses." She waved away Tracy's attempt to pay. "No, don't worry about it. Have a merry Christmas."

"Bye. Thanks for the cookie." Clara gave Katy a princess wave as they left the bakery behind. "I like that lady," she said. "She looks like a pixie. Maybe she really is."

"A pixie who bakes. I like that idea. Anyway, she's very nice, isn't she?" An explanation of Down syndrome was more than the little girl would understand. Today she'd go with Clara's version. Katy did resemble a pretty little pixie.

Tracy pushed the cart away toward the nearest checkout line. Clara munched the gingerbread man, nibbling off the feet, the arms, and finally the head. By the time they reached the checkout stand, the cookie was gone, and she had a ring of gingerbread and icing around her mouth.

The checkout would put a dent in Rush's credit card account, Tracy mused as she wheeled the cart across the slushy parking lot. But Travis had passed on the word that the sky was the limit. She could only hope Rush had meant what he'd said.

"Where are we going now?" Clara asked as Tracy lifted her into the booster seat and waited while she fastened the straps.

"We're going to my house to wait for your dad. Would you like that?"

"Uh-huh. Have you got a Christmas tree?" Clara looked tired.

"No Christmas tree. But I've got something else you'll like."

"What is it?"

"It's a surprise. You'll see." Tracy pushed the cart to the nearest stand and climbed into her car. Her house was only a few minutes away. If Rush didn't show up soon, she would make a simple lunch. After that, if Clara wasn't ready for a nap, maybe they could make some cookies for her to take back to the ranch.

Rush, huh?

Ben's words, and his knowing look, lingered in her memory. Why did people keep trying to make her and Rush into a couple? They were just friends, and barely that.

But what would it be like, snuggling in front of the fire, feeling his arms around her, tasting long, delicious kisses?

Stop it! Tracy gave herself a mental slap as she pulled the car into the driveway. Fantasizing was a waste of time, especially when nothing was going to happen.

She helped Clara out of the car and carried her to the front porch. Then she went back for the shopping bags before opening the front door. "I have a big dog," she warned Clara. "His name's Murphy. He's old and gentle, so you don't have to be afraid of him."

"I'm not afraid of dogs. We've got a dog at the ranch. His name's Bucket. You saw him with Conner." Clara walked into the living room. Murphy, still in his bed, raised his head and thumped his tail. With a little murmur, she ran to him and wrapped her arms around his neck. "Hi, Murphy," she said, stroking the old pit bull's massive head. "Is he the surprise?" she asked, looking back at Tracy.

"Maybe part of it. But no, there's more. First, you need the bathroom. You haven't gone all morning. It's just down this hall. Okay?"

"Okay." Clara headed in the direction she pointed. "Don't worry, I don't need any help. I'm a big girl."

"Fine. Wash your hands when you're done."

"I know." She went into the bathroom. As the door closed behind her, Tracy's phone rang.

Tracy snatched the ringing phone out of her purse. The caller was Rush. "Hi," she said. "We just got home. Clara's been great, but wait till you get your credit card bill!"

He laughed, a sound that sent warmth flowing to the tips of her toes. "She's got expensive taste. Probably gets it from her mother. Is she doing all right?"

"Fine. She's in the bathroom right now. Do you want to talk to her?"

"No, that's all right. Just to you," he said. "I'm

here with a mare who's about to deliver, so I'll be a while yet, maybe another couple of hours. Sorry, I didn't plan on this. Can I impose on you a little longer?"

"It's no imposition," Tracy said. "Take as long as you need. I'm enjoying her."

"Thanks. I owe you big-time for this. I'd like the chance to repay you."

Tracy's pulse slammed. Was the man about to ask her out on a date? A mindless panic seized her. It was too soon. She liked him, maybe too much, but she wasn't ready. "No need to pay me back. I'm enjoying your little girl. And you've already done so much, helping me with my pets and fixing my sink."

"Well, then, maybe—"

An urgent voice in the background interrupted him. "Sounds like it's time. Gotta go," he said, ending the call.

Through the bathroom door, she could hear the toilet flush and the sound of running water. A moment later, Clara opened the door. "All done," she said. "Now can you show me the surprise?"

"In a minute," Tracy said. "I just talked to your dad. He won't be here until sometime after lunch. Wouldn't you like to put some of your new play clothes on now? We could play in the snow after we eat, unless you'd rather stay in and make cookies."

She shook her tiara-crowned head. "I want to see the surprise now."

"All right. Just follow me." Tracy led the way to

the laundry room door at the end of the hall. "Go on in," she said, opening the door. "Climb on the chair and look down into that big box."

Lifting the skirt of her princess gown, she put a foot on the cross brace of the chair and climbed onto the seat. Her breath caught as she saw the kittens in the box.

"Oh . . ." she whispered. "Can I hold them?"

"Is the mother cat with them?" Tracy asked.

"She is. She's feeding her babies." Clara giggled. "Oh, they're so cute! They're doing this with their little paws." She made kneading motions with her fingers.

"Let's leave the kittens until they've finished eating," Tracy said. "Then you can take them out of the box and hold them. For now, let's have some lunch. Do you like grilled cheese sandwiches?"

"Uh-huh."

"Come on, you can help me make them."

Clara climbed down from the chair and followed Tracy into the kitchen. "Do the kittens have names?" she asked.

"Not yet. Would you like to name them?" Tracy pulled a stool close to the counter and boosted her onto it.

"Can I really name them?" She spread soft butter on the bread slices Tracy had laid out.

"You can name them for now. When they go to new homes, their new owners might want to choose their own names."

"When do they go to new homes?"

"Not yet. They still need their mother. But in a

couple of weeks, when they're old enough to eat solid food, they'll be ready to go."

"That's so sad. Won't their mom miss them?" Clara helped Tracy lay the cheese slices on the bread.

"Maybe for a little while," Tracy said. "But she'll be all right. Mother cats don't keep their babies a long time like people do."

"What's the mom's name?" Clara watched Tracy lay the sandwiches on the heated skillet.

"She doesn't have a name. I just call her Mama Cat."

"But why doesn't she have a name?"

"Because I don't plan to keep her after her babies are gone."

Clara looked shocked. "But that would be mean, just to put her out. . . . She'd be so sad. And she might be hungry and cold."

Tracy was beginning to feel like a monster. Clara was right. She hadn't wanted a cat, but the sweet calico mother had found a home with her.

"You've got to keep her," Clara said as Tracy turned the sandwiches with a spatula.

"I know." Tracy sighed as one more chink opened in the armor she'd placed around her heart. "As long as she's going to be mine, would you like to give her a name, too? A for-keeps name this time."

Clara grinned and nodded. "Don't worry, I'll come up with a good one."

Tracy cut the sandwiches into triangles, put them on a plate, and poured two glasses of milk. Life was full of surprises. Just like that, because of a little girl's wisdom, a needy stray cat had become family.

When she'd agreed to help Rush and his daughter, she'd sensed that she was putting her fragile emotions at risk. Now that she'd learned the truth about their tragic relationship, those emotions were threatening to wash through her defenses and sweep her away.

But she couldn't let that happen. She'd had enough trauma in her life. The last thing she wanted was more.

Chapter 7

After lunch, Tracy spread a blanket on the living room floor and put the kittens on it so Clara could play with them. The mother cat took a break to eat and use the litter box before curling up in a nearby chair to keep an eye on her babies. Murphy slept on, undisturbed by the cats or the little girl's happy chatter.

At about six weeks, the kittens were old enough to play and explore. They climbed onto Clara's shoulders, chased a string, nibbled her fingers, and purred in her arms. The little girl was all smiles and giggles.

"Are they boys or girls?" she asked Tracy.

"It's hard to tell when they're so little. But I think the little tabby is the only girl. The rest are boys."

"I've got names for them," Clara said, making a cradle with her skirt and putting the four kittens in it. "The black one is Midnight. The orange one is

Ginger. The striped one is Tiger. And this one . . ."
She picked up the little white cat and kissed its
head. "This one is Snowflake, like my toy cat back
at the ranch. They look just the same. But this
Snowflake is real. I love them all, but I love him
the most."

"Those names are perfect," Tracy said. "Have
you thought of a good name for their mother?"

"Uh-huh. She has all the cat colors—white and
black and orange. So, I think you should call her
Rainbow."

"Rainbow. I like it." Tracy had been prepared to
accept any name, even a silly one. But Clara had
made a good choice.

Leaning over the chair, she stroked the calico
mother's soft fur. "How do you like your new name,
Rainbow?" she asked.

Clara laughed. "Listen to her. She's purring.
She likes it."

Rainbow jumped down from the chair, walked
over to Clara, and gave an insistent *meow.*

"I think she's telling you she wants her babies
back," Tracy said. "Let's put the kittens in their
box for now. We don't want them to get too tired."

They carried the kittens back to the laundry
room and lowered them gently into the box. Rainbow jumped in after them, and they all settled
down for a nap.

"Now what?" Tracy asked. "Would you like to
change your clothes and play in the snow, or would
you rather stay in and make some cookies?"

Clara yawned. "Could I rest a little bit first?"

"That sounds like a good idea. Would you like to lie down on my bed under a nice warm blanket?"

"Just for a little while." Clara sounded sleepy. Tracy guided her to the bedroom, helped her onto the bed, and laid a pretty, quilted comforter over her.

"How's that? Cozy enough for a princess?"

"It's nice." Turning onto her side, she noticed Steve's photo on the nightstand. "Who's that?" she asked.

"My husband. He died more than a year ago, but I keep the picture there to remember him."

"I saw another picture on your fireplace. Is that him, too?"

"Yes, with me and Murphy."

"I'm sorry he died. You must be really sad."

"I am, but only sometimes," Tracy said. "Now close your eyes and rest. If you need anything, I'll be close by. Just call me."

When Clara didn't reply, she tiptoed out of the room. A few minutes later, when she checked, the little girl was fast asleep.

Entertaining a four-year-old had taken a lot of energy. Tracy was ready for a nap herself. But Rush would be showing up soon. Surely, he'd have called if he was going to be much longer.

She'd tidied the kitchen and living room and was kneeling beside Murphy's bed, scratching the old dog's ears, when she heard a rap on the door. She pushed to her feet and hurried across the room to answer it.

Rush stood in the doorway, moisture glistening on his dark hair and on his down parka. When Tracy glanced past him, she saw that the sky had darkened with clouds, and a soft, light snow was falling.

"I'm glad you heard my knock," he said. "I didn't want to ring the bell in case Clara was napping. She used to go down about this time."

"Good thinking. She went to sleep a few minutes ago. You might want to leave her for a while." Tracy stepped aside to let him in and closed the door behind him.

"Actually, I was hoping you'd say that." He slipped out of his damp parka and hung it on the coatrack near the door. "It's been a while, Tracy. I can't thank you enough for taking Clara at the last minute. It can't have been convenient. I understand that you might've had other plans."

"Not really," Tracy said. "Shopping with her was fun. But she's a little fashionista. She refused to settle for anything less than exactly what she wanted." She pointed to the Shop Mart bags that were piled on the floor at the end of the couch. "And before I forget, here's your credit card." She fished in her purse, found the card, and handed it to him. "We put some mileage on it today."

His laugh was deep and real. Tracy felt its warmth trickling through her like mulled cider on a cold day. "That doesn't surprise me," he said. "And don't worry about running up my balance. Making that little girl happy is at the top of my list."

Tracy turned away to hide a surge of emotion. So much love for a child who wasn't even his. What a great father he would be to his own children when the time came.

All the more reason to keep her distance.

Recognizing a friend, Murphy hauled himself to his feet and ambled over to meet Rush. "Hello, old boy, let's see how you're doing." Rush rubbed the elderly dog's ears while he examined his eyes. "No change there."

"But he's walking better, isn't he?" Tracy asked hopefully.

"A little, maybe. He does seem more comfortable, but at his age, you can't expect miracles." Rush ran a hand down the bony old back. "Good boy. You can go back to bed now."

Tracy didn't want to talk about where Murphy's condition was leading. "Are you hungry? I make a killer grilled cheese sandwich—especially the grown-up version."

"Thanks. I'll bet you do." He followed her into the kitchen and seated himself at the table, watching her as she assembled sliced bread, butter, bacon, chopped green peppers, and a thick slab of aged, sharp cheddar.

"Your daughter loved the kittens," she said, making conversation. "I think they wore each other out playing. Don't be surprised if she asks you for the white one."

Rush shook his head. "If she does, I'll have to say no. I'd like to give her a pet, but she wouldn't be able to take it home with her. Andre, her new father, is allergic." He caught himself, as if realizing he might have revealed too much.

It was time for Tracy to stop pretending that she didn't know the truth. She turned to face him.

"Clara told me what happened back in Phoenix," she said. "There were things she didn't understand, and I had to piece her story together, but I know that you found out she was another man's child. That must have been terrible for you."

He exhaled, as if relieved that she knew. "It was. Still is. I tried to get joint custody, or at least visitation rights, but between my ex's pricey lawyers and the fact that I'm not even Clara's blood relative, I didn't have a prayer. I thought it might be best to leave her and hope that she'd forget me. But now . . . it might have been kinder if I'd refused to take her."

"She's never forgotten you," Tracy said. "Let me pass on something she told me in the car. She said that Andre was her father, but that you would always be her daddy."

"Oh, hell." His jaw tightened as he struggled to control his emotions. "Let's talk about something else while you finish that sandwich."

"Yes, good idea." She stacked the layers of the sandwich and laid it on the heated griddle. The butter sizzled. Aromas of bacon and melting cheese drifted through the kitchen. "How's the Christmas tree business doing?" She turned the sandwich over to toast it on the other side.

"Now there's a safe subject. For what it's worth, between what the ranch sells and what we take to Hank's lot, it's doing fine. We should clear enough cash to fix up the house and have enough left over to cover the ranch expenses till spring." He looked down at the sandwich Tracy had set in front of him on a plate, with a linen napkin. "Wow, this looks good." He took a bite. "And it tastes like heaven. You do make a killer cheese sandwich, lady."

"I've got cold beer. It's good with grilled cheese." She took a can of Bud Light out of the fridge, popped the tab, and set it next to his plate. Then she sat down across from him.

"I could get used to this." He looked across the table, his eyes meeting hers, holding her gaze for a beat too long. "But something tells me I'd better not take things like this for granted."

Tracy tore her gaze away. "Another good idea," she murmured.

"I know you've resisted my repaying you for your help. But at least let me bring you one of our trees. This place could use a little Christmas cheer."

"That's very kind of you." Tracy felt the chill in her own voice. "But I gave up on Christmas after Steve died. It just didn't seem worth celebrating alone."

"I understand." At least he wasn't pushing the tree idea. "But how about dinner, or even lunch, no strings attached? There's a nice place on the way to Cottonwood Springs. Good steak and ribs."

"Yes, I know it. Logs and a big fireplace. Steve and I used to go there. It was our favorite place."

A shadow of frustration passed across his face and vanished. He was really just trying to be nice, Tracy told herself. Maybe she was being rude.

"Then here's an offer you can't refuse," he said. "The day after tomorrow is Saturday, the day of the weekly brunch at the bed and breakfast. Francine's cooking is sheer artistry—all you can eat, eggs and pancakes that literally float off the plate. I was planning to take Clara. We'd love to have you along as our guest."

Tracy had heard of the Saturday brunch at the B and B, as it was called. It was a popular gathering place for the whole town. Maybe that was why she'd never gone. She was a judge. How many people—those who'd been in her court—would see her and feel uncomfortable? Or was she just making an excuse because she didn't want to go alone?

"So how about it?" Rush asked. "Just brunch in a friendly place, with Clara along. No strings."

"That won't stop the gossip when people see us together," Tracy said. "Doesn't that bother you?"

Leaving the sandwich unfinished, he shoved his chair back from the table. "Tracy, I don't give a damn about the gossip," he said. "All I want is to do something nice for you. If that's too much of an imposition, I'll forget it."

She'd pushed him too far, and for no good reason, Tracy realized. He wasn't even asking her for a date, just breakfast with him and his daughter. The least she could do was apologize and say yes.

"No, it's all right," she said. "It's a very nice invitation and I'll accept it. It's just that being a judge in a small town . . ."

"This is the twenty-first century. You're not going to get a scarlet *A* on your chest if you have breakfast with a respectable man and his daughter. And you don't need to keep punishing yourself because you lost a husband you still love. I just want to be your friend, that's all, Tracy."

She glanced down at her hands for a moment, knowing the next move was up to her.

"Thank you for that trip to the woodshed," she said. "I could use a friend. Now please finish your lunch."

He moved his chair closer to the table once more. "Thanks. This is too good to go to waste. For what it's worth, the same goes for you."

"No comment." She lowered her gaze a moment to hide the hated blush. "What time should I be ready on Saturday?"

"The place gets crowded around nine o'clock. How about eight-thirty? That should give me time to finish the chores and have Clara ready."

"Good luck getting her into her new clothes. She's still in her princess gown."

"She'll be fine."

"She's a darling little girl," Tracy said. "I can tell she still loves you. According to her, Andre doesn't give her much attention."

"That doesn't surprise me. I don't know Andre very well, but he strikes me as something of a narcissist. Everything's about him. Now shut me up before I get carried away."

"What about her mother?"

"The two of them just went off on a cruise and left Clara with the hired help—over Christmas. Something about working on their marriage. I think that says it all. I tried to get visitation rights, but the two-bit lawyer who was all I could afford told me it was a lost cause. That's why I want to make the most of this surprise visit. I can't count on seeing her again until she's eighteen. As things stand, all I can do while she's here is give her a few happy memories."

When Rush had finished his lunch, Tracy carried his plate to the sink. She'd promised herself that she wouldn't get involved in Rush's problems. But his situation was more than unfair. It was tragic. Maybe there was nothing she could do. But at least she could research Arizona child custody laws in case there was some loophole Rush's second-rate lawyer had missed.

She wouldn't tell Rush what she was doing—not unless she found a real breakthrough. Otherwise, getting his hopes up would only be cruel.

Rush had risen from his place at the table. "You've put in a long morning helping me out. I should probably get Clara and give you a break. How long has she been asleep?"

"Maybe forty-five minutes. Is that enough time for a good nap?"

"It used to be. Show me where she is. I'll wake her."

"She's on my bed. You know the way."

"Yes, I do, thanks to your cat." He strode down the hall. When Tracy caught up with him, he was standing in the open bedroom door, as if hesitant to step inside. As Tracy looked past his shoulder she saw Clara asleep on the bed in her princess dress, partly covered by the quilt. Her eyes were closed, her lashes like dark velvet against her porcelain cheeks, her mouth a small pink rosebud.

"Now there's a sleeping beauty," he said softly. "I'm just grateful she's not old enough for Prince Charming."

"She's beautiful," Tracy said. "For now, her daddy can be her Prince Charming."

Or you could be mine if things were very different. Tracy willed the thought from her mind.

At the sound of voices, the little girl opened her eyes. "Hi, Daddy," she said.

"Hello, princess." Rush walked to the bed and picked her up. "Ready to go home?"

"Uh-huh. But first, put me down. I want to show you something."

As soon as her feet touched the floor, she was pulling at his hand, leading him on down the hall to the laundry room, and opening the door.

"Look, Daddy! Look in that big box!" She pulled him over to the box. Rush pretended to be surprised.

"Wow! Aren't they something!"

"I gave them all names," Clara said. "The babies are Midnight, Ginger, Tiger, and Snowflake. I love Snowflake best of all."

"What about the mother?" He gave Tracy a questioning glance.

"She has a name, too," Tracy said. "So, I guess that makes her officially my cat. Tell him what it is, Clara."

"I named her Rainbow 'cause she has all the cat colors," Clara said.

"Rainbow." Rush reached into the box and stroked the mother cat's head with a fingertip. "That's a perfect name."

"Tracy says that the kittens will need new homes soon. Do you think I could have Snowflake?" The hope in her big brown eyes would have melted a heart of granite. Tracy saw the sadness in Rush's gaze as he shook his head.

"I wish I could say yes, honey," he said. "But you can't take a cat home to Phoenix because Andre is allergic. And if we tried to keep Snowflake at the ranch, I don't know how well he'd get along with Bucket. That dog can be pretty rambunctious, even if he only wants to play."

Clara sighed. "Will you think about it, Daddy?"

"I'll think about it, but thinking might not be enough." He swept her up in his arms and carried her to the window. "Look! More snow! Who wants to go home and play in it?"

"Me!" Clara was easily distracted.

"I've got an idea," Tracy said. "Why don't we put on your new snow clothes here, before you leave? Then you'll be all dressed for the weather. Come on, you can choose what you want to wear."

"Yay!" She bounded into the living room where the shopping bags had been left and began dumping everything on the couch. After she'd chosen what she wanted, Tracy helped her change into a pink turtleneck shirt with a cat on the front, a blue fleece vest, and jeans. While Rush helped her with her socks and snow boots, Tracy folded the leftover clothes, including the princess costume and sneakers, and put them back in the shopping bags.

In her new outfit, Clara twirled like a miniature fashion model. "Do I look like a cowgirl now, Daddy?" she asked Rush.

"You look like the prettiest cowgirl in Texas," he said. "Now let's get your new parka and your mittens on, so we can go home and play in the snow."

"You'll need to get the booster seat out of my car," Tracy reminded him. "The doors are unlocked."

"Thanks for remembering. I'll do that when we go outside," he said.

Clara let him help her into her coat and pink kitty mittens. But she seemed distracted, as if she had something else on her mind. "Daddy," she said at last. "There's snow right outside. If we play here, Tracy can play with us. I bet she'd like that, wouldn't you, Tracy?"

Tracy had been looking forward to curling up on the sofa with a cup of hot herbal tea and a good book; but how could she say no?

"Tracy?" Rush gave her a knowing look. "If you feel like you've had enough—"

"No, it's fine. Go on out the kitchen door to the backyard. I'll get my coat and boots and join you."

Rush transferred the booster seat from Tracy's car into the Hummer. He and Clara were pelting each other with handfuls of powdery snow and laughing when Tracy came out onto the back porch. Rush was glad to see her. Having lived most of his life in Arizona, he had a lot to learn about playing in the snow.

Not to mention that she looked stunning in her scarlet wool coat and knit cap, with snowflakes swirling around her.

"I want to make a snowman!" Clara called out to her. "Can you show us how?"

Tracy came down the porch steps to join them. Picking up a handful of snow, she blew on it, scattering the flakes into the wind. "For snowman building, and things like snow forts and snowball fights, you need the kind of snow that sticks together," she said. "This snow is too fluffy. But I can show you some other games to play. Have you ever made snow angels?" She paused, glancing at their puzzled faces. "Watch. I'll show you."

She was already a snow angel, Rush thought. Her cheeks were becoming flushed with cold. Wind fluttered tendrils of golden hair around her face as she tromped to a fresh patch of snow, turned back toward them, grinned, and toppled over to land flat on her back.

For an instant, Rush was alarmed. Then he heard her laugh. "Just watch." She moved her arms up and down and her legs in and out, making a pattern in the snow. "Wow," she said, sounding a little breathless. "I haven't done this since I was in grade school! Now, somebody has to stand at my feet and pull me up."

Still laughing, she reached up for him. He caught her gloved hands, anchored his feet, and easily pulled her up. There, where she'd lain in the snow, was the imprint of a round head, sweeping wings, and a long skirt. "See?" Tracy said, "A perfect snow angel."

Clara clapped her hands, jumping up and down. "I want to make one, too!"

"Okay, I'll help you. Take my hands and lean back." Holding the small, mittened hands, Tracy eased the little girl onto her back in the snow. "Now, go for it!"

Clara had watched Tracy, so she knew what to do. She giggled, sweeping the snow with her arms and legs.

"Ready?" Tracy asked.

"Ready." She let Tracy pull her up. "Look!" she pointed, laughing. "It's a little snow angel. Like me."

"You did a great job. Are you cold?" Rush asked her.

"Kind of. But it was fun. Now it's your turn, Daddy. Make a big snow angel."

Rush hadn't planned on this. He was taller and heavier than Tracy or Clara. He would fall hard, and the snow wasn't deep enough to cushion the landing. But there was no way out except to be a good sport. As Clara and Tracy cheered him on, he found an undisturbed patch of snow and took a deep breath.

"Timber . . ." he shouted, as he keeled over backward and crashed like a fallen tree to the snowy ground. Slightly dazed, he lay still for a few seconds, watching the snowflakes swirl out of the pewter sky.

"Make an angel, Daddy!" Clara urged.

Rush moved his arms and legs, pushing away the cold snow with Clara laughing and cheering him on. "A little more! That's perfect, Daddy!"

Rush lay still. "Now, which one of you is strong enough to pull me up?" he joked.

"Hang on." Leaning over him, Tracy held out her hands. Rush gripped them as she braced her feet. Tracy might not be strong enough to lift him, but Rush knew that if he tried to help by getting his legs under him, that would spoil the snow angel for Clara.

Tracy met his eyes and nodded. Yes, they had to give it a try.

"Here goes," she said. "One . . . two . . . *three.*" On the count of three, she flung her full weight backward, straining to pull him to his feet. He was partway up when her boots slipped on an icy spot. She lost traction and might have toppled onto her rump if he'd let go, but his firm grip pulled her the other way. She pitched forward, landing on top of him. They collapsed together in the snow, laughing.

From somewhere beyond his sight, Clara was shrieking with laughter. But Rush's awareness was fixed on Tracy—her womanly curves pressing his body, her lovely lips so close to his that, if they'd been alone, he would have been tempted to kiss her.

Her hat had fallen off, freeing her hair to tumble around her face. Snow sparkled on her lashes; laughter danced in her hazel eyes.

Damn, but she was beautiful!

Rush knew that he wasn't ready to fall in love. He had too many unhealed wounds for that. But he wanted her—wanted her with a hunger he could feel in every part of his body.

And there wasn't a blasted thing he could do about it.

She rolled her weight off him and rose to her knees. Snow clung to her hair and her clothes. "I'm afraid there's not much left of your snow angel," she said, brushing away the snow almost too energetically.

"That's fine with me, as long as you're all right." He scrambled to his feet, heedless of the pattern in the snow. "Did I hurt you?"

"No . . . not at all." She sounded shaken. Had the fall scared her, or had she felt the same stirrings that he had—and been unsettled by them?

But never mind. Either way, he'd be a fool to assume anything.

"Do it again, Daddy!" Clara clapped her hands. "Make another snow angel!"

"Not on your life!" He picked her up, swung her high in his arms, and set her down as she giggled.

"Hey, your dad's snow angel doesn't look that bad," Tracy said to Clara. "Look at it. The skirt is a mess where he had to get up, but the head and wings are fine. I'll bet you and I could fix it. Want to try?"

Rush watched them work, patting and furrowing the snow. The two of them seemed so comfortable together, laughing and talking. Tracy would make a wonderful mother, he found himself thinking.

It had occurred to him to wonder why she had no children from her marriage. Maybe it was because she'd wanted to focus on her legal career. But that was none of his business.

The finished angel skirt was nothing to brag about. Mostly they'd just made it bigger. But Clara seemed satisfied, and that was all that mattered.

"All done, Daddy," she said, surveying their work. "Now we've got three angels—a mom angel, a little girl angel, and a big, messed-up dad angel. A family of angels." The way she looked from Rush to Tracy sent a message that couldn't be missed. Lord, was his little girl matchmaking too?

"I think that's enough snow games for now," Tracy said. Something told Rush she'd gotten the same message.

"We need to be going," he said. "Clara's getting cold. We'll just get her things from the house and be on our way."

"Can I say good-bye to Murphy and Rainbow and the kittens?" Clara asked.

"If you hurry. Stomp the snow off your boots so you won't track it into Tracy's kitchen."

"Okay!" She dashed for the house.

Tracy fell into step with Rush as they followed her across the yard. "Thanks for everything," he said. "She loves it here. I'm afraid she'll be begging me to let her come back."

"That would be fine," Tracy said. "She's delightful. We had a great time together."

"Are we still on for breakfast on Saturday?"

"I suppose so. I may be saying that against my better judgment, but I'm a woman of my word."

"Don't worry, you'll have fun."

They entered the house to find Clara standing

next to the box, holding the white kitten. "Be a good kitty, Snowflake." She kissed the kitten's velvety head. "Remember that I love you."

Rush swallowed the lump in his throat as he gathered up the shopping bags. "Come on, Clara, it's time to go," he said. "Put the kitten down and say thank you to Tracy. We'll see her Saturday morning when we go to breakfast."

Clara gave the kitten one more kiss and lowered it into the box with the others. "I'm coming, Daddy," she said. "Thank you, Tracy."

"You're very welcome," Tracy said. "We had fun, didn't we?"

"Uh-huh. Can I come again?"

"Sure, when it's a good time for both of us," Tracy said. "I'll see you two on Saturday"

Clara turned to go, then suddenly stopped. "Tracy, we forgot. You were going to help me write to Santa Claus."

"Next time," Tracy said. "Or maybe your dad can help you. Don't worry. We'll make sure Santa gets your letter."

Rush herded the little girl outside and boosted her into the Hummer. She waved at Tracy as they drove away. He could tell she'd had a good time. So had he. But when he thought about where all this was going, he could see nothing ahead but heartache. When the holidays were over, Clara would go home to a self-centered mother and an indifferent father, and probably a new set of caregivers. He might not see her again for years.

And what about him? Losing his little girl a second time was going to rip his heart out. And the prospect for anything lasting with Tracy wasn't much better. The beautiful judge was still wedded to her late husband. He would try to show her a good time. But he couldn't—and wouldn't—compete with a ghost.

For now, all he could do was make the most of every day, until the time came, as it surely would, when he'd be left with nothing but memories.

Chapter 8

Tracy stood on the front porch and watched the Hummer pull away from the curb. Clara waved at her through the rear side window. Smiling, Tracy waved back.

As the Hummer vanished into the swirling snow, she brushed the moisture from her coat and went back inside. Murphy raised his head and wagged his tail, greeting her as if she'd been gone for hours. Dropping her coat and sinking to her knees, she wrapped her arms around the old dog and pressed her face against his neck, inhaling his warm, familiar doggy aroma. A tear dampened her cheek.

Why did love have to hurt so much?

And why, when she knew the hurt would come, had she been foolish enough to open herself to more?

On Saturday, Rush and Clara would come by to take her to brunch at the B and B. If she had any sense, she would make an excuse, tell Rush that she was sick, or that she'd changed her mind. But that wouldn't keep Clara from begging to see the kittens. As long as the little girl was in town, Tracy would be trapped—a helpless passenger on the one-way train to heartbreak.

By Saturday morning, the storm had passed. A warm front had moved in, bringing sunny skies and snow melt. Water dripped from the eaves of the houses. Cars in the street splashed melting slush under their tires.

Tracy was waiting when Rush came to the door to pick her up. He steadied her on the slippery pavement as he helped her into the Hummer, where he'd left Clara, who was wearing her new jeans and vest.

"Did our snow angels melt?" Clara asked as Tracy fastened her seat belt.

"If they haven't already, they will," Tracy said. "The snow's going fast."

"Can we make more angels when it snows again?"

"*If* it snows again," Rush said, starting the engine.

"What if it doesn't snow?" Clara asked.

"Whatever the weather does, all we can do is make the best of it."

"But what if there isn't any snow for the parade?" Clara asked. "How will the horses pull the sleigh?"

"We can keep the sleigh on its flatbed trailer," Rush answered patiently. "The horses can pull it that way."

"But it wouldn't be real," Clara said. "Not without snow."

"It's too soon to worry about that," Tracy said. "The parade is two weeks away. There's plenty of time for another storm to move in."

"It's got to snow. It's just got to." Clara was quiet for a moment. "What's brunch?"

"What's *what?*" Rush was caught off guard by the sudden change of subject.

"You said we were going to brunch. What's that?"

Laughing, Tracy came to his rescue. "It's like breakfast and lunch put together—a late breakfast or an early lunch."

"Oh. Br . . . unch." Clara giggled. "Will I like it?"

"I know you like bacon and eggs and pancakes," Rush said. "Don't worry, you'll like it. And you'll get to meet some nice people, too."

"Can I tell them about the kittens, Tracy? You said they'd soon need new homes."

"That's not a bad idea," Tracy said. "Sure, go ahead and tell people if you want to."

"Okay. But I won't tell them about Snowflake. He's the one I love."

Rush glanced at Tracy, a dismayed look on his face. His precious little girl was setting herself up to have her heart broken.

The Branding Iron Bed and Breakfast was located in an old remodeled house just off Main Street. Most of the parking places were taken, but Rush managed to catch someone leaving and steer the Hummer into the empty spot. As he helped Tracy and Clara out of the vehicle, and the three

of them went up the sidewalk together, Tracy battled an attack of self-consciousness. This was a
small town. There was bound to be some gossip
when people saw her with Rush. But if that both-
ered her, she mustn't let it show. She would smile,
enjoy her meal, and leave as soon as possible.

Mouthwatering aromas surrounded them as
they opened the door. Inside, the spacious dining
room was decked out for Christmas with a glittering tree, small wreaths on the tables, and glowing
white lights strung from the ceiling. Traditional
Christmas music played in the background, turned
low enough to allow for conversation. Buffet tables
along the far wall were laden with warming pans
and trays of fruit, breads, and pastries that looked
and smelled heavenly.

Pretty Jess Marsden, the sheriff's wife, who ran
the place with her mother, took Rush's credit card
and showed them to an open table. "Nice to see
you, Tracy and Rush. And who is this young lady?"

"I'm Clara. Do you want a kitten? I know who
has some. They're really cute." Clara had her pitch
ready.

Jess smiled. "I hadn't thought about it," she
said. "But if I find anybody who'd like one, I'll
send them over."

"Wait! Somebody's got kittens?" Jess's mother,
Francine, bustling past with a pitcher of juice,
stopped in her tracks. "I've been pining for a cat
since my old Sergeant Pepper crossed the rainbow
bridge last summer. He was a ginger tabby. I'd love
another one like him."

"You may be in luck." Tracy spoke up. "The kittens are at my house. One of them, the feistiest one, is a little ginger. They're still nursing, but they should be ready to take home by Christmas."

Francine's smile broadened. "A little ginger, hmm? And feisty. I like that. Boy or girl?"

"He's a boy," Clara said. "And my daddy will give him free shots."

"Well, that wraps it up!" Francine said. "Save that precious boy for me, and let me know when I can come and get him." She hurried away, humming a Christmas tune.

"See? That was easy," Clara said.

"And Ginger will have a great home," Rush said. "Francine loved that old cat of hers. She'll love her new cat, too. Come on, let's get some food before you give away any more kittens."

At the buffet table, they loaded their plates with airy scrambled eggs, hash browns, bacon, sausage, and pancakes topped with strawberry sauce and whipped cream. When they returned to their table, cups of steaming coffee and a glass of orange juice for Clara were waiting for them.

"Good?" Rush asked Tracy.

"Mmm-hmmm." She was eating, but she nodded. Her hazel eyes sparkled, reflecting the Christmas lights that decorated the ceiling overhead.

"I told you it would be good." Rush liked watching her enjoy herself. And he liked being good to her. Tracy could use more of that, he mused. She needed to know that she wasn't alone, and that somebody cared about her—even if she might not return his feelings.

"Hey, slow down, princess." He patted Clara's shoulder. He'd remembered her as a picky eater, but this morning she was devouring her breakfast as if every bite might be her last. Rush knew enough to savor times like this. All too soon they would be over, maybe for good.

He'd had a reality flash last night when Cecil had called him from Oklahoma. Annie's father had survived the stroke but would be disabled for the rest of his life. He and Annie's mother wouldn't be able to manage without help.

"I e-mailed our resignation to Sonya," Cecil had told Rush. "And I let her know that you've taken Clara for the holidays."

"What did she have to say about that?" Rush had asked him.

"As you can imagine, she wasn't pleased."

"So, are they coming home early?" The dreaded question needed to be asked.

"No. They know Clara's in good hands. But I gave her your contact information. As soon as they're back, you'll be getting a call from her to arrange for Clara's return."

Rush had thanked the good man, ended the call, and lain awake for the rest of the night. Some ties were stronger than blood. For the first three years of her life, he'd been the only father Clara had ever known. How could he just hand her back to her parents and walk out of her life again?

If she never forgave him for that, he wouldn't blame her.

"I'm getting full." Clara's voice broke into his thoughts.

"I believe I am, too," Tracy said. "Thank you, Rush, for inviting me this morning. It's been a treat—even though we may have turned a few heads."

"Is that so bad?"

She laughed. "Maybe not. I could use a little scandal in my life."

"That's the spirit." He wouldn't mind creating a little scandal with her, Rush thought as he helped Tracy and Clara on with their jackets. Taking her out in public this morning with his little girl had felt almost like they were family. With her on his arm, and Clara holding his hand, he'd felt ten feet tall.

But he'd be a fool to believe anything would come of it. Tracy wasn't his woman. Clara wasn't his child—at least not biologically or legally.

"Can we go to Tracy's house?" Clara asked as he helped her into her booster seat. "I want to play with the kittens."

"You can go another time—but only if Tracy invites you. Anyway, we've got plans for today. Conner's offered to take us on the four-wheeler, out to where the Christmas trees grow. You'll have a fun ride, and you can play with Bucket. He likes to go along, too."

"Can Tracy come with us?"

"If she's got time, and if she wants to." He glanced at Tracy, who was in the front seat. She gave a subtle shake of her head. "But Tracy's got other things to do. She's one busy lady." Had he said the wrong thing? He didn't want Tracy to feel unwelcome; but Clara's attachment was in danger of becoming a problem.

Tracy looked back at Clara and gave her a smile. "Thanks for inviting me, but I do have a lot to do. I have a stack of briefs to read for the court—that's part of my job. I was also planning to make treats for my neighbors, do laundry, and work on my computer. Another time, all right? And don't worry, I'll invite you to play with the kittens soon. You did a great job of finding Ginger a home this morning."

Thanks. Rush mouthed the word as he climbed into the driver's seat. She returned a silent nod. He should have known Tracy would understand. That was just one more thing he liked about her.

They pulled up in front of Tracy's house. "Thanks again for taking me to brunch, Rush," she said. "Don't bother getting out to help me. I'll be fine."

She'd opened the door and was about to climb out when Clara spoke up.

"Tracy, will you promise me something?" she asked.

"Maybe, if it's a good promise. Tell me what it is."

"Well . . ." Clara paused, taking a deep breath before she plunged ahead. "I know people will want the kittens. But will you save Snowflake for me? I know Daddy said I couldn't keep him, but maybe something will change. Please, Tracy, promise you won't give him away." There were tears in her voice.

Tracy hesitated, but Rush knew she wouldn't

refuse. "All right, I promise for now," she said. "But if you can't keep him, he's going to need a home. I'll save him for you until Christmas. All right?"

"All right." Clara's sigh made it clear that she'd hoped for better terms. "But you promise for sure?"

"Yes, for sure." Tracy climbed out of the Hummer. "Thanks, you two. Have a good time on the ranch."

Rush drove, holding his tongue until they reached Main Street. There, the traffic forced him to slow down. Clara lowered the window partway so she could look at the holiday lights and hear the Christmas music that was coming over the loudspeakers. This morning the song was "Joy to the World."

"Clara," he said, "do you think that was fair, making Tracy promise to keep Snowflake for you?"

"She didn't say no, Daddy."

"She didn't say no because she's nice and she doesn't want you to be sad. But you know that you don't have any way to keep a kitten. What if Snowflake misses the chance for a good home because you won't let Tracy give him away?"

"I know what you told me," Clara said. "But sometimes, if you believe, special things can happen at Christmas. Annie called them miracles. I'm going to believe really hard. If I do, maybe a miracle will happen."

Rush sighed, knowing better than to crush her childish faith. This holiday season, he needed his own miracle. But he'd long since stopped believing in such things. Anything special that happened would have to be up to him.

* * *

Tracy was about to take off her jacket and hang it up when she remembered that she needed to take Murphy outside. The old dog had raised his head when she came inside, but he was still in his bed.

She whistled softly. "Come on, Murphy, time to go out."

With effort, Murphy hauled himself to his feet. Head down and tail drooping, he followed her out the kitchen door to the backyard. Was he moving more slowly than he had yesterday? Was he in pain? She watched as he finished his business and hobbled back to be let inside. When he hesitated at the stoop, she helped him by lifting his hind-quarters.

His food bowl was in the kitchen. He took a few bites, then wandered back to his bed and closed his eyes. Tracy stroked the massive head, fighting tears. Rush had been right. Soon she would need to start thinking about the next step. But how would she know when it was time? Where would she find the strength to let her beloved dog go?

Her gaze wandered to the photo on the mantel. The memory of that day on the beach with Steve and Murphy replayed in her mind every time she looked at it—Steve laughing under his baseball cap, Murphy wet from the sea, tongue lolling, his face wearing that goofy dog grin. Murphy was no longer the same dog. But he was all she had from that wonderful day. When he was gone, there would be nothing left but the photograph and the memory.

And she would be alone.

There was still time, Tracy told herself. Maybe after Christmas, she'd be ready to face what had to be faced. For now, she would focus on keeping busy.

She gathered up the laundry, sorted it, and loaded the washer with darks. Glancing down into the box, she saw the kittens, curled together in a warm, sleepy ball. Rainbow was spending less time with them now, and they'd started to climb the sides of the box. Soon they'd be getting out, exploring the house, and eating their first solid food. Then it would be time for new homes. Ginger, the boldest of the four, would be a perfect cat for Francine. She could only hope the others would be just as lucky.

Reaching down, she tickled Snowflake's silky white belly. He opened his eyes, yawned, and went back to sleep. He was the sweetest, calmest, and most affectionate of the kittens. No wonder Clara loved him best. And what a shame it was that there was no way for her to keep him.

The thought of Clara reminded Tracy of her promise. And the promise reminded her of something else she'd resolved to do. Leaving the laundry room door open for Rainbow, she crossed the hall to the small spare bedroom she used for an office. The legal briefs were on her desk, waiting to be read, but they could wait. Right now, she had something else on her mind. Something personal.

Maybe there was nothing she could do for Rush and Clara. But as a lawyer, she would at least have the background to know something useful when she saw it. Or, if Rush's case turned out to be hopeless, at least she'd be able to say she'd looked.

Sitting at her desk, she put on her glasses, logged into her computer, and googled the website for Arizona child custody laws.

The trail to the Christmas trees led along the boundary of the pastureland and over a low hill. In the backseat, Rush hung on to Clara to keep her safe as Conner's ATV swayed and bumped over the rough ground. The melting snow had left puddles that splattered upward under the wheels. Clara squealed with laughter as the icy water splashed her face.

Bucket sat in front, next to Conner, his nose to the breeze. When a startled jackrabbit leaped out of the way and bounded off across the flat, the fool mutt was off the seat like a rocket, tearing through the sagebrush to give chase. Minutes later, he came trotting back, mouth grinning, tongue lolling, and leaped back onto the empty seat.

Conner laughed and scratched the dog's shaggy ears. "Got away from you, did he, old boy? Maybe you need to chase something slower."

"Conner, does Bucket chase cats?" Clara's small voice was drowned out by the engine. Rush was close enough to catch the question, but Conner hadn't heard.

"Wait till we stop." Rush spoke into Clara's ear. He knew why she was asking. She was still hoping for a way to keep the white kitten. Much as he wanted to make her happy, Rush couldn't see any way to make her wish come true.

The ATV slowed atop the low hill that hid the pine-carpeted hollow from the road and from the rest of the ranch. Last year, Conner and Travis had discovered the trees, planted years ago by the ranch's former tenants. Together, they'd come up with the idea of Christmas Tree Ranch. By the time Rush joined the partners last year, the Christmas tree venture was already underway. His good credit and the income from his veterinary practice had lent the ranch much-needed financial stability. And the ranch had given Rush a home and a new start.

Rush had never believed in miracles. But the trees, which seemed to appear out of nowhere, were a miracle in themselves.

"Look!" Clara was bouncing with excitement. "It's a forest! A whole forest of Christmas trees!"

Rush had to hold her in place as Conner drove the ATV over the brow of the hill and down into the hollow where the trees grew. Conner pulled onto a level spot, where he'd left the half-loaded trailer, and turned off the engine. Bucket jumped down from the seat and raced off among the trees, where he loved chasing birds and squirrels.

"I'll bet you don't have trees like this in Phoenix, do you, Miss Clara?" Conner teased.

"Last Christmas, Annie and Cecil put up a fake tree," she said. "I like real trees better. They smell nice." She took deep breaths, inhaling the fragrance of pine. Rush hadn't told her about losing Cecil and Annie, who'd been there for her since she was a baby. She was bound to be upset. He would need to find a time to break the news.

"Can we get a tree for the house?" Clara asked.

Conner answered before Rush could respond. "Maybe, but only if we have leftover trees that don't sell. That means we'll have to wait. Last year we sold them all."

Clara frowned. "How long will we have to wait?"

"Maybe till Christmas Eve. We sell a lot of trees. People come from all over the county to buy them here and in Hank's lot."

"Who's Hank?"

"He's the man who—"

"He's the man who sells our trees at his store." Rush shot Conner a warning glance. To reveal that Hank was the parade Santa would devastate this child who still believed.

"But look at all these trees!" Clara gestured toward the lush green forest. "Can't you just cut one down for the house?"

"It's not that simple," Conner said. "There are a lot of trees, and we've planted more. But it takes at least eight years to grow a nice Christmas tree. These trees need to last until the new ones are big. If we cut too many too soon, we'll run out."

"Oh." Clara nodded, although Rush suspected that Conner's explanation had been too much to grasp.

"But can't we just have a little tree—like this one?" She ran to a tree about her own height, a healthy-looking volunteer that had likely sprung from seed. Wrapping her coat-clad arms around it, she gave Conner a sad-puppy look that would have softened a cast-iron girder. "Poor little tree. It isn't very big or really pretty. Nobody will want it for a Christmas tree. Think how sad it must feel. Please . . ."

Rush had to bite his cheeks to keep from laughing. Poor Conner. He didn't stand a chance.

Conner sighed. "Well, all right, I guess it wouldn't hurt to cut it for a Christmas tree. But I don't know what you'll do for decorations. We've got lights, but we're using those outside. There's nothing else."

She turned her soulful, brown eyes on Rush. "We can buy some, can't we, Daddy? It's just a little tree. It won't need a lot of decorations."

"Sure. A string of lights and some tinsel shouldn't cost much. We'll go shopping tomorrow. Then we can decorate the tree."

Conner caught Rush's eye, grinned, and shook his head. Two strong men had met their match.

"Conner, I've got a question," Clara said as Conner readied his power saw to cut down her tree.

"Anything for you, princess," Conner said. "Ask away."

"Is Bucket friends with cats? Do you know?"

"Hmm," Conner said, thinking. "I don't know that he has any cat friends, if that's what you mean. I've never seen him hanging out with a cat."

"No, I mean, if he saw a cat, what would he do?"

"Probably chase it. That's what he does with most things."

"But would he hurt it?"

"He'd have to catch it first. But Bucket isn't mean. I don't think he'd know what to do with a cat if he caught it."

"So you don't know for sure, do you?"

"Nope. Sorry." Conner revved the motor on the chain saw to test it. "Travis might know. He got Bucket from the old man who had him first. You're sure you want this tree?"

"Uh-huh. I mean, yes. Thank you, Conner."

Conner felled the small tree with a single stroke and set it aside. While he was cutting more trees to load onto the trailer, Rush took Clara for a walk, down along the rows of trees. The afternoon sun had melted the snow. Crows, jays, and small brown sparrows flitted among the pine trees, filling the air with their calls. A squirrel, probably flushed and treed by Bucket, scolded in the distance.

"Daddy, do you like Tracy?" Clara asked.

"Sure, I do. She's nice. Do you like her?"

"Uh-huh. I like her a lot. But she seems so sad. She told me her husband died."

"I know that," Rush said. "It can take a long time to get over losing someone you love." *I know. I lost you.*

"Do you think she'll get married again?"

"Maybe. But not till she's through being sad."

"You're sad, too, Daddy. I can tell. But I've got it all figured out. You and Tracy could get married."

Rush stifled a groan. He should have seen that coming. "I don't think Tracy's ready to get married," he said. "Neither am I."

"But think how nice it would be. We could live in her house, and I could have Snowflake, and nobody would be sad."

"So you've got it all figured out, have you?"

"Uh-huh."

"Listen, honey." He laid a hand on her shoulder. This wasn't going to be easy. "By the time you're older, you'll learn that you can't just make people do what you want. I would love to keep you with me forever. But I have to follow the rules. And the rules say that when your mom comes back from her cruise, I have to send you back to Phoenix. And you can't take Snowflake with you. You already know why."

"I know. It's 'cause Andre's allergic. I hate the rules! They're mean and stupid!" She kicked at a rock.

Rush wanted to kick at a rock, too. Or maybe a boulder. The news he'd been holding back would make her feel even worse. But putting it off wouldn't make it any easier.

"I've got some more news," he said, forcing the words. "I'm afraid it's going to make you sad."

"I'm sad now." Her head was down, her feet dragging.

"Cecil called me last night. Annie's father is still sick. Cecil and Annie will need to stay in Oklahoma to take care of him and Annie's mother."

"Stay?" Startled, she looked up at him. "For how long? Forever?"

His silence answered her question. Tears welled in her eyes.

"You'll be all right," Rush said. "Your mom will find somebody new to take care of you. Somebody nice, I'm sure." He hoped he could promise that, at least. But Annie and Cecil had been like family. They had loved her. In Clara's life, they were irreplaceable.

"Why can't Mom take care of me herself?" Clara demanded. "Or if she's too busy, why won't she just let me stay with you?"

Rush knelt beside her and hugged her close. "Those are very good questions," he said. "I only wish I had good answers. But you're a big girl, you're growing up, and you have people who love you. You'll be fine."

The way she stood against him, stiff and unyielding, told Rush she had her doubts. She was afraid for the future, and he couldn't say he blamed her.

Just then, Bucket came trotting out from among the trees, his tail up, his coat tangled with mud and pine needles. Catching sight of Rush and Clara, he picked up a stick from the ground and came bounding toward them, wanting to play.

"Here you go, boy." Rush picked up the stick the dog had dropped at their feet and held it out to Clara. "Want to throw it for him?"

"I can't throw very far," she said. "Will you help me?"

"Okay." He handed her the stick and stood behind her, holding her arm as the dog danced and wagged. "I'll count to three. On three, let go. Here goes. One, two, three . . ."

The throw was awkward at best, only sailing about ten feet, but Bucket didn't seem to care. He shot after it, catching the stick in midair. Prancing, he carried it back for another throw.

"Try it yourself this time," Rush said. "You'll do fine."

Clara took the stick and threw it as high and hard as she could. It soared upward, arced, and came down about a dozen feet away. Again, Bucket caught it in the air. Grinning his doggy grin, he came bouncing back.

Clara picked up the stick he'd dropped at her feet and raised her arm to toss it again.

"At least somebody's happy," she said.

Chapter 9

Tracy took off her glasses and rubbed the bridge of her nose. She'd spent most of the afternoon online, searching for any glimmer of hope that might give Rush legal access to the child he loved as his own.

Most of what she'd found was discouraging. In cases where no formal adoption had taken place, precedence would be given to the biological parent, especially if proven by DNA. As a former stepparent with no blood relationship to the child, Rush was no more than a caregiver.

As Clara's natural parents, Rush's ex-wife and her husband had the legal right to bar Rush from seeing Clara until she became an adult.

Fairness didn't enter into the law. Neither did the motives of the parents—which Tracy guessed to be plain, mean-spirited selfishness. Rush's case looked hopeless.

But then, as she was about to give up, she'd found it—one small loophole. Tracy's pulse had leaped when she'd come across the paragraph. But as she read through each line of text, once and then again, she'd realized that, under the present conditions, the loophole was useless. As long as Clara's parents remained together, there was nothing Rush could do.

With a sigh, she logged off the computer, laid down her glasses, leaned back, and closed her eyes to rest them. The question, now, was how much should she tell Rush about what she'd learned.

Telling him what he already knew would be a waste of time and would only frustrate him. But what about that faint possibility, that dim spark of hope she'd just discovered? Should she share it with him, or would that only be cruel, like showing a pitcher of water to a thirsty man without giving him a drink?

For now, she would keep what she'd learned to herself. In fact it might be best not to tell him she'd done research at all. She could always tell him later if the need arose. Meanwhile, it might not be smart to let Rush know how much she cared about him and his little girl.

Something soft brushed her arm. Startled, she blinked and sat up. Rainbow had jumped onto the desk and was gazing at her with curious golden eyes. The weeks since Tracy had taken her in had transformed her from a skinny, bedraggled stray into an elegant cat, with a sleek body and long, silky fur.

Now, with a plaintive *meow*, she rubbed her head against Tracy's hand, wanting to be petted. "Hello, Rainbow," Tracy said, scratching her behind her ears and under her chin. "Taking a break from your babies, are you?"

A purr rumbled in Rainbow's throat and quivered down the length of her body. "Mmmm, I can tell that feels good." Tracy stroked along her back, down to the base of her tail, sending the cat into ecstasies of purring.

Tracy, who'd never had a cat before, had been surprised to discover how calming they could be. Keeping Rainbow had been a good decision. But no more kittens. She would hold Rush to his promise to spay the mother cat once her babies were weaned.

She was about to untangle herself from the cat and stand up when her cell phone rang. The caller was Maggie.

"Hi, Tracy." Maggie's voice was as cheerful as the call of a spring meadowlark. "I'm sorry we missed you at the B and B this morning. Travis and I arrived after you left, but somebody mentioned that you and Rush had been there."

"I'll bet they did," Tracy said. "I had a feeling that if I showed up with Rush and Clara, tongues would wag."

Maggie chuckled. "Don't worry. This is a small town. In a day or two you and Rush will be old news. Anyway, that's not why I'm calling. Tomorrow's Sunday, and since Christmas Tree Ranch will be closed for business, and the guys have been working so hard, I wanted to bring them some lasagna and garlic bread for a nice sit-down dinner. I'd love to have you come."

Tracy's first impulse was to make an excuse. But

Maggie was trying to be her friend, and she needed good friends. If she ever wanted to be happy in this close-knit little town, she would have to stop living like a hermit outside of work.

"Thanks, I'd be happy to come," she said, measuring each word. "But only if I can bring something. How about a salad or dessert—or both?"

"Your choice. Either or both. We'll be gathering at five o'clock. Does that work for you? I can't wait to meet Rush's little girl."

"You'll love her. And five o'clock is fine."

Maggie paused, as if torn between ending the call and asking one more question. Curiosity won. "Tracy, you and Rush—are you, you know, a couple?"

Tracy sighed. She should have expected this. "Heavens no, we're just friends. If people are saying that we're together, that's plain wrong. We're not even dating."

"I understand. But what I'm saying is, maybe you should be. Rush is a great guy, and I know he likes you. According to Travis, the divorce really put him through the grinder. I've heard how much he loves that little girl. He deserves a second chance at a family, with children of his own. So do you. In fact, I think the two of you would make wonderful parents."

"Oh, Maggie—" For the space of a heartbeat, Tracy was tempted to share her secret. But she swiftly thought better of it. Nothing stayed secret for long in Branding Iron.

"I'm sorry," Maggie said. "Did I say too much? I'm known for putting my foot in my big mouth."

"No—oh, no," Tracy protested, fighting a flood of emotion. "You caught me off guard, that's all. But it's far too soon to be talking about any kind of future with Rush, especially when part of me is still married to Steve."

"I'm sorry. As usual, I overstepped."

"No, you meant well, Maggie. But now you know better. I'll see you tomorrow at five o'clock."

"Wonderful. See you then."

Tracy ended the call and pressed her hands to her face. Maggie was a good person, and she'd spoken with the best of intentions. But it had been all Tracy could do to keep herself from cancelling the dinner invitation. What if Maggie had said the same things to Rush? What if Rush was hoping for the loving family Tracy could never give him?

How could she face him and his friends at dinner, knowing what a fraud she was?

Being with Rush made her feel warm and safe. If she allowed her emotions free rein, she could even love him. But it would be a love built on empty promises and doomed expectations—a love that, in the end, would leave them both hurt and bitter.

But tomorrow night was only a dinner with friends. She could handle that.

Tracy forced herself to think about what she could bring. A salad would be easy. And to go with lasagna, maybe a light dessert like a fruit sorbet—but no, she'd be feeding three hungry, hardworking men. Chocolate was the only way to go.

After taking stock of what she had on hand, she made a list of ingredients to buy. By now it was getting dark. With the sun gone, the air had turned frigid. Shop Mart was open on Sundays. Tomorrow morning would be soon enough to pick up what she needed.

That done, she took Murphy out to his favorite tree, gave him his medicine, scooped out Rainbow's litter box, and checked on the kittens. After that it was time to end the day with popcorn and a good movie.

Living alone had its perks. But as she settled in to watch the newest mail-order DVD, with the bowl of popcorn in her lap and Rainbow purring next to her on the afghan, she found herself missing the warm weight of an arm around her shoulders, the sound of deep-voiced laughter in her ear, and the roughness of a stubbled chin brushing her cheek. But that wasn't all. The house was too dark and quiet, too much the same as always. She missed the soft glow of lights, the scent of fresh pine, the subtle excitement of seeing wrapped packages, and the sound of a choir singing traditional carols on the radio.

For the first time since Steve's death she was missing Christmas.

The big-box store opened at 10:00 on Sundays. Tracy drove into the lot at 10:15, early enough to get a good parking spot. The sky was cloudy, the morning wind warm enough to usher in a storm. Would it be snow? When it came to Texas weather, there was no telling what the next day would bring.

She tested the cart to make sure the wheels were

quiet before pushing it toward the produce section, where she selected lettuce, spinach, toma-
toes, avocados, poppy seed dressing, and a small
bag of croutons.

She had most of the ingredients for the chocolate cake she'd planned, but she picked up a disposable pan that she could leave at the ranch, as
well as cream cheese for the icing. After getting a
few more items she needed at home, she headed
for the checkout stand.

Rounding the end of an aisle, she nearly bumped
into Rush, who was pushing a cart with Clara inside.
This morning she was wearing her princess costume.

"Hi, Tracy!" Clara gave her a grin. Rush greeted
her with a smile and a strangely sexy twitch of his
eyebrow.

"Hello, Your Highness." Tracy gave the little girl
a deep curtsy.

"We've got a Christmas tree," Clara said. "We're
going to buy some decorations."

"She wanted to wear her princess dress so people would recognize her," Rush said.

"I'm sure they will," Tracy said. "We've never
had royalty in Branding Iron before."

"I've been telling people about the kittens," Clara
said. "But remember your promise. You mustn't give
Snowflake away."

"I'll remember," Tracy said. "So, for now, we just
need homes for Tiger and Midnight, right?"

"Right." Clara gave the royal wave to a passing
shopper, who smiled and waved back.

"Maggie says you're coming to dinner today," Rush said.

"That's right. It was nice of her to ask me."

"And it was nice of you to accept. We'll all be glad to have you there, especially the princess. You've become her favorite person."

"Daddy," Clara said, "after we shop, can I go to Tracy's house and play with the kittens?"

Rush met Tracy's eyes and gave a slight shake of his head. "Maybe another time. Tracy probably has things to do. And this morning we need to go home and decorate your tree."

"But the kittens are getting big. Soon it'll be time for their new homes."

"Tomorrow would be a good day for me," Tracy said. "But you'll have to ask your dad first."

"Please, Daddy!" Clara's pleading expression was irresistible.

Rush frowned, then nodded. "I've got some appointments tomorrow morning. Barring an emergency, I should be able to pick her up around noon. Would that be too long?"

"It would be fine," Tracy said. "As long as she doesn't get bored."

"I won't get bored." Clara tugged at her father's sleeve. "Please, Daddy!"

"We'll see. You'll have to promise to behave yourself and not pester Tracy for things you can't have."

Like the white kitten. Tracy knew what he meant. "I was just about to get in the checkout line," she said. "I'll see you later, for dinner, okay?"

"Okay. Let's get shopping, princess."

Tracy watched him walk away with Clara waving and smiling in the cart. Sooner or later, Rush would find the right person and marry her. Whoever she was, she would be one lucky woman. Tracy sighed. Too bad that woman wasn't going to be her.

At this early hour, the checkout line was short. Tracy made it to the register in a few minutes and paid for her purchases.

The bagger was a young man she recognized. Daniel, nice looking with dark eyes and hair, had Down syndrome. Last year, when his family was new in town, he and Katy had discovered each other. Now they were sweethearts. There'd been talk of a wedding, but for now they lived with their families and spent as much time together as possible.

"Can I help you to your car?" he asked Tracy as he put her bags in the cart.

"Thanks, Daniel, but I can manage fine," Tracy said.

"Please let me help you," he said. "I need to ask you something."

"Of course." Tracy let him lead the way to her car, pushing the cart. What could this nice young man possibly want to ask her?

"I hear you have kittens," he said.

"I do. They'll be ready for new homes by Christmas."

"I want to give Katy a kitten," he said. "I already asked her mom. She said it would be okay. Are any of the kittens girls? I think Katy would like a little girl cat."

"There's one girl," Tracy said. "She's a little tabby. So cute. Katy would love her."

"She sounds perfect." He grinned as he lifted the bags into the trunk of Tracy's car. "Would you save her for me? I can pay you."

"No, the kittens are free. And Dr. Rushford will give them shots—and I'll send a little bit of food with her, and some litter," Tracy added as an afterthought.

"Will you tell me when I can pick her up?"

"It'll be a few days before Christmas. Do you know where I live?"

"My dad will know. I don't drive, but he can bring me."

"Wonderful. I'm so glad Katy will be getting one of the kittens."

Tracy drove home with a smile on her face. Two of the kittens, Ginger and Tiger, would soon go to good homes. Only Midnight was still available—and Snowflake, too, if Clara couldn't find a way to keep him.

Her heart ached for the little girl and for Rush. But there was nothing she could do—despite what she'd learned online.

By the time she got home, made the cake and salad, and did some things around the house, it was time to get ready for dinner. She knew no one would be dressed up, but she put on clean jeans, black boots, and a new black sweater. After freshening her makeup and curling the ends of her hair, she added small silver earrings.

Why should it matter how she looked? Tracy

asked herself. But she knew the answer to that question. She wanted to appear at her best for Rush.

As she checked her reflection in the dresser mirror, Steve's photo on the nightstand seemed to gaze at her with sad blue eyes. *It's only paper*, she told herself. But she couldn't shake a prickle of guilt. The love of her life was gone, and here she was, with his picture still on display, primping to impress another man.

A man who would never be hers.

Never mind, she told herself, as she slung her purse on her shoulder and carried the cake and salad out to her car. She would go to dinner, be a good guest, make pleasant conversation, and leave. That would be the end of it. . . .

Until tomorrow, when Rush brought Clara to play with the kittens.

The December sunlight was already fading as she took the south highway and found the turnoff to Christmas Tree Ranch. Tracy switched on her headlights, feeling the bumpy surface beneath her tires as she drove past the ancient cottonwoods that lined the left-hand side of the road. Their branches were bare now, their tops black tracery against the deepening indigo sky. She parked next to Maggie's old Lincoln Town Car. The lights were on in the house, the breeze cool on her face as she stepped out of her vehicle, balanced the cake and salad in her arms, and mounted the front steps to the porch.

Rush opened the door before she could find a way to knock. "Here, I'll take that." He ushered her inside and eased the rectangular cake pan out of her grip and set it on the counter. "That looks downright decadent," he said, looking at the cake. "You're a woman who knows the way to a man's heart—or maybe three men's hearts tonight." He leaned close to Tracy's ear as she set the salad bowl on the table. "And you look pretty damned decadent yourself, lady," he whispered.

Tracy felt the heat creep into her face. Rush hadn't flirted openly with her before. Maybe he was doing it to impress his friends.

The table was set with six mismatched place settings. Maggie was just taking the lasagna and foil-wrapped bread out of the oven. The aroma was intoxicating. "Hey, you're just in time," she said. "And your salad looks yummy. Give me a couple more minutes, and it'll be time to sit down."

Clara, dressed in her new ranch clothes, came dancing down the hall with a clean, fluffy dog at her heels. "Doesn't Bucket look beautiful?" she exclaimed. "Travis and I gave him a bath in the tub! Boy, was he dirty! Come and see our Christmas tree, Tracy!"

She took Tracy's hand and tugged her into the living room, where a three-foot tree was set up on a wooden crate in the far corner. Lights, tinsel, and miniature ornaments, almost enough to bury the tree, decorated every branch and twig.

"Isn't it the prettiest tree ever?" Clara asked. "I decorated it all by myself."

Tracy smiled. It was impossible not to respond to the happy little girl. "I have some good news," she said. "Tiger has found a home. She's going to be a present for Katy, the girl who gave you the gingerbread cookie."

"Yay!" Clara clapped her hands. "So now there's just Midnight. Midnight's the playful one. He's so cute. He'll find a home soon."

And there's one more. But Tracy decided against mentioning Snowflake's uncertain future. That would only spoil a joyful moment.

"I want to show you something else." Clara ran to the blue tent, unzipped the flap, and slipped inside. She emerged holding a fluffy white toy cat with blue glass eyes. "This is Snowflake," she said. "I got him for my birthday. I have to keep him in the tent so Bucket won't use him for a dog toy. Here, you can hold him."

Tracy took the life-sized stuffed animal and stroked its silky fur. She recognized the exclusive brand, which she'd seen in high-end stores.

"I love him," Clara said. "But he's not as much fun as a real cat. That's why I love the real Snowflake more."

"He's beautiful," Tracy said. "Now you'd better put him back where he'll be safe."

"Come and get it!" Maggie called from the kitchen.

As they gathered around the table, Rush boosted Clara onto the box that had been added to her chair. When they were all seated, Clara recited a murmured grace. Then the bread and salad started around the table, while Maggie cut squares of lasagna and doled them out with a spatula. Bucket disappeared under the table to wait for a spill or a handout.

Seated across the table from Tracy, Rush stole furtive glances at her. Tonight she looked so tempting that it was all he could do to keep from devouring her with his eyes.

They'd been playing games since the night she'd called him about her cat—and Rush was getting tired of it. He wanted her, pure and simple. If she couldn't get over her late husband, maybe it was time somebody gave her a nudge in the right direction.

As things stood, he had nothing to lose by trying. At best, he could move the relationship forward. At worst, she would freeze him out and slam the proverbial door in his face.

At least she'd shown up tonight, looking like a sexy angel. If that was a signal, he was ready to take a chance. Get the lady alone, and the next step would be up to him.

"Rush?" Maggie's voice startled him. He realized he'd tuned out the buzz of conversation.

"I'm sorry, Maggie, did you ask me something?" he said.

She gave him a knowing smile. "I was just telling Clara about the Cowboy Christmas Ball a week from Saturday. It's a lot of fun. You should plan on taking her."

"Is it a real ball, like in *Cinderella*?" Clara asked.

"Sort of," Maggie said. "Only it's for cowboys, and it's a lot more fun. The whole town will be there."

"Can I wear my princess dress?"

"Honey," Maggie said, "you can wear anything you want to."

"That princess dress needs a trip to the cleaner's first," Rush said. "Remind me to drop it off."

"Hey, I remember that Christmas Ball from last year," Conner said. "The food was great, and I had a blast—must've danced with every single woman there, and some of the married ones."

"I know," Travis teased. "I was waiting for you to get beat up by some woman's jealous husband."

"Well, what about you two?" Conner gave Maggie a wink. "You were so wrapped up in each other that I was afraid the sheriff was going to haul you off for indecent conduct."

"You were there, too, weren't you, Rush?" Maggie asked.

"He was," Conner said. "But all he did was stand around. He didn't even dance."

"I was looking for somebody," Rush said, glancing at Tracy. "Somebody who never showed up."

"I've never been to the ball," Tracy said. "Steve's—my late husband's—law firm always had their annual party that night. And last year, as I'm sure you'll understand, I didn't feel much like celebrating."

"Well, this year, you're going!" Conner said. "And I'm getting in line for the first dance."

"Not if I get there ahead of you," Rush said.

Tracy glanced down at her plate, causing Rush

to wonder if she was being pushed too far and too fast. "We'll see," she said. "I recall that the rule is traditional Western dress, with long gowns for the women. I don't have anything to wear, and no time to get something made."

"Not to worry. I've got a couple of extras," Maggie said. "I'll bring them by your house, and you can choose one. You might have to baste up the hem and tighten the sash, but you'll be right in style. Before the ball, there's a class to teach first-timers the dances, but I can show you the basic steps when I bring the gowns."

"Thanks, that's awfully nice of you." Tracy still sounded hesitant, but nobody could say no to Maggie.

"Can you show me, too?" Clara asked.

"You bet. I'll even show you a few steps after dinner."

Maggie cleared away the emptied dinner plates while Tracy cut big squares of chocolate cake and served them on paper plates.

Conner speared a generous forkful and tasted it. "Mmmm! Now this is what I'd call a perfect ending to a perfect meal. Which one of you lovely ladies would be willing to marry me and make me the luckiest man in the world?"

Tracy looked startled, but Maggie was used to Conner's banter. "Sorry, Conner," she said. "If we took you out of circulation, the good women of Branding Iron would tar and feather us."

"Well, it was worth a try," Conner said. "Let me know if either of you has a change of heart. Meanwhile, I'll take seconds on that cake."

"Don't worry, there's plenty left, and I'm planning to leave it here." Tracy passed Conner another slice. "Anybody else?"

Maggie shook her head. "One more bite and I won't fit into my ball gown."

"I'm full," Clara announced. "I want Maggie to teach me to dance."

"In that case," Conner said, "I volunteer Travis and me for cleanup duty." Turning aside, he gave Rush a private wink. The situation was beginning to feel like a conspiracy, Rush thought. But if it offered him a chance to be alone with Tracy, he was all for it.

"I guess that leaves me to take Bucket out and check the stock," he said. "Want to come along, Tracy? It's a nice evening for a walk."

She hesitated. His breath stopped. But then she smiled. "Why not? I could use some fresh air."

"I'll get your coat," he said.

By now, dusk was deepening to night. Emerging in the darkness, stars twinkled above the distant hills. The breeze was light and moist.

With her hands thrust into her pockets, Tracy strolled across the yard with Travis. Bucket trotted alongside them, his shaggy ears on full alert. The single security light, mounted on a high pole, cast long shadows across the ground.

"Thank you for inviting me tonight," she said, making conversation. "It did me good to get out and enjoy a meal with nice people."

"Thanks. I'd like to take credit, but it was Maggie who invited you," Rush said. "I need to thank her, for that, and for talking you into coming to the Christmas Ball."

"Maggie's good at talking people into things, isn't she?" Tracy remembered Maggie's phone call and her pitch that she and Rush should become a couple. Maggie had meant well, but there were secrets she didn't know.

"Maggie's a master of persuasion," Rush said, chuckling. "That's why she's the mayor. Now, if you'll come to the ball as my date, I'll really have a lot to thank her for."

"As your *date*?" Tracy wasn't dating yet. Didn't he understand that?

"Well, technically it would be *our* date, since we'd be taking Clara. If I could walk into the gym with two beautiful girls on my arm, I'd be the envy of every man there."

So it wasn't a real date. That made the decision easier. "All right," Tracy said. "You, me, and the princess. It sounds like good, old-fashioned fun."

"Thank you." He sounded relieved. "I'd like us to spend more time together, Tracy. If that doesn't suit you, you can always say no. But it won't stop me from trying."

Tracy didn't reply, but she could feel her emotions pulling her one way, then the other. It was as if she'd been handed a wrapped gift—a gift she was afraid to open.

They had reached the pasture fence. Rush took a flashlight out of his pocket and used its powerful beam to scan the pasture. There was an open shelter for the cattle along the side fence, but tonight, most of the cows and their large calves were still grazing. He took the time to locate all of them. "All present and accounted for," he said.

His hand rested on the small of her back as they followed Bucket toward the barn. The contact sent forbidden tingles through Tracy's body but she didn't pull away. Being touched by him awakened needs that were too powerful to name.

The barn was dark inside. Rush's flashlight illuminated a wall of hay bales stacked along the back and a row of stalls on either side. The air smelled of hay and the warm, pungent aroma of horses.

Something large snorted and moved in the shadows. Rush trained the light into a roomy box stall. A massive silver-gray draft horse nickered and came toward the gate. "Here, you old beggar." Rush fished a carrot out of his pocket and laid it on the palm of his hand. The horse took it almost daintily, crunching with its big teeth.

"This is Chip," Rush said. "His brother in the next stall is Patch. They pull Santa's sleigh in the Christmas parade." He moved on to the neighboring stall. The horse that thrust its head over the gate for a treat had a white patch on its forehead.

"They're magnificent," Tracy said. "Can I pet him?"

"Go ahead. These two are as gentle as lambs." Rush guided her hand to the horse's neck.

Tracy stroked the satiny coat, feeling the solid muscles beneath. "Beautiful," she whispered.

"So are you." His hand cupped her chin, tilting her face upward for a long, dizzying kiss.

Chapter 10

The kiss triggered a surge of sensual heat—a heat that flowed like a spring thaw through Tracy's body, warming every part of her. Her arms slid around Rush's neck, pulling him down to her, deepening the contact of his lips on hers.

He kept the kiss tender, almost gentle—but that slow-burning flame was kindling a blaze inside her. She stretched on tiptoe, hungry for more.

Whoa! the warning voice in her head cried out. *You're not ready for this. You can't make a fool of yourself the first time a man kisses you. . . .*

Tracy forced herself to listen. It made sense to be cautious. There were red flags going up all over the place—her grief over Steve's death, Rush's recent divorce, and the fact that she wouldn't be able to give him children. And that was just to name a few.

Summoning her will, she tore herself free and spun away from him. They stood face to face, both of them breathing hard.

"Tracy—" he began.

"No. I'm sorry. I can't do this, Rush. I'm not ready."

One dark eyebrow lifted. His mouth tightened. He shook his head, visibly bringing his frustration under control. "Tracy, I don't know whether to believe your words or believe that sensational kiss. I think you're readier than you say you are. But if you feel pressured, I'll do my best to be a gentleman and respect that."

"Thanks." *So why am I aching for him to kiss me again?*

"Still friends?" she asked, knowing she sounded like a fool.

"Friends," he said. "Can I drop Clara off tomorrow? And will you still be my date to the Christmas Ball?"

She forced herself to smile. "Why not—if we can pretend this never happened?"

"No problem. If you're not ready, you're not ready. But don't expect me to wait too long."

"That's just the problem. I might never be ready. There are things you don't know—" Should she tell him? Now would be the time. Waiting would only make things more painful.

"Then let's give it time," he said. "For now, we can be friends and enjoy a few laughs together. If anything changes, fine. If not . . ." He shrugged. "That's life for you. Now let's get back in the house before my partners get the wrong idea."

With Bucket tagging behind them, he ushered her back inside through the kitchen. Conner and

Travis were loading the dishwasher. "Back so soon?" Conner asked, glancing up.

"Nothing's going on out there," Rush said.

"Since I've already got my coat on, I should probably be getting home," Tracy said. "Thanks for your company. It's been a great evening."

"And I'll thank you with every scrumptious bite of that leftover chocolate cake," Conner said.

When Tracy walked into the living room, Maggie and Clara were practicing dance steps in front of the Christmas tree.

"Thanks again for inviting me, Maggie," she said. "Clara, I'll see you tomorrow. You can play with the kittens and help me make cookies."

"And if it's a good time, I'll come by after work and bring you the gowns," Maggie added.

"I know how busy you must be," Tracy said. "If it's too much bother—"

"Nonsense, it'll be a pleasure," Maggie said. "I'll call you when I'm on my way."

"I'll walk you to your car." Rush opened the front door for her and lent an arm to help her down the rickety steps. Tracy walked beside him in silence. "Are you all right?" he asked. "If I spoiled a nice evening, I'm sorry."

"No need to apologize," Tracy said. "If I were a different woman, I'd be thanking my lucky stars for a man like you. But there are things—"

"Hush." He opened the driver's-side door and held it while she slipped behind the wheel. "If you were a different woman, Tracy, I wouldn't be here. I'll see you tomorrow."

With that, he closed the door and stepped back from the car. As Tracy switched on the headlights and drove out of the gate, an aching lump rose in her throat.

Why did life have to be so complicated?

When she undressed that night, Steve's handsome face smiled at her from its leather frame. *It's only paper. It isn't really him,* she told herself as she buttoned her cotton pajamas. Yet she couldn't help wondering what her husband would think if he knew she'd been kissing another man—and liking it.

Except for practical things like finances, insurance, and the house, they'd never discussed what she should do after he was gone. Would he want her to spend the rest of her life in mourning, or would he want her to move on and find happiness with someone new?

But no—that wasn't the question she should be asking herself. It wasn't what would Steve want her to do. It was what did *she* want to do?

After turning out the light, she lay in the darkness, remembering the heart-stopping sensation of Rush's lips on hers. It had been all she could do to pull away from him. But a kiss was one thing. A lifetime was something else. And the most vital question of all lay between them, unasked and unanswered.

The next morning brought a drizzling rain, dashing the hope for snow. Before breakfast, Tracy took Murphy outside in her rain jacket. She had to help him to his favorite tree and back inside, where she dried his coat with a towel so he wouldn't chill.

At 8:30, Rush brought Clara to the front door. "Thanks again," he said. "Sorry I can't come in. I'm already late for my first appointment. But I'll see you when I pick Clara up."

Then he was gone, splashing water beneath his boots as he strode down the sidewalk. He had barely met her eyes. Had last night made him uncomfortable? But that wasn't like Rush. He was just in a hurry, Tracy told herself.

Clara made a beeline for the laundry room. Tracy could hear her laughing through the partly closed door. "Come see!" She ran back to Tracy, tugging her hand. "The kittens can climb out of the box! Ginger was the first one, and now they're all doing it!"

"Wow, they're supercharged." The kittens were exploring the laundry room, scampering, creeping, and pouncing. "Where's Rainbow?" Tracy asked.

"She's eating." Clara brightened. "Maybe the kittens can eat some food, too. They've all got teeth."

"Let's find out." Tracy had bought a few cans of wet kitten food. In the kitchen, she opened one, scooped out the tuna-flavored mix, and spread it on a small paper plate. Keeping Rainbow distracted, she let Clara set the plate on the floor of the laundry room.

The kittens came running to check out the intriguing new smell. They sniffed, licked, nibbled, and became tiny carnivores. Their little tails quivered with pleasure as they devoured their first meat. "They love it!" Clara was giggling and clapping. "Look, they want more."

The kittens were licking the paper plate, scratching it with their paws and looking up at Clara. "Can we give them another can?"

Tracy hesitated. "Let's wait. Too much food before they're used to it could make them sick. And they'll still be drinking Rainbow's milk for a while."

"Does that mean they'll soon be ready for new homes?" The excitement was gone from Clara's voice.

"They still need to stop nursing, and I'm hoping Rainbow will teach them to use the litter box. But they're growing up. It won't be much longer."

"Oh." Clara picked up Snowflake, held him close to her shoulder, and rubbed her cheek against his velvety white head. She looked as if she were about to cry. "But I don't want them to go." A tear trickled down Clara's cheek. "I thought it would be fun to find them new homes. But now I want them to stay here. And I want them to stay little. Rainbow will be so sad without her babies."

"Oh, Clara." Tracy gathered the little girl close, kitten and all. "Cats grow up fast. It's what nature intended. And Rainbow might be sad for a day or two. But if we give her plenty of love, she'll be fine."

"Will she have more kittens?"

"No. I'm going to let your dad fix her so she won't have more. She can be just a happy, healthy cat."

"Oh." Clara sounded uncertain. "Why not let her have more kittens? They're so cute. And how is Dad supposed to fix her?"

"Those are good questions for your dad," Tracy said, letting her go. "You can ask him."

Clara kissed Snowflake and put him on the floor again. "I still want to keep him. You won't give him away, will you?"

"I promised to wait, remember?"

"I just wanted to make sure."

"Well, for now would you like a job?" Tracy said. "These kittens are curious. Now that they're out of the box, they'll want to run all over the house. You can follow them and make sure they don't get into trouble or get lost. Okay?"

"Okay." Clara gave her a tentative smile. "Sure."

"When they get tired and hungry, they can go back to their mother."

"What if they can't get back in the box? It'll be hard if they're tired."

"You're right. How can we make it easier?"

"I know!" Clara said. "We can cut a door in the box."

"Good thinking. Your dad would be proud of you." The words reminded Tracy of Rush's heart-breaking situation. He was Clara's dad in every respect but one—the one that counted with the law.

Using a kitchen knife, Tracy cut a round hole in the front of the cardboard box, just big enough and low enough for Rainbow and the kittens to go in and out without having to climb. "Perfect," she said. "That was a great idea, Clara. Now you'd better go and look after those kittens. They've already made it into the hall."

Following the kittens around the house kept Clara entertained for more than an hour. By the time Rainbow called her little family back to the box, they were ready for warm milk, a family snuggle, and a nap.

Tracy made sure they were all in the box, then closed the laundry room door to keep them from wandering out. "Good job," she said to Clara. "Now, do you want to help me bake cookies? We'll make plenty, so you and your dad can take some back to the ranch."

Tracy had expected the little girl to be excited. But Clara only shook her head. "What is it?" Tracy asked. "Making cookies will be fun."

"I know," Clara said. "But you promised to help me write a letter to Santa. If we don't do it today, he might not get it in time for Christmas."

"That's right, I did promise you, didn't I?" Tracy said.

"And promises are more important than cookies."

"Wise words. Are you sure you're only four years old? Sometimes you talk like you're about fifty."

Clara giggled. "I'm not fifty. That's really old. Have you got some nice paper?"

"I think so. But we could do the letter on my computer. That would be easier. We could even send Santa an e-mail."

"They might not have e-mail at the North Pole," Clara said. "Anyway, I think Santa would rather get a real letter."

"Okay," Tracy said. "I've got some paper in my desk."

Tracy kept a box of light blue linen stationery with matching envelopes in the back of a drawer. She took it out and carried it, along with a pen, to the kitchen table, where Clara had taken a seat. "Will this paper do?" she asked.

"Blue is nice," Clara said. "I think Santa will like that."

Tracy sat next to Clara, laid a sheet of paper on the table, and poised the pen. "Ready? I'll write whatever you say."

"Okay." Clara paused, thinking. "Dear Santa Claus . . ."

Tracy printed the words. Clara watched her form the letters. "I wish I could read," she said. "I know I'll learn in school, but that's not for a long time."

"You could learn now. All you need is someone to teach you. Maybe your dad could take you to the library and find you some easy books." Tracy held the pen and waited for Clara to go on.

"Dear Santa, I hope you get this letter on time." She paused. "Got that?"

"Just about. You might want to slow down a little." Tracy finished printing the line. "Next?"

"I have been very good this year." She spoke slowly, enunciating each word. "Here is what I want for Christmas."

"Got it."

"What I want most is a white kitten. A real kitten, not a toy. His name is Snowflake. I believe in you, Santa. Can you please make a miracle and get him for me?"

Tracy muffled a sigh as she wrote the words. She should have seen this coming.

"I want another miracle, okay, Santa?" Clara was getting warmed up now. "I want to be with my dad—I mean my daddy, not my father. Maybe he could get married. Then we could live in a house, and I could have Snowflake."

"You're asking for a lot, Clara," Tracy said.

"I know." Clara's big brown eyes shone with a child's faith. "But if I don't ask, how will Santa know what I want?"

"That's a good question," Tracy said. "But what if the miracle's too hard for Santa? What if he has to say no?"

Clara's hopeful expression faded. She gazed down at the table for a moment before she replied.

"Then I'll be really sad. But Santa wants to make kids happy. He'll try."

"Then I guess that's all we can hope for," Tracy said. "Is there anything else you want to tell Santa?"

Clara thought for a moment, then nodded. "Write this," she said. "I know you'll do your best. When I see you in the parade, I'll wave at you. I'll have on a red coat, so you'll know it's me. Love . . . and then my name."

Tracy finished writing. "You can sign your own name," she said, handing Clara the pen.

Clara signed with big, crooked letters. "Now let's put it in an envelope," she said. "Can you help me fold it?"

Tracy showed her where to fold the page so it would fit in the envelope. Then she addressed it to Santa Claus at the North Pole. "Anything else?" she asked.

"I just need to lick it." Clara took the envelope, slicked the flap with her tongue, and held it shut. "Now it needs a stamp," she said.

"Oh, dear." Tracy remembered that she'd used the last of her stamps to mail her bills. "I'm all out of stamps. Leave the letter right here on the table. When your dad comes, he can take it to the post office and put a stamp on it there."

"What if he forgets?"

"We can remind him," Tracy said. "Now, how about helping me make those cookies?"

It was almost noon by the time Rush finished his last appointment. As he drove back to Tracy's house, the thought of being with her again triggered a subtle quickening of his pulse. He remembered last night, holding her in his arms, feeling her slender curves pressing his body as he kissed those heavenly lips. She'd tasted a little like the chocolate cake they'd both had for dessert. He'd found himself wanting second helpings, and thirds.

Not that it had ended well. He should have known that Tracy would back off. But, damn it, he could tell that she'd liked kissing him. And she was going to like it even more the next time it happened.

Was he falling for her? It felt like it—and it felt good. For the first time in recent memory, he felt like taking a chance. If he ended up getting his heart stomped, at least he could say he'd enjoyed the ride.

He parked in front of her house, took the front steps two at a time, and rapped lightly on the front door. He heard the sound of her quick, light footsteps before the door opened. The warm air that rushed out wrapped him in the aromas of sugar, vanilla, and cinnamon.

Tracy stood in the doorway, wearing an old-fashioned apron over her jeans and a dab of flour on her nose. She looked good enough to devour, like a woman-shaped sugar cookie.

It took all the self-control he could muster to keep from sweeping her into his arms and kissing her till she whimpered. They had the start of a good thing here. He didn't want to spoil it by rushing when she wasn't ready.

"Shhh!" She put a finger to her lips as she let him in and closed the door softly behind him. "Clara's asleep. She wore herself out chasing kittens and making cookies."

"That's fine." He wandered toward the kitchen, taking note of the old dog snoring by the fireplace. "I hope you baked a few of those cookies for me."

"Have all you want. I was just making some coffee." As he took his seat, she put a saucer and a napkin on the table, along with a plate of warm sugar cookies shaped like stars and bells and Christmas trees. "We were going to ice them, but Clara was too tired."

"That's fine with me. I like them better plain."

He sampled a star cookie. The first bite melted in his mouth. He was about to take another bite when he noticed the blue envelope lying on the table. "What's this?" He picked it up and read the address. "Did Clara write Santa a letter?"

"With my help. The post office will send it to a place with that address. I was going to mail it, but I didn't have a stamp."

"We've got stamps at the ranch. I can take this home and put it in our mailbox. I still need to buy her some presents. What did she ask for?"

"Nothing you can get at Shop Mart, I'm afraid." Tracy poured two mugs of coffee and set them on the table before she sat down.

Rush was slipping the letter into his jacket when he realized the flap was loose. He took a closer look. Clara, it appeared, had licked off enough adhesive to keep the envelope from sealing.

"I can get you a new envelope," Tracy said.

"Don't bother. I'll tape this shut before I mail it." Rush paused, wondering what was in the letter. "Do you think she'd mind if I looked?"

"Since you're the closest thing to her Santa, I think you should," Tracy said. "But don't expect it to resolve anything."

Rush slipped the folded page out of the envelope, smoothed it on the table, and read the words his little girl had asked Tracy to write. The kitten was no surprise. Even that would be a problem. As for the rest . . . Rush struggled to ignore the rising lump in his throat. "Damn," he muttered.

Tracy shook her head. "I understand, and I'm sorry."

Rush folded the letter again and put it back in the envelope.

"Give it to me. I've got some glue." Tracy stepped to the cupboard and found a small bottle of white glue. She squeezed a thin line along the flap of the envelope and closed it. "There. It might be just as well if she doesn't know you read the letter."

Rush slipped the envelope into his pocket. "I'd do anything to keep her with me, even part-time. But she doesn't understand how impossible it is, let alone the reason why."

"I think she understands more than you realize. That's why she asked Santa for miracles." Tracy refilled his coffee cup. "Can't you appeal to your ex-wife? Surely she wants her daughter to be happy."

"I tried. But Sonya wanted to create a new family with Andre as the only father and me totally out of the picture. She insisted that having two fathers would only confuse her little girl."

"But you've got Clara now."

"That was a fluke. When she gets home from her cruise, Sonya will probably throw a full-scale hissy fit, and the next person I hear from will be her lawyer."

Tracy was looking at him as if she had something to say. Her lips parted. Then, with a slight shake of her head, she pressed her mouth into a tight line.

"What is it?" Rush asked.

"Nothing. Don't worry about it."

He would have pressed her for more, but just then Clara walked into the kitchen, yawning and rubbing her eyes. Her face lit with a happy little smile when she saw him. "Hi, Daddy. Did you see the cookies we made you?"

"I saw them and tasted them. They were yummy. Thanks."

Clara looked at the table. "Where's my letter?"

"I've got it in my pocket," Rush said. "When we get home to the ranch, I'll put a stamp on it. Then you can put it in the mailbox."

"Can't we take it to the post office? Santa will get it faster that way."

"Sure. In fact, I was planning to take you to Buckaroo's for burgers and shakes. The post office is right on the way." Rush glanced at Tracy. "You're invited, too," he said.

She shook her head. "Thanks, but Maggie is coming by later to bring me her spare ball gowns. I've got things to do before then."

"There'll be another time." Rush masked his disappointment with a smile. There never seemed to be enough time for the two of them. "I hope you'll take a rain check."

"Certainly. Here's a box of cookies to take home and share with your partners."

"Thanks. And thanks for helping out this morning." He took the cookies from her, knowing the busiest season at the ranch was just beginning. Travis and Conner were going to need his help. He'd have little time for the woman whose company he'd come to crave. "Get your coat, Clara."

"Can I say good-bye to the kittens first?"

"If you don't take too long."

She raced back to the laundry room and disappeared inside, leaving Rush and Tracy alone.

"Thanks again," he said, wishing he could say more. He'd already begun to dream of a future with her, raising a family here in Branding Iron and growing old together, enjoying their grandchildren. . . . But it was far too soon to bring that up. The dream would have to wait.

"Good luck with Christmas," she said. "You're going to need it."

"Thanks," he said. "The next couple of weeks are going to be crazy at the ranch, but I'll call you."

"It's fine. I understand. I'll be here."

"Come on, Clara," he called. "I promised to help Travis and Conner this afternoon. We need to go."

"Okay." She closed the laundry room door and came skipping back down the hall. "You should see those kittens, Daddy! They're already getting out of the box and eating food. They're so cute, and Snowflake is the cutest one of all!"

Rush helped her with her coat. "Let's go. Burgers and shakes are waiting." He ushered her out the door, pausing to give Tracy a backward wave.

Tracy stood at the window and watched them drive away. Had she made a mistake by not telling Rush what she'd learned online? Since there was nothing he could do, would it be fair or cruel to give him a glimmer of empty hope?

For a moment, when he'd talked about losing Clara, she'd been tempted to tell him. But then Clara had awakened and come into the kitchen, settling the question for now. Sooner or later, especially if they parted company, he would need to know. But she would wait for a better time.

Making cookies with Clara had been a riot, but the kitchen was a disaster site of unwashed bowls, cups, and cookie cutters, spilled flour, broken eggs, and sticky spots on the floor. Maggie had mentioned that she might get off work early. Tracy knew that Branding Iron's mayor wouldn't mind a messy kitchen. Still, she couldn't help wanting to make a good impression.

Summoning her energy, she flung herself into loading the dishwasher, wiping up spills, taking out the trash, and mopping the floor. From there, she moved on to tidying the house, fluffing a pillow, dusting a table, putting a magazine away. By then her phone was ringing. Maggie was on her way.

Minutes later, when Tracy answered the door, Maggie breezed in with her arms full of gowns. "I hope one of these will do," she said, laying them over the back of a chair. "I'm a big girl, at least two sizes larger than you are, so it might take some stitching. Do you sew?"

"Nothing fancy. I don't have a machine, but I can thread a needle and baste a hem."

"That'll do." Maggie said. "Heavens, it smells wonderful in here."

"Clara and I were baking cookies this morning, before Rush picked her up. I put a box aside for you to take home. Would you like to have some, with a cup of coffee?"

"Let's try the gowns first." Maggie slipped off

her jacket and tossed it on the coatrack. "I was just going to leave them, but I've got some time and, if you don't mind, I thought it would be fun to see how you look in them. I brought all three of mine, just in case."

"These are beautiful." Tracy lifted each gown from the stack. "Did you make them yourself?"

Maggie laughed. "Hardly. There are women in town who make their Christmas money sewing Western ball gowns. But you have to get your order in a couple of months early. You might want to think about that for next year."

Tracy sighed. "Maggie, I have no idea whether I'll even be here next year."

Maggie looked startled. "But you and Rush— everyone who knows you both is hoping you'll get together. The two of you make such a great couple. What's wrong?"

"Nothing right now. But there are . . . complications."

"Anything you want to talk about? You can count on me to keep things to myself."

"I appreciate the offer, but I've got a lot to work out," Tracy said. "For now, you can help me try on these lovely gowns." She scooped them up in her arms and headed back toward her bedroom.

Following her, Maggie passed Murphy, dozing in his bed. The old dog raised his head and thumped his tail as she bent to pet him. "Hello, old guy. You're a sweetheart, aren't you?" She rose. "I didn't know you had a dog, Maggie."

"He was Steve's dog. Steve had him longer than he had me."

"He's precious," Maggie said. "I like dogs."

"I've got cats, too, if you're interested."

"I know about the kittens. But as I mentioned before, I'm not a cat person. If you have any that aren't spoken for, I'll spread the word."

"There's just one, not counting the white one Clara has her heart set on. He's a little black boy. Full of mischief. Somebody's bound to love him."

"If you want, I can put up a notice at work."

"Thanks. I'll write one for you. I promised Clara I'd save the white one until Christmas. She's hoping for a miracle. But if she can't keep him, he'll be available, too." Tracy spread the three gowns on her bed. "Oh, these are gorgeous. I can't believe you're letting me borrow one."

Maggie gave her a smile. "What are friends for?"

The words touched Tracy with unexpected sweetness. She'd needed a friend—and the friend she'd needed had pushed through her resistance and found her.

Chapter 11

All three of the gowns were traditional Old West–style, with high necks, long sleeves, and nipped-in waists. "I have to wear a corset to look good in mine," Maggie said. "Something tells me you won't need that."

Tracy slipped the first dress over her head. It was a sky blue calico with little yellow flowers and a wide ruffle at the bottom that trailed on the floor when she walked. Maggie stood behind her as she studied her reflection in the full-length mirror.

"Great color on you," Maggie said. "But it's too big in the waist, and that ruffle would take forever to shorten. Try the green."

Maggie unzipped the back of the dress, helped Tracy out of it, and handed her the deep jade green gown with black piping. Tracy held it up in front of her. "I don't need to try this on," she said. "This is *your* gown, Maggie. It's your color and cut to fit your curves. I'll bet you look just stunning in it."

"I just brought it for fun, and to give you a

choice." Maggie smiled. "All right, one gown to go, and I've saved the best for last. I wore this when I was in high school, and it's hung in the back of the closet for years. It doesn't fit me anymore, but I'm betting it will almost fit you." She lifted a lavender gown, trimmed with ecru lace, from the bed.

"I don't know what I was thinking, with that color and my red hair," she said, slipping the gown over Tracy's head. "But it'll be perfect on you."

Tracy gazed at her reflection as Maggie zipped the back of the lavender gown. She looked like someone from a long-past time, with the gauzy fabric floating around her and the high lace collar framing her face.

"Yes!" Maggie took Tracy's hair, twisted it into a high pompadour, and held it there for effect. "Perfect," she said. "You'll just need to take up the hem a few inches. Since I'll never get into it again, it's yours."

"Thank you! I can't believe you'd give me this. I love it!" Tracy twirled in front of the mirror. "Now, what do you say we take it off and go have some cookies?"

"That sounds wonderful. And I've just got time before I need to go."

Maggie helped her out of the gown and waited while Tracy dressed in her jeans and sweatshirt. Her gaze fell on Steve's photo, next to the bed. "I still remember him," she said. "I didn't know him very well, but he was a real gentleman, and so good-looking." She gave Tracy a knowing look. "You mentioned complications with Rush. Does Steve happen to be one of them?"

Tracy sighed as she laid the lavender dress carefully over the back of a chair. "I'm afraid so. But there's more involved than that. With Steve, it's a matter of when to let go and move on. And yes, I'm having trouble with that. But there are other issues, things I can't change."

Maggie gathered up the two remaining gowns. "Let me put these by the front door, where I won't forget them," she said. "Then we can go in the kitchen."

"I'll make a fresh pot of coffee," Tracy said.

"That sounds wonderful." Maggie strode back to the living room and laid the gowns on the chair nearest the door.

In the kitchen, Tracy started a fresh pot of coffee. "Come see the kittens while we're waiting," she said. I know you're not a cat person. Neither was I until the little pregnant mother showed up on my doorstep."

"Okay, but don't try to give me one." Maggie followed her down the hall to the laundry room, where they found Rainbow in the box, nursing her four kittens. "All right, I admit they're pretty cute," she said.

"It's the white one Clara wants," Tracy said.

"I know. Travis says that kitten is all she talks about."

"Did Travis tell you why she can't have him?"

Maggie shook her head.

"She can't take the kitten home to Phoenix because Andre, her father, is allergic. And she can't keep the kitten at the ranch because of Bucket."

"Bucket? No way," Maggie said. "I knew the man who gave him to Travis. Bucket was raised with an old cat who eventually died. They were best friends. Bucket should be fine with a cat. But the kitten would have to stay inside at the ranch. Coyotes, foxes, hawks, and owls would all be after him. And that white coat would make him an easy target."

"Thanks, I'll pass that on to Rush. Not that it'll make much difference if Clara can't stay with him."

Should she tell Maggie what she'd learned about the loophole she'd discovered online? No, Tracy decided, the first one to be told about it should be Rush. "It smells like the coffee's ready," she said. "Let's go sit down. I hope you like home-made sugar cookies."

"I love homemade sugar cookies." Maggie followed her back to the kitchen and took a seat at the table. "It smells like Christmas in your house. But it doesn't look like Christmas."

"Just call me Scrooge," Tracy said. "I used to do a tree and hang lights on the porch, but after Steve died, I boxed up all the decorations and put them in the attic."

"Maybe it's time to get them down," Maggie said as Tracy poured her coffee and put a platter of cookies on the table between them. "Surely Rush and Clara will be spending time here. Think how much they'd enjoy having a nice tree. And you wouldn't have to decorate it alone. They could help you, or at least Clara could. She'd love that."

"Yes, I suppose so." Tracy stirred creamer into her coffee.

"You really should do it. I can see how much Rush likes you. I know he misses being part of a family, especially at Christmas. And this year, with his little girl here, you could make it special for them. Like family."

Tracy could feel something crumbling inside her. "Don't," she whispered. "I know you mean well, Maggie, but just don't, all right?"

Maggie's lips parted in a little gasp. "Oh, no, I'm sorry, Tracy. Me and my big mouth. What did I say that was wrong?"

"Nothing, really. It's not your fault." Tracy felt the dam that held back her emotions giving way. "It's just that . . . I can't do the family thing with Rush. I can't even go through the motions, pretending. It would be a lie."

"I still don't understand," Maggie said.

"I know that Rush wants a family of his own. When I see how he is with Clara, I can just imagine what a great dad he'd be with his own children. But I can't give him what he wants."

"Are you sure?" Maggie's hand reached out and rested on her arm.

"Steve and I tried for years to have a baby. Nothing worked. The doctors checked us both out. He was fine. The problem was with me and only me. Maggie, I can't give Rush the family he deserves. I can't have children."

Maggie's eyes were wells of sympathy. Her hand tightened on Tracy's arm. "And you haven't told Rush?"

"It's never come up. There's never been a good time. And I'm afraid that when Rush finds out, especially after my keeping it from him this long, he'll walk away."

"That doesn't sound like the Rush I know. I certainly won't tell him. But I think you should." Maggie paused. "Do you love him?"

"I could if I let myself. That's why I need to tell him the truth, even if it means losing him, which it probably will."

"Tracy, there's more than one way to become a parent," Maggie said. "There's always adoption. And there are new medical procedures—"

"And there are attractive, fertile women in this town who'd jump at the chance to do it the old-fashioned way. In all fairness, I should step aside and give them a chance. After what happened with Clara, Rush deserves children of his own."

Maggie glanced at her watch, finished her coffee, and rose from her chair. "I need to go," she said. "But give Rush the benefit of the doubt. Tell him. The longer you wait, the harder it will be."

Tracy walked her friend to the door. "Call me anytime you need to talk," Maggie said, gathering up the spare gowns. "I mean it. I'm here for you, Tracy."

"I know you are. Thank you so much." Tracy hugged her and watched her drive away. Maggie was right. She'd already kept her secret from Rush for too long. She had to take a chance. She had to tell him.

But when would she find the time and the courage?

A few days had passed since Rush had mailed Clara's letter to Santa. He'd taken her into the post office with him, bought stamps, and let her drop the envelope into the slot. "Do you think Santa will read it?" she'd asked him.

"Santa reads everything," he'd replied. But even if Santa were real, with the power to fly through the air and deliver presents to every child on earth, there was no way he could give Clara what she wanted for Christmas.

Rush had racked his brain trying to figure out a way to make her happy. Bringing the kitten to the ranch wasn't out of the question, especially since Travis had passed on Maggie's news that Bucket would be fine with a cat. But Clara wouldn't be able to take Snowflake back to Phoenix, and that would break her heart.

As for the rest, short of begging Sonya on his knees, which Rush was prepared to do, his hands were tied.

With Christmas a little more than two weeks away, the season peak that could make or break the tree business was upon the ranch. People from all over the county were swarming to Hank's tree lot or out to the ranch to buy fresh, fragrant trees that had been cut within the past few days. Keeping the supply in stock was a full-time job for the partners, and Rush had his vet practice calls to make as well.

Fortunately, Clara had made friends with the family on the neighboring ranch. Jubal and Gracie McFarland had a nine-year-old daughter, a two-year-old boy, a baby, and a little white poodle that Clara had loved on sight. The McFarlands were happy to include her in their lively family while

Rush was working. And Rush would repay them the next time one of their animals needed care.

Busy as he was, Rush called Tracy almost every day, even if the call was little more than a quick hello. They hadn't seen each other since the day he'd picked up Clara at her house. He found himself missing her even more than he'd expected to. That was why, when a midday cancellation came up, Rush jumped at the chance to spend some time with her.

"How about a quick lunch date?" he asked when she picked up his call. "The crowd at Buckaroo's should be thinning out by now."

He sensed a beat of hesitation before she replied. But when she said, "Hey, that sounds great. I'm starved," he dismissed his worry.

"I'll be by in about ten minutes," he said.

Buckaroo's, a burger and pizza joint on the corner of Main Street, had a down-at-the-heels look about it. The bulbs on the string of Christmas lights above the counter were dulled with smoke and grease, and the aging speakers that blared country Christmas music needed replacing; but there was comfort in the sameness of the place. And the food was always good.

The lunch crowd had cleared, giving Rush and Tracy their choice of booths. They slid into the one in the farthest corner, where they could talk.

"So, have you found homes for the kittens?" he asked, making small talk as they sipped sodas and waited for their pizza.

"All but Snowflake. Maureen, from work, called me yesterday. Her little granddaughter wants a kitten, so Midnight is spoken for. Just like that. They're so cute. I'll miss them when they're gone."

"But you're keeping the mother?"

"Oh, yes. Rainbow has found a place in my heart. She even caught the mouse that startled me under the sink."

"You could keep Snowflake, too. The cats would keep each other company. And at least Clara would know where he was."

"I've thought about that. Snowflake would be safer with me than on the ranch. But Rush, there has to be a way for Clara to keep him."

"She asked for a miracle. That's what it's going to take."

"Couldn't Andre just take allergy pills, or stay away from the cat?"

"Maybe. But Andre isn't the accommodating sort. Everything has to revolve around him and what he wants. He was the one who insisted that I be kept away from Clara. Didn't want the competition." Rush gave himself a mental slap. "Sorry, I promised myself I wouldn't put him down. He is Clara's father, after all."

Just then the server appeared with their pizza. Tracy had said she was hungry, but she nibbled at the single slice she'd put on her plate as if forcing herself to eat. Something, Rush sensed, was wrong. He'd suspected it earlier but dismissed the thought. Now the worry returned.

"Is everything all right?" he asked her.

"Fine. Just a lot on my mind, that's all."

"I've missed you," he said. "I told you I was going to be busy for the next couple of weeks, and

I have been. But that doesn't mean I haven't thought about you. I hope you understand."

"Oh, I do. It's not that at all."

"But it's something, isn't it? I can tell. Does it have anything to do with me?"

"Yes and no."

He reached across the table and captured her hand. "I've never told you how I feel, because you've said you weren't ready for anything serious," he said. "But I've tried to show you how much I care about you, Tracy. If I'm pushing you where you don't want to go—"

"No, it's not even that." She was on the verge of tears, Rush could tell. "It's not you. It's me."

The old breakup line hit Rush like a punch below the belt. He felt as if he'd had the breath kicked out of him, but he was determined not to show it. "Have I taken too much for granted?" he asked. "Are you having second thoughts about us? Is that what you're trying to tell me?"

Tracy shook her head. "Please don't ask me anything else. There's something I haven't told you, that's all. I'll tell you in the car."

Neither of them felt like finishing the meal. Rush left a tip on the table, helped her with her jacket, and held the door as they went outside. Cloaked in a silence that matched the dark clouds spilling over the distant hills, they crossed the empty parking lot and climbed into the Hummer. The inside was still warm. There was no need for Rush to start the engine and turn on the heater.

"Here?" he asked. "Or do you want me to drive?"

"Here, I guess," she said.

Rush felt his gut clench as he waited. He should have known that the budding relationship with this woman was too good to be true. When she dumped him, as he was sure she was about to do, he would take it like a man. But it would hurt like hell.

"I'm listening." He paused. "It's all right, Tracy. Whatever it is, I'll handle it."

She took a breath. Rush could sense her anguish. At that moment he would have done anything to fight her battles, charge to her rescue, ease her pain.

But then she spoke.

"Hear me out, Rush. I've seen what a wonderful father you are to Clara. And I can imagine how loving you'd be with children who were your own flesh and blood, children nobody could take away from you. You deserve to have those children with a woman who can give them to you. No matter how much I might care for you, and you for me, I'm not that woman."

Rush reeled inwardly as the truth dawned—a truth he'd never considered, let alone expected.

"Steve and I tried for years to have a baby." Her voice trembled as she continued. "We never did. It took a doctor to prove that it wasn't his problem, it was mine. I won't go into details, but I can't get pregnant. Not ever."

He found his voice. "Tracy—"

"No, there's nothing you can say. I should've told you sooner, but it was so personal. And I didn't know I would come to feel this way about you."

"What way?"

"Never mind. It doesn't matter anymore."

The Hummer was getting chilly inside. Rush turned on the engine and dialed up the heater. Outside, a cold wind blew dry leaves against the windshield.

"Damn it, Tracy, listen to me. Do you think that's all I care about? Sure, having a family is important to me. But there's more than one way to get one. I couldn't love Clara more if she'd been born to me. And I'd feel that way about any child I took in as my own."

"You're saying that now," Tracy said. "But you need time to think about it. There are some lovely women in Branding Iron. Some of them already have children and could have more. Maybe you should try dating them."

"So what are you saying?" She was getting to him. Rush could feel his frustration building. "If you're trying to break up with me, just do it. Don't use an antiquated excuse that makes me look like Henry the Eighth."

Tracy's hands clenched in her lap. "All I'm saying is that we should spend some time apart—time for you to decide whether you want a relationship that won't give you the family you deserve."

"Or give you time to realize that it doesn't matter."

"Fine." She turned away and gazed ahead, through the windshield. "At least we're in agreement about something. I think it's time you took me home."

Rush drove the short distance to Tracy's house with her sitting in silence beside him. His head was still spinning. What else could he have said? Nothing, he realized. Of course, he'd rather have children of his own flesh and blood. But if having a woman he could love meant doing things differently, he could live with that. Plenty of happy couples did.

All he could do was back off and hope Tracy would come around to his way of thinking. One thing was certain—he wasn't about to come around to hers.

He pulled the Hummer into her driveway. She opened her own door and slid off the seat.

"Tracy."

She turned back to look at him. He saw the gleam of tears in her eyes.

"Call me if you want to talk, or if you need anything," he said. "I mean it."

She shook her head. "We both need time." With that she slipped to the ground, closed the door behind her, and fled into the house.

Rush drove back to the ranch. A sooty bank of clouds moving in from the west added to the gloom of the day—the kind of clouds that brought icy rain or thin, powdery snow that would blow away on the wind.

He battled the urge to pick up his cell phone, call Tracy, and try to put this nonsense to rest. But no, he had to respect her wishes to be left alone. All he could do was keep busy and hope for the best.

* * *

Even with the tree-selling season past its peak, the partners were working long hours. Late buyers still flocked to the ranch and to Hank's tree lot for their fresh trees. The thought of the cash flowing in was enough to keep the partners in good spirits, but the pace was exhausting. They were all anxious for the coming holiday, when they could rest and celebrate a profitable season.

Rush had cut back his veterinary practice to emergency calls only, so he could help at the ranch. It helped to keep busy. Still, every spare moment found him thinking about Tracy. A week had passed since he'd let her off at her house. Still she hadn't called.

Clara had begged him every day to take her to Tracy's to see the kittens. It had been hard, telling her he was too busy. But he was doing his best to keep her entertained.

She was still spending time with the McFarlands. She also enjoyed playing with Bucket and "helping" with the tree sales when customers came. Rush had checked out a big box full of picture books and easy readers from the library. With a little instruction in the basics, Clara was learning to read. They read together every night before she went to bed. Rush cherished every moment of these times, knowing they would never come again.

Busy as he was, the thought of Tracy was never far from Rush's mind. Did she miss him? Had she come to realize that as long as they had enough love, they could find a way to have a family? True, they hadn't spent enough time together to develop a solid relationship. But he'd sensed from the beginning that he and Tracy were meant to be together. He could only hope that she felt the same way.

He'd fantasized about his future family with her. Now the picture he imagined had changed—their children, not alike or like them, perhaps of different races, maybe even with special needs. The only constant was that they would all be loved.

He yearned to call her and hear her voice, but every time he reached for the phone, he checked himself. She'd asked him for time. He would give it to her.

It was after midnight, a week before Christmas, when Rush's ringing phone woke him out of a sound slumber. As his sleep-blurred vision focused on the display, his heart slammed. The caller was Tracy.

"What is it?" He was instantly wide awake.

"It's Murphy." She was sobbing, barely able to speak. "He's in pain. I think he's dying. I don't know what to do."

"Stay with him. Comfort him as much as you can. I'll be right there."

He flung on his clothes and boots. After pausing to wake Travis to tell him where he was headed, and to make sure Clara would be looked after, he grabbed his keys and raced out the front door.

Outside, it was snowing. Thick flakes swirled out of the night black sky, cloaking the world below in white velvet. Rush scarcely noticed the storm as he sprinted toward the Hummer and cleared the windshield with a sweep of his hand. Heedless of the snow, he started the engine with a roar, backed out of the drive, and shot down the lane to the highway.

Minutes later, he pulled up to the curb in front of Tracy's house. Before getting out of the vehicle, he reached back for his medical bag. Included in its contents was an injection kit for putting animals out of their suffering. If he needed to use it, he could only hope that Tracy would allow him to do the right thing.

Through the closed front blinds, he could see the glow of a single lamp. He opened the unlocked door and stepped into the living room.

Dressed in faded flannel pajamas, Tracy was huddled on the floor next to the unlit fireplace. The old dog lay in his bed, not curled as usual, but on his side, with his head in her lap.

As Rush walked in, she raised a tear-stained face. Her eyes were swollen from weeping. "Thank you for coming," she said. "He seemed all right when I went to bed, but when I woke up in the night, I found him like this. He flinches if I touch his body, and he's barely breathing."

"Let's see what I can find out." Rush used the stethoscope in his bag to check Murphy's heart and lungs. His pulse was thready, his breathing the barest broken whisper.

"Can you do anything for him?" Tracy asked. "I know he must be suffering."

Rush laid a hand on her shoulder, his touch as

light and gentle as he could make it. He could feel
her trembling.

"I think Murphy is telling you it's time to go," he
said. "How it happens is up to you. We can put him
to sleep, or we can wait for as long as it takes."

"How long?"

"Not long. Maybe a few hours."

"Isn't there anything you can do to save him?"
she pleaded.

"Even if there was, I wouldn't be doing the old
boy any favors. His body is failing. Take your time,
Tracy. Either way, I'll support your decision."

Tracy stroked the old pit bull's massive head.
Rush could feel her anguish. The dog was more
than a beloved pet. He was her last living tie to the
husband she still mourned.

Her throat moved as she swallowed and took a
breath. "He's suffering. It would be selfish to put
him through this any longer."

"You're sure." It wasn't a question.

She nodded, fresh tears flowing down her cheeks.

Rush prepared the IV for the injection. "Don't
worry. It'll be painless. He'll just go to sleep."

Tracy held the dog, stroking and kissing his
head as Rush shaved a small patch of skin to insert
the needle. "Good boy," she whispered, watching
his eyes close. "Go to Steve. Run to him. He's waiting for you."

By the time she'd finished speaking, Murphy
was gone.

Rush gave her a little time before he spoke. "You
can't bury him, especially in this weather. The vet

clinic in Cottonwood Springs can cremate the body. I can bring you back the ashes if you want."

Silent, lips pressed together, she nodded.

Rush wrapped the dog's body in a lightweight plastic tarp, carried it outside, and laid it in the rear of the Hummer. When he came back to the house, Tracy was sitting on the floor where he'd left her, next to the empty dog bed.

"Come here, Tracy." He reached down, caught her hands in his, and pulled her to her feet. She swayed slightly, then leaned forward and let him pull her into his embrace.

"Hold me," she whispered.

Rush knew better than to speak. His arms tightened around her trembling body. He cradled her against him, holding her as if he never wanted to let her go again.

Chapter 12

He held her close as she cried softly against his chest. Her body quivered with muffled sobs. Her tears soaked into his flannel shirt. Some might say it was a lot of grief for an old dog that had lived out its time. But Rush knew better. Tracy wasn't just weeping for a cherished pet. She was crying for a memory, her last living connection to the man she'd lost.

He could only hope that, once she let herself heal, she'd be able to move on—to him.

He did his best to calm her, massaging her back through the flannel pajamas, brushing his lips along her hairline, and whispering little phrases of comfort.

"It's all right, Tracy . . . Cry it out . . . you'll be fine."

He could feel her struggling to bring herself under control. Little by little, the crying ebbed until she rested quietly against him.

"Are you all right?" he asked.

She nodded. "I will be."

"You're shivering. Are you cold?"

"A little." Her teeth chattered as she spoke. With the heat turned down for the night, and no fire in the fireplace, the room was chilly.

He glanced at the mantel clock. "It's barely one o'clock in the morning. You belong in bed. Come on. I'll tuck you in."

"I don't know if I can sleep."

"At least you'll be warm. I'll stay if you want me to."

He guided her down the dark hall to her bedroom. She'd left a bedside lamp on, the light turned low. Rush smoothed the rumpled covers, turned them down, and tugged them over her as she slipped into bed.

"Don't go," she said, looking up at him.

Rush knew better than to take her words as an invitation to make love. She was grieving, and she didn't want to be alone. That was all.

He sat on the far edge of the bed, pulled off his boots, and stretched out on top of the covers. When she didn't speak, he turned onto his side and wrapped an arm around her. "All right?" he asked.

He felt her nod. "All right," she whispered. "Thanks for understanding."

He laid his cheek against her hair, feeling its silken warmth as she relaxed against him. Love swelled his heart. He would do anything for this woman, to protect her, provide for her, and make her happy. She might take time to come around, but he would wait—for as long as it took, he would wait. Tracy was worth it.

After a while she slept, warm and secure in his arms. Rush lay awake, holding her, listening to her breathe and filling his senses with the sweet, sleepy aroma of her skin. Turning his head, he could see the luminous dial of the clock on her nightstand. He wouldn't allow himself to stay past dawn, to risk creating a wave of gossip.

When the digits flipped over to 4:30, he stirred, eased himself away from her, and sat up. She opened her eyes, gazing up at him, still muzzy from sleep.

"I need to go," he said.

"I know," she whispered. "Don't worry, I'll be all right."

"I'll see to Murphy and call you later." He bent and kissed her, feeling the warm response of her lips. Resisting the urge to stay and taste them again, he picked up his boots and carried them into the living room. After pulling them on, he found his medical bag, where he'd left it next to the fireplace. He glanced around for his coat before he remembered that, in his haste to get here, he'd left it at the ranch.

Locking the front door behind him, he stepped out into a world of white. Fresh snow, six inches deep and still falling, blanketed the roads and walks, the lawns, the houses and trees, and the cars.

Snow. This time it was deep enough and cold enough to last for weeks. Branding Iron was going to have a white Christmas.

*   *   *

Tracy rose at 6:00 and turned up the heat in the house. She was tempted to crawl under the covers again until the place warmed up, but she was too restless to sleep. Wrapping her warm robe over her pajamas, she pattered barefoot into the kitchen to make coffee.

The sight of Murphy's empty bed by the fire-place almost undid her. Tears welled in her eyes. She blinked them away. *He's with Steve now,* she told herself. *They're together. They're happy.*

After she got dressed, she would roll up the bed and take it out to the trash. Then she would box the leftover canned food and save it as a treat for Bucket.

Last night she had shut Rainbow and her kittens into the laundry room. Now, from the other side of the door, she could hear a chorus of meows. When she opened the door, the four kittens came charging out into the hall, looking for any trouble they could find. Rainbow followed more sedately, pausing to rub against Tracy's legs and purr a greeting. Tracy picked her up and snuggled her close, kissing the heart-shaped orange spot on her head. "I guess it's going to be just us girls," she said.

When Rainbow meowed, Tracy put her down to round up her active babies. Only then did Tracy glance out the window and see the snow. Her breath caught. Overnight, the snow had trans-formed the world into a white fairyland. Trees had become lacework, the ground a glittering carpet, untracked except for Rush's half-buried boot prints, leading to the curb where he'd left the Hummer.

The whole town had been waiting for Christmas snow. This had to be a sign of something good, she told herself as she headed back to the bedroom to get dressed.

The patchwork quilt where Rush had lain beside her still bore the imprint of his weight. She remembered how tenderly he'd held her, and how he'd kissed her good-bye that morning. She'd kissed him back, and everything about it had felt right.

Steve's photograph still smiled at her from its place on her nightstand. It was only paper, she reminded herself again. And it was time to put it away.

After wrapping the photo in a spare pillowcase, she lifted the lid of the cedar chest at the foot of the bed and slipped it inside. For now she would leave the beach picture taken with Murphy in its place on the mantel. But later on, that would be put away, too. It was time she looked to the future.

If fate and heaven willed it, her future would be with Rush. She wanted to believe what he'd told her about creating a family. But what if he changed his mind? What if he realized that he wanted to father his own children, with a woman who could make it easy?

Tracy gazed out the window at the falling snow. *Believe,* a voice inside her whispered. *Take a chance. Trust your heart.*

But what if her heart was wrong? What if she was about to get it broken again?

* * *

For the next hour, Tracy forced herself to sit at her desk and tackle the rest of the legal briefs she'd put off reading. She would need to be familiar with their contents when the court took up its business again after the first of the year. Today, she also needed a way to keep her mind occupied.

It was almost 10:00 when Rush called to let her know he'd made the drive to Cottonwood Springs and left Murphy's remains at the clinic. The ashes would be ready in a couple of days.

"How about some breakfast before I head home?" he asked. "Even on a weekday, the B and B serves up a good plate of bacon and eggs."

"I don't think I'm up for going out in public," Tracy said. "But how would you like to lend me Clara for the day? I could use some cheering up, and she's the most cheerful person I know."

"That would be great!" he said. "She's been asking and asking. But are you sure you're up for a day with a four-year-old?"

"I think a day with a four-year-old is exactly what I need."

"She'll be over the moon when I tell her," Rush said. "I'm just getting into town. I'll head straight home and have her at your door in about an hour. Oh—and thanks. Things are crazy busy at the ranch, especially with the snow. Think sleigh rides."

"I'm thinking more like snow angels, and maybe a snowman. Have her bring her warm clothes. I'll see you soon."

Tracy ended the call and grabbed Ginger, who

was headed into the broom closet. Midnight and Tiger were chasing a spider they'd scared out from behind the stove. Snowflake, the quiet, snuggly one, was enjoying a tongue bath from his mother. She would miss the kittens when they were gone. But at least the place would be quieter.

By now she had a half dozen people on a waiting list in case the original adoptions fell through. Several people wanted Snowflake, but Tracy remembered her promise to Clara. She would save the white kitten, at least until Christmas.

Pulling on her coat and boots, she went outside to shovel the walks and the driveway. The snow was deep, but not heavy, and the hard physical work felt good. The snow was still falling. By the time Tracy finished shoveling, the areas she'd cleared first were already coated with white.

When she rolled up Murphy's bed and carried it out to the trash, the familiar scent of his tired old body brought tears to her eyes. But she forced herself to keep moving until the job was done. The woodpile was by the kitchen door, sheltered from snow by the overhang of the roof. She gathered logs and kindling and carried them inside to make a fire in the fireplace. Clara would enjoy its cheery warmth.

After rounding up the kittens and luring them back into the laundry room with food, she laid the fire with wood and crumpled newspaper. The logs were just beginning to burn when the front door-bell rang. Tracy hurried to answer it.

Rush and Clara stood on the threshold, snow-flakes glistening on their coats and hair. Rush was carrying a wreath of fresh pine boughs. "We brought you a present," Clara said.

"You're supposed to hang it on the outside of your door," Rush added. "But we thought maybe you'd rather hang it inside, for the smell. I brought a hanger. It goes over the top of the door."

"Come on in." Tracy stepped aside for them to enter. A chilly breeze blew in behind them. The glorious fragrance of fresh-cut pine flooded the room. Tracy inhaled, deeply. "Oh, my, it smells like Christmas!"

Rush took the hanger out of his coat pocket. It was designed with a bent metal piece, flat and thin enough to fit over the top of a door, with a longer hook at the bottom for a wreath.

"Inside or outside, up to you," Rush said.

"Oh, inside. Definitely inside."

While Rush hung the wreath on the door, Clara wandered over to the fireplace and stood looking down at the empty spot where Murphy's bed had been. Sad-eyed, she turned back to Tracy. "Daddy told me that Murphy went to heaven," she said. "I'm sorry, Tracy. I bet your husband was happy to see him."

"I'm sure they were happy to see . . . each other." Tracy's voice stumbled over the last words.

"Are you sad?" Clara asked.

"Yes, I am," Tracy said. "But I'll get better. That's why I invited you to come, to help me get better."

"I'll try. Where are the kittens?"

"In the laundry room. You can let them out. They've been needing somebody like you to play with them."

Clara scampered down the hall to open the laundry room door. Rush had finished hanging the wreath. Its fragrance scented the air, spreading through the room. Tracy walked over to the door where he stood. "Thank you," she said. "For the first time in two years, that wonderful aroma makes me feel like it's Christmas." *And so do you.*

"Well, you said you didn't want a tree. But I didn't think you'd mind a nice wreath—at least for the fragrance. It's a Christmas thing."

"Can you stay?"

He shook his head. "If I'm one minute late getting back to the ranch, Conner will have my head. It's crazy time at Christmas Tree Ranch. Thanks again for taking Clara."

"She'll be good for me."

"And you're good for me."

She was looking up at him when he bent, caught her waist, and kissed her. The kiss, meant to be a quick good-bye peck, lingered, deepened, went on and on as their hungry lips clung.

"Oh, wow!"

They broke apart. Clara stood at the entrance to the hallway, a kitten cradled in each arm. "Does this mean you're getting married?" she asked.

Rush laughed. "Right now, all it means is that we really, really like each other. Get used to it."

With that, he was out the door and gone.

Hot-faced, Tracy turned back to Clara. The little girl was grinning. "I'd like it if you married my dad," she said. "Then you could be my mom."

"You already have a mom, Clara," Tracy said.

"I have two dads. I could have two moms."

Tracy shook her head. "Never mind. Did you have breakfast?"

"Uh-huh. I ate three whole pancakes. Travis made them."

"Okay, you can tell me when you're hungry for lunch. I know you're playing with the kittens right now, but what else would you like to do?"

"Can we play in the snow?"

"It's still coming down out there. Wouldn't you rather wait till it stops?"

"No. It'll be like playing inside a snow globe. I saw one in a store once. It was so beautiful with the snow coming down." Her small face brightened. "Let's go out now, before it stops."

There was no way Tracy could win that argument. Dressed in warm parkas, boots, and gloves, they raced outside into clouds of swirling white. The snow on the ground was deep enough to reach Clara's knees. She stumbled and floundered through it, giggling ecstatically as she fell backward, making angel after angel.

"You make an angel, too," she told Tracy. Tracy fell on her back in the snow. Fanning her arms and legs, she made a perfect angel. Then she tried to get up.

"Oh, no," she moaned, "I'm stuck!"

Clara squealed with laughter as Tracy thrashed and struggled to her feet, her angel spoiled. "Can we make snowballs?" Clara asked. "We could have a snowball fight."

"We could try." Tracy tried shaping a handful of snow into a ball. It fell apart. The snow was too soft. "I guess we'll just have to throw snow," she said, tossing a handful at Clara's coat. Clara grabbed some snow and tossed it back. By the time it struck Tracy, it had broken into powder.

"I guess we can't make a snowman, either," Clara said.

"We can try in a day or two, when the snow's had time to settle," Tracy said. "But I know a fun game. It's called Fox and Geese—or Goose, I guess." Letting Clara follow her, she broke a circular trail in the snow, with cross trails leading from one side of the circle to the other. "Okay, you're the fox, and I'm the goose. We can only run on the trails, and you have to catch me. Go!"

Tracy started running in miniature steps around the circle. Catching on fast, Clara chased her. When the "goose" was nearly caught, Tracy turned onto a cross trail and got away. After a few such maneuvers, she let Clara catch her. "Now I get to be the fox," she said. "Run, goose!"

By the time they'd played the game for ten or fifteen minutes, Tracy was out of breath and Clara was getting cold. "Time to go in." She picked up the little girl and carried her to the porch, where they stomped the snow off their boots and brushed it off their clothes. As they opened the door and stepped inside, the lush fragrance of the pine wreath surrounded them. It really did smell like Christmas.

"That . . . was . . . fun." Clara's teeth chattered as Tracy helped her out of her coat and boots.

"Sit here by the warm fire while I make us some hot cocoa," Tracy said. "When we're warmed up, it'll be time to play another game—it's called Find the Kittens."

The four kittens had scattered in all directions. Rainbow, curled in a chair by the fire, watched in quiet amusement as Clara and Tracy searched. It was as if she were saying, *Go ahead and look. I know where they are. I could find them in a minute.*

Midnight was under Tracy's bed, his black fur blending with the shadows. Ginger had climbed into an open kitchen drawer. Tiger was under the desk in Tracy's office. Snowflake was asleep on the furry white rug in the bathroom, almost invisible until he opened his eyes and meowed.

Clara put the kittens in the chair with their mother. They snuggled together, a bundle of purring contentment.

Tracy made grilled cheese sandwiches and tomato soup for lunch. They sat at the kitchen table, talking and eating. "I wish I could stay here forever," Clara said. "I love the snow and the ranch. I love Daddy's friends and Bucket. And I love being here at your house."

"Your parents would miss you if you stayed here."

Clara shrugged. "My mom might. But she could have another baby. Andre wouldn't miss me much at all."

"We can't always have what we want." Tracy's heart ached for the little girl.

"I know," Clara said. "I have to go home to Mom and Andre. And I know they won't let me bring Snowflake. I wrote to Santa just to ask him. But he can't really bring me what I want. He can bring toys and stuff, but he can't make people change."

Tracy reached across the table and squeezed her hand. "You're a wise girl," she said. "And whatever happens, you're going to do fine."

"Can I ask you something?" Clara said. "You don't have to say yes."

"Go ahead."

"If I can't have Snowflake, could you keep him? That way I would know he was happy with his mom. And Rainbow wouldn't be lonesome."

"I think that's a lovely idea," Tracy said. "But let's wait and see what happens."

"Is that a no or a yes?"

"It's a yes, if nothing better works out. Okay?"

"Okay." Clara ate in silence for a few minutes, then changed the subject.

"I know something we can do after lunch. My friend, Gracie McFarland, showed me how to make Christmas cards. Have you got any paper, and some markers or crayons?"

"I think so," Tracy said. "The paper is just white. Will that be okay?"

"Uh-huh. I want to make cards for everybody."

Tracy had plenty of white copy paper in her office. The packet of washable markers hadn't been used in a while, but when she tested them, all the colors worked. By the time she'd found what she needed and carried everything into the kitchen, Clara had finished eating. They cleared the table, wiped it off, and got ready to work.

Clara took a sheet of paper and folded it in half.

"See," she said. "Now it's a card. You make a picture on the front and you write on the inside."

"Can you write?" Tracy asked.

"A little. But it's kind of hard. I'll make the picture, and you can write what I tell you. Okay?"

"Okay. Let's do it."

"This one's for my dad." She used the green marker to make a squiggly Christmas tree. "Now you write," she said. "Merry Christmas to Daddy, from Clara."

Once they got started the cards went fairly quickly. Each picture was different—a dog for Travis, a horse for Conner, a star for Maggie, a cat for her friend Gracie, and other pictures for the rest of the McFarland family. She even made cards for Cecil and Annie who'd taken care of her in Phoenix. The inside messages were all the same except for the names. Her artwork wasn't bad for a four-year-old's, but best of all, she was having fun.

"Are you going to make cards for your parents?" Tracy asked.

"They're on the big boat. They can't get my cards there." Clara shook her head and kept on drawing.

On the last card, she drew a big brown dog with wings on his back. "This card is for you," she said. "It's Murphy. He's an angel now."

Tracy blinked away a tear.

By the time the cards were finished, Clara was yawning. "Time for a rest," Tracy said. "Would you like to lie down on my bed?"

"Uh-huh. Can I take Snowflake with me?"

"All right. Just be careful. Pick him up gently so Rainbow will know she can trust you."

Clara tiptoed over to the chair, eased the white kitten away from the others, and gathered him into her arms. Rainbow raised her head. "Don't worry, Rainbow, I'll bring him back," she said.

Tracy walked with her back to the bedroom, helped her onto the bed, and covered her with the small quilt. A few minutes later, when she went back to check on her, Clara was fast asleep with Snowflake curled in the spoon of her body.

Moving quietly, Tracy went into her home office and sat down at her computer. Something Clara had said earlier had given her an idea for a gift.

A quick search on her computer brought up just what she wanted—a beautiful snow globe with Santa and his sleigh inside. Using her credit card, she chose express shipping and placed the order. The snow globe would be something that Clara could have in Phoenix. When she made the snow swirl, she would be reminded of Christmas Tree Ranch and the people who loved her.

It was after 3:00 when Rush parked outside Tracy's house and climbed the front steps. Between cutting and hauling trees, grooming the sleigh-ride trail, repairing the harnesses, and polishing the hardware on the sleigh till it gleamed, he ached in every joint and muscle. The snow was a blessing to the ranch. But the popular sleigh rides, which would continue through the New Year if the snow lasted, doubled the season's workload.

He rapped lightly on the door, hoping that Clara would still be napping. This morning's brief time with Tracy hadn't been enough.

She opened the door, dressed in jeans and a faded sweatshirt, her hair loose and her face glowing. Just seeing her smile made the drive on treacherous roads worth his time.

He was head over heels in love, and it felt damned good.

Stepping inside, he closed the door softly behind him, shed his coat on the floor, and caught her in his arms. Their kiss was long and sweet, leaving them both hungry for more. But what they really wanted would have to be saved for another time.

She stepped back with a mischievous smile. "I see you still have your head," she said.

It took a beat for him to remember what he'd said about Conner that morning. "Just barely," he said. "I threatened him with mutiny if I didn't get a break. How's Clara?"

"Still napping. I think we wore her out."

"Yes, I saw the snow angels and the Fox and Geese game. I haven't played that since I was a kid." His gaze wandered to the couch and the fire. "Now that looks inviting. I can't stay long, but I've been fantasizing about you and that couch and that fireplace all day."

"So have I," she said. "But first, come down the hall with me. You need to see something." She touched a finger to her lips. "Not a sound, now."

Walking quietly, he followed her down the hall to her bedroom. The door stood partway open.

From where he stood, Rush could see Clara sleeping like a little dark-haired angel, with her arm around the white kitten. The sight of her raised a lump in his throat. There was nothing he wouldn't do to make that little girl happy. But considering what she wanted, she might as well have wished for the moon.

He followed Tracy back to the couch and settled her next to him with her head on his shoulder. The fire lent a cozy glow to the room. Rush rested his boots on the hearth and let the tension of the day ease out of him.

"I can get you something to drink," Tracy said. "Would you like a beer?"

"Don't you dare move," he said. "I could stay just like this forever."

Tracy snuggled closer. "Clara spent half the afternoon making Christmas cards for everybody. You, Travis and Conner, Maggie, the McFarlands . . . I think she even made one for Bucket. I put them in a bag for her to take home. Don't let her forget them."

"I won't." Rush sighed. "Damn it, I wish I could give her what she wants. I hate to see her heart broken on Christmas morning when Santa doesn't deliver her wish."

Tracy stirred and looked up at him. "But she understands that it's only a wish, Rush. That's what she told me today. She's not expecting it to come true."

Rush gave her a surprised look. "Then why did she write the letter?"

"She wanted to tell Santa her wish. But as she

said to me, Santa can only bring toys and things. He can't make people change."

"Damn, I had no idea," Rush said.

"She's a very wise little girl. You should be proud of her."

"I am." Rush shook his head. "I was just wondering how two people as shallow as Sonya and Andre could have produced a child like Clara."

Tracy squeezed his hand. "She had you to give her a good start. And she had Cecil and Annie. She made cards for them, too. If you have their address, maybe you could help her mail them."

"I do, and I'll be happy to. Cecil and Annie would love those cards." Rush sat in silence for a long moment, gazing into the fire.

"Are you all right?" Tracy asked. "You look perplexed."

Rush exhaled slowly. "I'm fine. It's just that I've wasted time beating myself up because I couldn't give Clara what she wanted. Now I need something real to give her. I want her to remember this Christmas forever. Something tells me I'm going to need your help."

"Of course, you'll want to give her presents to open," Tracy said. "I could take her to the mall in Cottonwood Springs. Maybe she'll see something she wants there. Meanwhile there'll be things going on all week. We've got the parade coming up on Saturday, with the Christmas brunch in the morning, and the Christmas Ball that night. And she can always have fun in the snow on the ranch. You could even—"

She broke off as Clara emerged from the hall,

trailing the quilt and cradling Snowflake in her arms. "What are you and Tracy talking about, Daddy?" she asked, still sounding sleepy.

"We're talking about ways to have fun," Rush said. "And I just thought of one. How would you and Tracy like to go on a sleigh ride?"

Chapter 13

Tracy drove herself to the ranch that evening. Rush had offered to come to town and pick her up for the sleigh ride. But she knew the partners would be busy with last-minute preparations. The roads had been plowed, and her old Mercedes had new all-season tires. The short drive wasn't a problem.

She swung the car through the gate, parked, and lifted out the pan of cinnamon rolls she'd made. The front porch and yard were hung with lights, and Christmas music was playing on the boom box.

By now, most families in town had bought trees, but a few were still looking, their children enjoying the free hot chocolate and marshmallows roasted over a small bonfire. The partners had hired two local teenagers to tend the fire, serve the hot chocolate, and supervise the marshmallow roasting.

It was Rush who opened the front door for her. "Hey, come on in. Ladies with treats are always welcome here. Are you ready for a moonlight sleigh ride?"

"Ready." Tracy laughed as Clara came bounding into sight, bundled into layers of warm clothes.

"Can we go now?" she demanded. "And can Bucket come with us?"

"That's fine with me," Rush said. "I'll bet Bucket's already waiting for us in the sleigh. Tracy, do you mind sharing the ride with a smelly, wiggly dog?"

"The more the merrier," Tracy said. "Let's go."

They trooped out the door to the backyard, where the sleigh was waiting with Conner at the reins and Bucket next to him on the driver's bench. The sleigh rides for customers wouldn't start until tomorrow. Today the partners had made an afternoon trial run with the sleigh and horses. But they needed to make another run by moonlight, with passengers, to test the trail again, and to re-accustom the Percherons to nighttime sounds and shadows that might startle them.

Tonight, Conner, the most experienced driver, would handle the team. Rush, Tracy, and Clara would ride in the sleigh. Travis would keep an eye on business at the house.

The ride would take them across the pastures, over the hill to the tree forest, and back again for a round-trip of about forty minutes—plenty of time on a chilly night.

Rush helped Tracy and Clara into the sleigh and tucked a warm quilt around them before he climbed onto the seat beside them. They sat with Clara in the middle, keeping her warm from both sides.

"Ready?" Conner glanced back over his shoulder, grinning.

"Ready!" Clara said.

"Okay," Conner said. "Before we start I need to tell you a couple of things. People on these sleigh rides tend to make a lot of noise. I need you to get the horses used to the ruckus so they won't be scared next time. Shout, sing, hoot, and holler, anything you want to. Understand?"

"You said a couple of things. What else do we need to know?" Tracy asked.

"Just a word of caution." Conner winked. "Last year there were three marriage proposals on these sleigh rides. And some of the couples got so passionate that I didn't dare look back at them. There's something about being out here on a beautiful moonlit night that brings out the romance in people. If that happens to you, don't say I didn't warn you."

Clara giggled. "You can kiss her, Daddy. I won't look."

Conner whooped with laughter. "Here we go!" He clucked his tongue and slapped the reins lightly on the horses' backs. The traces tightened as the massive animals pulled, moving the sleigh effortlessly over the packed snow. Bucket kept his balance on the driver's bench next to Conner, ears pricked, nose sniffing the air.

The night was cold and clear, the stars like a spill of diamond dust across the ink black sky. The rising moon hung low in the sky, casting a golden glow across the snowy landscape.

The horses moved at an easy walk, their hooves all but silent on the snow as the sleigh glided along.

Tracy was entranced by the peace of the night, broken only by the snort of a horse, the faint swish of runners, and the faint jingle of harness bells; but it wasn't meant to last.

"I don't hear any hootin' and hollerin' back there," Conner called to them. "Come on, folks, let's have some noise!"

"I've never been much of a hootin' and hollerin' type," Tracy confessed to Rush in a whisper.

"Then how about we sing? Come on now." Rush broke into "Jingle Bells," his voice a deep, musical baritone. Clara joined in, then Tracy. Once she got warmed up, it became fun. After "Jingle Bells," they sang their way through "Here Comes Santa Claus," and "Up on the House Top." They'd just started on "Jolly Old St. Nicholas," when a startled jackrabbit leaped out of a sage clump, almost under the front hooves of the horses.

The two huge animals snorted, stamped, and reared, yanking at their harnesses. As the sleigh rocked, almost tipping, Rush flung himself protectively in front of Clara and Tracy, holding them in place on the seat.

A less skilled driver than Conner might have lost control of the team. But within seconds, working the reins and talking in a soothing voice, he managed to calm the horses and avoid a dangerous spill. As the sleigh swayed to a halt, they all took a breath of relief.

"Are you all right?" Conner asked his passengers.

"We're fine," Rush said. "But where's the dog?"

Conner swore under his breath. Evidently, Bucket

had caught sight of the rabbit as it bounded off across the snow. He'd leaped off the sleigh and gone rocketing after it. By the time Conner had quieted the horses, he was almost over the next hill, a distant dot against the moonlit snow.

"Bucket!" Conner shouted at the top of his lungs. "Come back here, you blasted mutt!"

Bucket didn't respond.

"What can we do?" Clara was close to tears.

"All we can do is keep going and hope the fool dog comes back," Conner said.

"What if he doesn't come back? We can't leave him out here. It's too cold." Clara had started to cry. "He'll freeze. Or the coyotes will get him. I know about coyotes. They could kill him."

Tracy gathered the little girl close, wrapping her in her arms. "Don't worry, Clara," Rush said. "Bucket knows where we are. When he gets tired of chasing that rabbit, he'll come back and find us. You'll see."

Conner nudged the horses to a brisk walk. As the sleigh moved ahead, Tracy heard a sound, faint with distance but unmistakable. She clutched Clara tighter, making sure the little girl's ears were covered so she wouldn't hear. Rush glanced toward her. As their eyes met, they heard the sound again. Tracy shivered, a chill creeping up her back.

It was the haunting cry of a coyote.

Coyotes were no threat to the horses or the people in the sleigh. But a full-grown coyote could kill a dog like Bucket. If she heard their calls, out there in the darkness, Clara would be terrified for him.

Thinking fast, Tracy spoke up. "I know what we can do. Let's sing again, as loud as we can, so Bucket will hear us and come."

It was Rush who began the song, his rich baritone ringing in the darkness. "*Silent night . . . holy night . . .*"

Tracy and Clara, then even Conner, joined in. Now the night was anything but silent as the sleigh glided up the rise that overlooked the tree forest. Minutes had passed. Still there was no sign of Bucket.

At the crest of the hill, Conner paused the horses. In the hollow below, the pine trees spread like a dark carpet, snow glittering on their branches.

Suddenly Conner hushed the song and pointed down into the hollow. Standing in the sleigh for a better view, Tracy followed his gaze. Her lips parted in wonder. Rush stood beside her, holding Clara high so she could see.

In a moonlit clearing at the edge of the trees, two dark shapes were romping in play. One of them was Bucket. The other was a small coyote.

"It looks like a young one, probably a female," Rush whispered in Tracy's ear. "She could be looking for a boyfriend. Bucket can't be much help on that account, but look how much fun they're having."

The two animals were tussling in the snow, rolling, and chasing each other in circles, all in the spirit of play. Watching them, it was hard not to smile. But if more coyotes showed up, Bucket would be in danger.

Conner gave a loud whistle. The young coyote

looked up at the sleigh on the hill, wheeled in her tracks, and raced off into the trees. Bucket hesitated, as if torn between chasing her and returning to his human pack.

"Bucket, come," Conner commanded. "Come on, boy."

Decision made, Bucket trotted up the hill and jumped into the sleigh. He was snowy, dirty, and smelled like eau de coyote, but his face wore a doggy grin. Clara jumped off the seat and flung her arms around him. "You bad dog!" she scolded him. "Now you're all wet and cold. Come up under the blanket and get warm."

She helped Bucket scramble onto the seat, then climbed up next to him and covered him with her end of the quilt. The wet dog reeked to high heaven, but he was shivering with cold, so keeping him covered probably wasn't a bad idea.

Tracy gave Rush a smile as he shifted to make more room on the seat. This sleigh ride hadn't turned out to be the romantic interlude they'd hoped for. But they'd shared an adventure, one that Clara would talk about for a long time to come.

Back at the ranch, they cleaned up. Clara's nylon parka and the quilt went into the washer. Rush offered to bathe the dog, with the help of Clara, who'd washed the dog before and knew what to expect.

"I'll help, too," Tracy said.

"No need. Bucket doesn't mind baths if the

water's warm." Rush piled some worn-out towels on the floor, herded the dog into the bathroom, and ran the tub, the only place to wash him in cold weather. While the tap was running, he filled an empty milk jug with fresh water for rinsing.

"Give me a break," Tracy teased. "It looks like fun."

"Come on, Daddy, let her help," Clara said.

Rush lowered Bucket into the warm water, then glanced up at Tracy. "All right, but if you get soaked, don't say I didn't warn you."

Tracy rolled up her sleeves and knelt next to the tub. Rush was secretly pleased that she wanted to help, but he kept that to himself as he handed her a plastic soft drink cup. "Okay, use this to scoop water on him while I soap."

"What about me?" Clara asked.

"Stay up by his head. Talk to him and keep him calm. And try not to get too wet." As Tracy began wetting Bucket down with bathwater, Rush lathered soap between his hands and rubbed it into the dog's wet, smelly fur.

"Ugh!" She wrinkled her nose. "He smells worse now than he did in the sleigh."

"Keep pouring water on him," Rush said. "Coyotes are smelly animals. They roll in whatever they can find to hide their scent. But I imagine that, to Bucket, that young lady coyote smelled like she was wearing perfume. We should probably keep an eye on him when he's outside. He might get it into his fool head to go looking for her again."

"Did you have fun, Bucket?" Clara scratched the dog's head. "Don't worry. We're not mad at you.

Just don't do that again." She paused, as if remembering something. "Daddy, did you ever find out if Bucket likes cats?"

"I never found anybody who knew." Rush added more soap to the thick fur around Bucket's neck.

"But I did," Tracy said. "I asked Maggie. She knew the man who gave Bucket to Travis. Bucket was raised with an old cat. He gets along fine with cats."

"See, Daddy! He does like cats!"

"Maybe so." Rush knew what Clara was thinking. "But that doesn't mean Bucket would be gentle with a kitten. He likes to play rough."

"Oh." Clara sighed. Rush hated to crush her hopes, but reality was what it was. A tiny kitten wouldn't be safe on the ranch.

After twenty minutes of soaping and rinsing, Bucket was fit for polite company once more. Rush pulled the drain plug and gave him a final rinse-off with the water from the jug. He was reaching for the stack of old towels when Bucket did what he always did after a bath—he shook his coat, flinging water in all directions.

Rush and Clara knew what to expect. They dodged out of the way. But Tracy was caught off guard. The water hit her straight on, soaking her down the front from her head to her hips.

As the shaking ceased, she knelt by the tub, her face frozen in shock. Water was dripping off her hair and running down her face, pooling in the hollow between her breasts and plastering her shirt to her body.

Recovering slowly, she looked down to assess

the damage. Her eyes met Rush's. He tried to hide his amusement, but lost the battle to the laughter that tugged the corners of his mouth and spilled over.

Her gaze took on a steely look. Something told Rush he was in trouble.

Her hand still held the plastic cup she'd used to pour water on the dog. The tub was emptying slowly. A few inches of dirty water remained in the bottom.

With a lightning move, she scooped a cupful of water and dumped it over his head. "Now it's my turn to laugh at you," she said. "See how it feels."

Her eyes sparkled with mischief as she spoke. She was beautiful, even like this, Rush thought, with her hair hanging in wet strings around her glowing face, her wet shirt clinging to her body, revealing every sexy, enticing curve.

Somewhere behind him, Clara was enjoying a giggle fit, reminding him that he and Tracy weren't alone. If they had been, Rush thought, he would have crushed her in his arms, devoured her with his lips, and turned his hands loose to possess all the sweet, forbidden places he'd yearned to touch.

As they gazed at each other, her eyes became dark pools of emotion. Her damp lips parted. The urge to kiss her, here and now, even with Clara watching, was a fever in him. He reached out . . .

That was when Bucket made his move. With no one paying attention to him, he clambered over the edge of the tub, raced out of the bathroom and down the hall, leaving a watery trail behind him.

With a half-mouthed curse, Rush grabbed a handful of towels and plunged after the dog, tackling him as he made it to the kitchen. Bucket wagged and grinned, enjoying the game as Rush toweled him dry. "Blasted hound," Rush muttered. "If there's a way to get into trouble, you'll find it."

By the time Travis and Conner ended the ranch business for the night and came inside, Clara was ready for bed, and Tracy was getting ready to leave. She'd given her hair and clothes time to dry, but everything smelled from the dog bath. She was anxious to get home, throw her clothes in the washer, and take a long, hot shower.

She'd spent some time helping Clara read one of the beginner books Rush had brought home from the library. The little girl had come a long way since the day Tracy had helped her write to Santa. By the time she started kindergarten next year, she could be reading well—at least she might be, if her Phoenix family gave her the help and encouragement she needed. Tracy made a mental note to buy some books as a gift for Clara along with the snow globe.

Clara would be going home sometime after Christmas, pending arrangements with her mother and Andre. When Tracy thought about her leaving, and what the separation would mean to both her and Rush, her heart ached for them.

Conner and Travis came in hungry. They pounced on the cinnamon rolls Tracy had brought, taking big bites and washing them down with cold milk. "These are heavenly!" Conner declared, reaching for his third helping. "Rush, if you let this woman get away, you deserve to have your head examined."

By now, Tracy had learned to ignore Conner's teasing. But she couldn't help wondering where things were going with her and Rush. In the weeks she'd known him, it was as if he'd brought her back to life—as if he'd freed her to feel emotions she'd believed to be buried forever.

And yet, how much did she know about this man? How much did he know about her? What hidden secrets were waiting to surface and tear them apart?

She would be wise to guard her heart and be prepared.

"It's time I was going," she said, zipping her parka. "Keep the rest of the cinnamon rolls. I'll get the pan later."

"Thanks," Travis said. "Believe me, they won't last long."

Clara ran to her for a hug and a good-night kiss. "I'll walk you out to your car," Rush said, grabbing his jacket off the coatrack. "You'll want to hang on to me. It's slippery out there."

He gave her his arm as they stepped out onto the front porch. A passing snow flurry had moved in from the west. Big, lazy white flakes drifted from the sky. They settled on Rush's dark hair as he guided her down the icy steps. Tracy clung to his side, feeling his solid strength. *I could get used to this,* she thought.

When they reached her car, he turned and took her in his arms. "Damn, that feels good," he muttered. "I could spend all night holding you like this, except—" He gave a rough laugh. "Just holding you wouldn't be enough."

Tracy understood. She closed her eyes and rested her head against his chest. Beneath the open front of his jacket, his shirt was damp from washing Bucket. "You smell like wet dog," she teased.

"So do you." His arms tightened around her. "Blast it, woman, when are we going to get some serious time alone?"

She looked up at him. "Something tells me it won't be until after the holidays. So we might as well relax and enjoy the fun while it lasts."

"Things will be crazy between now and this Saturday. I'd like to take you to the brunch, but we'll be busy getting the sleigh and the team to town for the parade. It'll be my job to load and unload the horses and drive their trailer."

"Why don't you let me pick up Clara and take her to the brunch? Then I can drive her to the parade."

"That's a nice thought," Travis said. "But I promised her a special surprise. For that, she'll need to be home with us Saturday morning. I can meet you on Main Street before the parade starts. We can watch it together before I have to go back and reload the horses."

"I'd love that. I've never watched the parade. You're sure you'll have time?"

"Once the sleigh's in line for the parade, I'll be free to come and meet you. I'll call you when I'm on my way."

"Well, then, I have another idea. Why don't I pick up Clara's princess costume and take her home with me after the parade? Once she's had time to play and nap, we can get ready for the Christmas Ball together. You know, sort of a girly thing."

"I like girly things." He nuzzled her hair. "Especially yours."

"But what do you think of my suggestion?"

"It's a grand idea. She'll love it. Then I can pick up my princess and my queen at seven o'clock and take them to the ball. I'll be the luckiest man there."

The snow was coming down harder now, swirling around them. He bent his head and kissed her—a slow, dizzying kiss that Tracy felt all the way to the tips of her toes. "You'd better get going," he said, opening the car door for her. Tracy slid into the driver's seat.

"Be careful on the road," he said, closing the door. "I love you, Tracy."

As she drove away, Tracy could see him in her rearview mirror, standing in the driveway with snow falling around him. Had he meant for her to hear him as he closed the door? Had he really said he loved her, or had she only imagined it?

She'd be a fool to believe what she'd barely heard, Tracy told herself. But the thought that the words might be true made her heart sing.

She turned on her wipers to clear the falling snow. "I love you, too," she whispered into the darkness. "I love you, Rush."

On Friday, Tracy picked up Clara at the ranch for a visit to the mall in Cottonwood Springs. Rush's Hummer had been missing when she arrived. He'd let her know earlier that he'd be gone, freeing and doctoring a bull that had been caught in a tangle of barbed wire half buried in the deep snow. "Wish me luck," he'd told her on the phone. "This isn't going to be an easy job."

As she drove north, Tracy tried not to think about the danger he could be in. A powerful bull, trapped and in pain, could do a lot of damage to anyone who got too close. Would Rush subdue it with a tranquilizer dart before cutting the wire? Would there be men to hold the huge animal with ropes? What if the bull got loose?

Never mind, she told herself. Rush knew his job. He would be fine. Meanwhile, he'd left her his credit card, with orders to have a good time and buy Clara whatever she liked.

"We've got a big mall in Phoenix." Clara spoke from the safety of her booster seat. "It's got a merry-go-round and a huge food court and a place to see movies."

Something told Tracy that Clara wouldn't be impressed by the modest-size Cottonwood Corners Mall. "Phoenix is a big city, so it can have a big mall. Cottonwood Springs is just a big town."

"So it doesn't have a very big mall."

"Right. But we can still have a good time looking in the stores and getting some lunch. Maybe you'll see something you'd like for Christmas."

"Maybe." Clara sounded skeptical. Tracy knew that what she really wanted couldn't be found in a store.

The mall was festively decorated, with Christmas lights and decorations. The strains of "Silver Bells" rose above the babble of shoppers and vendors. The air swam with the fragrances of cinnamon and peppermint.

In the center of the mall was a glittering Christmas tree. At its foot, in a red and gold velvet chair, sat the mall's Santa Claus. The line of children waiting to meet him stretched far down one wing of the mall. Tired-looking parents stood off to one side, waiting. Clara stopped, standing a few paces back to look.

"Would you like to talk to Santa?" Tracy asked.

The little girl shook her head. "He's not the real Santa. I can see his fake beard from here. And he looks tired. Let's keep going."

They passed a shoe store, where they found a pair of silver sneakers for Clara to wear with her princess costume. Coming out of the store, Clara suddenly pointed. "There! That's what I want to do." She ran toward a brightly painted photo booth. "Let's take pictures of us together."

Mugging and laughing in the booth, they took two strips of photos. "One for you and one for me," Clara said. "We can keep them to remember each other."

Tracy suppressed a murmur of dismay. Clara, with a wisdom beyond her years, was already preparing for the time when she'd go back to Phoenix and leave everyone she'd found here, maybe forever.

Racing down the mall, Clara stopped abruptly outside the window of a photo studio. "What does that sign on the glass say?" she asked.

Tracy read the sign out loud. "*Special: Christmas portraits while you wait.* That means you can go in and have your picture taken and get it back while you're here."

"I want to do that." Clara marched into the shop. "It's for my dad," she told the photographer.

Clara wasn't dressed up, but she looked adorable in her red Christmas sweater and jeans. After Tracy combed her hair, the photographer sat her in front of a Christmas scene to snap the picture. "I'll have it for you in about thirty minutes," he said. "I can put it in a frame if you like. I can even gift wrap it—after you've seen and approved it, of course."

While they waited, they had Chinese in the food court. By the time they returned to the studio, the portrait was ready. Tracy had it framed and wrapped, and paid for it with her own card.

"Can we go now?" Clara asked as Tracy tucked the wrapped picture in the shopping bag with the little silver shoes.

"If you're ready." Tracy had hoped Clara would see something that Rush could pick up later for a gift. But aside from the shoes, which weren't really a present, all she'd wanted were the photos.

Not long after leaving the mall, Clara fell asleep in her booster seat. Lost in thought, Tracy drove home. Clara was so young. She was bravely preparing for the day when she would have to go home to her parents. But how could she understand the full implications of that time—the idea that she might not be allowed to see Rush again for years, until she came of age?

Tracy remembered the nugget of hope she'd found in her online search. It might not be of any help now, but anything could happen in the years ahead. There were no guarantees, not even the promise that she and Rush would stay together. She needed to make him aware of it while she could.

She'd told herself that it would be cruel to give him false hope. But what could be crueler than no hope at all?

She had to tell him what she'd found. But first she would share what she knew with someone else—a wise friend who could advise her how to proceed.

She would talk to Maggie.

Chapter 14

Standing in the light of Clara's small Christmas tree, Rush unzipped the tent flap far enough to look inside. He checked on Clara every night before he went to bed. It was a tender moment, made poignant by his knowing that soon she'd be gone, maybe for years.

In the faint glow that shone through the fabric, she lay nestled in her sleeping bag. One arm snuggled her stuffed white cat, much as she'd cradled the real kitten at Tracy's house. The sight of her, sleeping so peacefully, was enough to tie his heart in a knot.

Tomorrow, the Saturday before Christmas, would be Branding Iron's day of celebration, with the parade in the morning and the Cowboy Christmas Ball that night. Christmas would fall on the following Wednesday. After that . . .

He tried to shove the thought aside, but it stayed to torment him like a buzzing, biting insect. He'd heard nothing from Sonya. He didn't even know for sure when the cruise would end. He only knew that after Christmas his days with Clara would be numbered. All he could do was make the most of each one.

On Saturday morning, Tracy rose early, fed the cats, and went outside to clear away the few inches of snow that had fallen in the night. The sky was clear, the air crisply cold but not frigid. The weather would be perfect for the parade.

The parade, scheduled to begin at 10:00, started at the high school parking lot, continued down Main Street to the last stoplight going south, then turned around at the intersection with the highway and went back in the other direction. Nobody minded that the procession went both ways. Seeing everything twice made the fun last twice as long.

By 9:15 Tracy was ready to go, dressed in a festive red sweater, jeans, boots, and her warm parka. Leaving the car on a side street, she walked the short distance to the city park, a good spot for parade watching.

Rush had arranged to meet her next to the World War II monument, a tall block of native stone with a flagpole on top and a bronze plaque listing the names of Branding Iron's veterans. The sidewalks along the parade route were already crowded, with people staking out the best spots. Even families from Cottonwood Springs—a bigger town, but with no parade of its own—enjoyed coming to Branding Iron for some old-fashioned Christmas spirit.

It was early yet. Tracy didn't expect Rush to

meet her until almost parade time. But as she strolled through the milling crowd, she spotted several people she knew. Maureen, the receptionist in the courthouse, gave her a friendly wave. "Can I come tomorrow and get that little black kitten?" she asked.

"Can you wait till later in the day?" Tracy asked. "Dr. Rushford is coming tomorrow to give the kittens their vaccinations. Then they'll be ready to go."

"Sure," Maureen said. "I'll call before I come."

Tracy sighed as she walked on. She was going to miss those kittens. Over the past week, they'd become little holy terrors, racing through the house, climbing on everything. But they were so cute and so much fun. Unless Clara got her miracle, Tracy realized she'd likely be keeping Snowflake. Clara would never forgive her if she gave the white kitten away. At least he was the calm one.

But he really belonged to Clara. Tracy knew it. Clara knew it. Maybe even Snowflake knew it.

Through the crowd, she could see Katy and Daniel walking hand in hand. Daniel would be picking up Tiger before Christmas. Sweet, loving Katy would adore the little tabby girl.

Only as they passed her did Tracy notice someone walking with them—a young woman she'd never seen before.

She appeared to be in her mid-twenties, slim as a willow, with long brown hair and striking dark eyes. But it was her clothes that drew Tracy's attention. She was dressed in faded jeans with tooled leather cowboy boots that came almost to her knees.

Over a black turtleneck, she wore a buckskin jacket that looked like something salvaged from a rock star, with trailing fringe on the yokes and sleeves, and exquisite beading down the front. A weathered Stetson shaded her face. On anyone else, the outfit would have been too much. But the young woman wore it with such elegance and flair that she made a stunning picture.

Tracy looked away for a moment. When she looked back, Daniel, Katy, and the mysterious stranger were nowhere in sight.

She glanced at her watch. Rush could be showing up any minute. She hurried back to the monument to find him waiting for her. He grinned and caught her hand. "Come on, the parade's about to start."

"Where's Clara?" Tracy asked.

"You'll see. Come on." He led her to a good vantage point, standing behind a family who'd brought chairs. The Christmas music on the public address speakers had gone silent. From up the street they could hear the beat of a snare drum as the flag came into sight, carried by the members of the American Legion. Everyone stood and placed their hands over their hearts. When the flag had passed, Rush moved behind Tracy and wrapped his arms around her. The feeling was pure joy, being with a man who wouldn't hesitate to show the whole town that she was his woman.

At a respectful distance behind the flag came a white convertible with local and visiting dignitaries—the lieutenant governor, the county commissioners, and Maggie, bundled into a dark green

coat. Catching sight of Rush and Tracy, she grinned
and blew them a kiss.

Tracy remembered their talk two days ago. Over
coffee and pie at Buckaroo's, she'd given Maggie a
copy of the obscure Arizona law she'd found online. "Rush needs to have this," Maggie had said.

"Maybe later," Tracy had replied. "Right now I
don't want to give him false hope. But somebody
else needs to be aware of this, in case I'm not
around later on. Sometime—maybe years from
now—it could be useful. Just not now."

"I can't say I agree." Maggie had frowned and
shaken her head. "I think you should just give it to
Rush. But I'll respect your decision and keep this
somewhere safe—for now."

The memory faded as she and Rush settled in to
watch the parade. The Branding Iron High School
Marching Band was playing Christmas music—
more than a little off-key, but nobody seemed to
mind. The local businesses had decorated simple
floats, some with pretty teenage girls riding on
them. Volunteers dressed as elves scampered along
the sidelines, throwing wrapped candies to the kids.

At the sound of sleigh bells, a stir of excitement
passed through the crowd. Children peered up
the street, some of them jumping up and down.
Parents lifted the little ones to their shoulders for
a better view.

Santa was coming.

Branding Iron wasn't much of a town, and the
Christmas parade was no grand spectacle. But the
Branding Iron Santa, in a real sleigh, pulled by
massive draft horses with real brass bells on their

harnesses, was pure magic. There was no better Santa in the state, maybe in the whole country. And now he was coming down the street, the sleigh gliding on a layer of hard-packed snow.

Standing on tiptoe, Tracy could see the sleigh. Hank, who'd taken over the job last year, was a magnificent Santa. Waving at the crowd, smiling at the children, he radiated genuine Christmas joy. Bucket, on his best behavior, sat beside Hank, wearing a miniature red cape and Santa hat.

Conner, in full cowboy gear, drove the team from the low front bench. Next to him, smiling and waving in her red parka, was Clara.

"Look at her! She's having the time of her life!" Tracy waved back, as did Rush. "What a wonderful idea! She'll remember this forever!"

"I hope so." There was a note of sadness in Rush's voice. Understanding, Tracy squeezed his hand.

After the parade, Rush handed Clara over to Tracy, who would take the little girl home, feed her, and give her a chance to rest before dressing for the ball.

Free now to work, Rush hurried over to help Conner lift the heavy harnesses from Chip and Patch. The huge geldings stood patiently as the buckles were unfastened, the collars lifted away. They seemed to know that warm, dry stalls and an extra helping of oats awaited them back at the ranch.

Conner, usually low-key, was as excited as Rush

had ever seen him. "Rush, I saw this girl in the crowd! Lord help me, I could've wrecked the sleigh looking at her. She knocked my socks off! Then she was gone, and there was nothing I could do."

Rush shook his head. "I can't believe this. You've always been Mr. Cool around the ladies. What's gotten into you?"

"If you'd seen her, you'd know. Brunette, dark eyes, long hair, wearing a Stetson and this ungodly fringed leather coat. I've never seen her before. Now it's almost like she was a mirage—like I imagined her."

"Well, maybe you'll see her at the ball tonight," Rush said. "Even if she's not there, you're bound to have a good time. You've never suffered from a lack of female attention."

"I know. But when I saw her, it was like being kicked by a mule. You and Travis have got your women. Maybe she's the one for me."

"Or maybe not." Rush laughed. "All I can do is wish you good luck."

They laid the priceless harness carefully in the bed of Travis's pickup and led the horses up the ramp into the big double trailer. Travis had taken Conner's Jeep to drive Hank home, where he would help him out of the Santa costume. Once the horses and their gear were put away, Rush and Conner would return with the truck to hitch up the flatbed with the sleigh and tow it home. After that, the partners could relax and look forward to the Christmas Ball.

Bucket was waiting for them inside the cab of

the truck. He greeted them with wags and dog kisses. "Good job today, boy," Rush said. "Come on, let's get you home."

By 6:15 that evening, rested, shaved, showered, and decked out in their finest Old West duds, the partners were ready for the Christmas Ball. Since Maggie needed to be at the gym early, Travis had already left to pick her up. Conner was going stag, but he'd offered to pick up some extra napkins, paper plates, and utensils from Shop Mart, so he'd left early, too. Only Rush remained to close up the house. He glanced around to give the place a quick once-over before leaving. Clara had left her pillow on the floor outside the tent, not a good idea with Bucket in the house. He unzipped the tent flap and tossed the pillow inside.

Now, where was Bucket? After that incident with the coyote, the partners had kept a close eye on the dog, only letting him out when someone was around. He must've slipped out the door when Travis or Conner left.

It was already dark outside when Rush stepped onto the front porch and turned on the light. "Bucket! Come here, boy!" He called and whistled, cursing silently as he listened in the stillness. He couldn't go and leave the blasted mutt outside. There was nothing to do but call Tracy, explain, and tell her he might be late.

He was reaching for his phone when Bucket appeared, prancing up the driveway as if he didn't have a care in the world. He wagged his tail, gave a little *yip*, and trotted up the steps, into the house.

"You old rascal," Rush scolded him. "I know you heard me calling, but you didn't show up till you were good and ready. No treats for you tonight." He checked the dog's food and water bowls in the kitchen and turned off the lights except for a lamp in the living room. Leaving, he made sure to lock the front door behind him.

Tracy and Clara were ready and waiting when Rush arrived. Clara, who opened the door for him, looked adorable in her freshly cleaned princess gown, with her silver shoes and sparkly tiara. Tracy had fixed her hair in fancy braids and even put a little dab of pink lipstick on her mouth.

Rush's pulse skipped when Tracy walked into the room. With her flowing, lace-trimmed lavender gown, upswept hair, and simple pearl earrings, she looked as if she'd stepped out of an old-time portrait. She took his breath away.

"Doesn't Tracy look beautiful, Daddy?" Clara asked.

"She looks amazing, and so do you." Rush picked the little girl up and waltzed her around the room. "With you two lovely ladies on my arm tonight, I'll feel like the luckiest man in town, maybe in the world. Shall we go?"

He made a courtly show of helping them both with their coats and escorting them outside. They'd decided to take Tracy's car instead of the Hummer. It would be easier for Tracy, climbing in and out with her gown, and Clara's booster seat was already buckled into the back.

It was barely 7:00 when they walked into the gym and presented their tickets at the door; but the festivities had already started. The buffet tables along one side of the room sagged with donated food—sliced ham and roast turkey with dressing, scalloped potatoes and baked beans, mountains of fresh homemade rolls, a sea of salads, cakes, and pies. No alcohol was the rule, but there were punch bowls and canned sodas in tubs of ice. Families in Western dress were lined up to heap their plates with food and find a place at the tables.

"Are you hungry?" Rush asked.

"I'm not hungry yet," Tracy said. "But I'm guessing you and Clara might be. Just get me a soda, and I'll save us a place to sit, while you go through the line."

They found a quiet spot at the end of a table. Tracy took a seat while Rush found a Diet Coke in the tub and had Clara run it back to her while he saved a place in line.

The gym was decorated for Christmas with a twelve-foot, specially ordered tree in the center. It was trimmed with colored lights, traditional ornaments, and paper decorations made by Branding Iron's schoolchildren. Strings of red and green crepe paper had been strung from the treetop star to the walls, to make a canopy above the dancers.

Right now, the dance floor was empty. The Badger Hollow Boys, a Nashville band that played for every Christmas Ball, had yet to make an appearance. Rush had seen their bus outside, so he knew they were here. But they would probably wait until

8:00, after the food rush had ebbed, before starting their first set.

Keeping a firm grip on Clara's hand, Rush surveyed the expanse of tables. A smile tugged at his lips as he spotted Conner, sharing a meal with Ronda May Blackburn. Petite and buxom, with blond curls and a turned-up nose, Ronda May might not be the prettiest girl in town, but she was pretty enough, and way out front in terms of determination. She had set her sights on Conner, and made up her mind to rope, tie, and brand him. Now that she had him cornered, she probably wouldn't let him out of her sight.

Conner's mystery woman didn't seem to be here. Too bad. Rush would have enjoyed the drama. And he would've enjoyed teasing Conner tomorrow.

He helped Clara fill her plate, got his own food, and made his way to the table where Tracy waited. By the time they'd finished their meals, the Badger Hollow Boys had walked out onto the makeshift stage and begun warming up.

A few minutes later, they broke into a lilting Texas two-step. Couples were already moving out onto the dance floor. Travis had captured Maggie for a first dance. Daniel and Katy were dancing slowly, looking into each other's eyes. Francine, in her red saloon girl costume, was strutting her stuff with a cowboy while Hank, who didn't dance, enjoyed watching her from the sidelines. Ronda May was tugging Conner in that direction.

Knowing Tracy would understand, Rush bowed low before Clara. "May I have the honor of this dance, my princess?" he asked.

Clara giggled and held out her hands. Rush picked her up in his arms, walked onto the floor, and began to dance with her. Clara's smile was like a sky full of stars.

As the music faded, he carried her back to the table. "There's a room down the hall where kids can play games and have fun," he said. "Would you like to go there while I dance with Tracy for a little while?"

"Okay." Clara looked hesitant. Rush realized that aside from the McFarland kids, she'd spent very little time with other children.

Tracy stood. "I'll go with you two. Don't worry, Clara, it'll be fine. We'll check on you in a little while."

They walked her down to the classroom where about fifteen kids were doing crafts, playing board games, and watching videos. The volunteers in charge greeted Clara warmly and seated her at a table with two little girls who were making necklaces out of colored macaroni.

"Do you think she'll be all right?" Rush asked as they walked back down the hall.

"She'll be fine. It'll be good for her," Tracy said. "Now, what do you say we do some dancing?"

They made it back to the gym in time for a slow waltz. Holding Tracy in his arms and drifting with the music was as close to heaven as he'd ever been, Rush thought. He wanted a life with this woman and the special family they would find a way to create. It was too early in the relationship to propose, but he would do his best to keep things headed in that direction.

The music ended, and the guitarist of the Badger Hollow Boys stepped up to the microphone. The antiquated P.A. system in the gym was hard to understand, but he seemed to be introducing a new performer. The audience applauded as a figure walked onstage.

Long dark hair, topped by a weathered Stetson, stunning dark eyes, and that fringed, beaded rock star coat . . .

Rush almost laughed out loud. Unbelievable. It was Conner's dream woman.

"I saw her today," Tracy whispered. "She was watching the parade."

Rush guided Tracy toward the foot of the stage. "Conner saw her, too. Come on, I want to watch this up close."

With his arm around Tracy, Rush scanned the dance floor until he spotted his partner. Conner was staring drop-jawed at the stage. Ronda May was tugging at his arm, wanting his attention and not getting it.

The music started, the bass guitar pumping out a throbbing beat. The stunning singer leaned over the mike and broke into a cover of the old Patsy Cline hit "Walkin' After Midnight."

The audience, who'd stopped dancing to listen, applauded wildly. As the clapping faded, she gave them a smile, nodded to the band, and began to sing "Jolene."

She was pretty good, Rush conceded. Not Patsy Cline or Dolly Parton good, but good enough for Branding Iron on a Saturday night. She'd chosen great songs, and the audience seemed to love her.

Rush kept an eye on Conner. With Ronda May hanging on to him like an anchor, the man was visibly suffering. It was a pleasure to watch him.

The mystery woman sang two more songs, then walked off the stage and vanished. As the applause faded, the band took up a lively dance tune. Ronda May had pulled Conner back onto the dance floor. Short of shoving her away—and he was too much of a gentleman for that—Conner was helpless to go after the woman who'd cast a spell on him.

"We should check on Clara," Tracy said.

They walked back up the hallway to the room where the children were being entertained. When she saw them in the doorway, Clara ran to meet them.

"Look at the necklace I made!" Eyes sparkling, she showed them the string of macaroni that hung around her neck. "I'm making a bracelet now. And I have a new friend. Her name's Brandy."

"It sounds like you're having a good time," Tracy said. "Are you ready to go home yet?"

"Do we have to go now? I want to stay and play a little longer. Okay?"

"Okay," Rush said. "We'll give you another half hour. By then it'll be past your bedtime."

He caught Tracy's hand as they hurried back down the hall. "Another half hour to dance with you. Let's not waste a single minute of it."

By the time they went back to get Clara, she was tired. Her new friend had already gone home, so she didn't mind leaving. Rush carried her outside. By the time they made it to Tracy's car, she was almost asleep.

At Tracy's he transferred the booster seat to the Hummer and buckled Clara into it before he turned back to Tracy. She melted into his arms for a lingering kiss. "This was a perfect evening," she murmured.

"Yes, it was. Thank you." He kissed her again for good measure. "I'll see you in the morning when I come to vaccinate the kittens."

"I'll have breakfast ready for you," she said.

He left her and drove back to the ranch, humming Christmas songs along with the radio. Things couldn't have gone better tonight. Dancing with Tracy in his arms had been a dream. He was already looking forward to seeing her tomorrow. And Clara had enjoyed a grand time, too.

A smile tugged at his lips. He could hardly wait to hear what Conner had to say about finding his dream woman.

Travis's truck and Conner's Jeep were still gone from the driveway. The house was as he'd left it, with the porch light on and no sign of activity inside. Clara was awake. He could hear her unfastening her safety belt. He climbed out of the Hummer and went around to lift her out of the booster seat.

"Come on, princess, time for bed." He carried her up the steps, opened the front door with his free hand, and stopped short, frozen in shock.

By lamplight, the living room was a disaster. Clothes and bedding spilled out through the open tent flap and lay strung across the floor. Hunks of scattered white fuzz clung to the furniture and the rug.

"Oh, no!" Clara raced into the room when he put her down. "No, no, no!"

She picked up something off the floor that looked to Rush like a lumpy white rag. His heart sank as he recognized it. It was the ripped outer covering of Snowflake, her beloved toy cat.

Bucket!

But even then, Rush knew that this mess wasn't Bucket's fault. It was the nature of a dog to scatter, play, and chew on things. The real fault was his own. In his hurry to leave tonight, he had left Clara's tent flap unzipped, with Bucket alone in the house.

Clutching the ragged remains of her favorite toy, Clara began to cry—not just her usual sniffling sobs, but a full-blown wail of childish grief that went on and on.

Heartsick, Rush gathered her into his arms and held her until her wails became quiet sobs. "It'll be all right, sweetheart," he murmured. "We'll go shopping tomorrow. I'll buy you a new cat."

"But a new cat won't be the same! It won't be Snowflake. He was mine. He was special." She looked up at Rush, her eyes swollen, her face stained with tears. "It was Bucket, wasn't it? I'm so mad at that dog!"

Rush sighed and patted her small, quivering back. "Bucket was just playing. He didn't know any better. If you want to be mad at somebody, be mad at me. I was the one who let Bucket in the house and forgot to zip your tent."

She stared up at him, her eyes brimming. "Oh, Daddy."

"I'm sorry," he said. "So, so sorry. I'll do anything to make it up to you."

But even as he said the words, Rush knew there was nothing he could do.

Bucket came slinking into the room, head down, tail drooping, as if he knew he was in trouble. Bits of white stuffing clung to his muzzle. "Look at him, Clara," Rush said. "You can tell he's sorry for what he did. Can you forgive him?"

Clara looked down at the guilty dog. "Maybe later. But I need to stay mad at him for a while."

"And me? Do you need to stay mad at me, too? If you do, I'll understand."

She gave him a stern look. "Is it okay if I stay mad at you, too? I'll still love you. I'll just be mad."

"Sure. Just tell me when you're through being mad." He gave her a quick hug. "You've had a long day. Let's get you ready for bed."

He helped her out of the princess costume and laid it over a chair. While she was getting into her pajamas and brushing her teeth, he gathered up her scattered clothes, folded them, and put them back in her suitcase.

After he'd tucked her in and zipped the tent flap, he finished picking up the fuzzy remnants of the toy cat. Then he sat by the tent for a time, until he could be sure Clara was sound asleep.

After checking on her one last time, he wandered back to his room. Sitting on the edge of the bed, he worked his cowboy boots off his tired feet. The day had been so good. It was a life lesson, he supposed, that his own mistake had added a sad ending.

He had just stretched out in bed and was drifting off to sleep when his phone rang. Without switching on a light, Rush turned over and reached for it. It could be Tracy, calling to say good night. But it was more likely somebody with a sick or injured animal.

"Hullo," he muttered. "This is Dr. Rushford."

"Rush." The all-too-familiar voice seemed to drop his heart into his stomach. He sat up and swung his feet to the floor.

"What is it, Sonya? Where are you?"

"I'm home. I'm back from the cruise," his ex-wife said. "We need to have a talk."

Chapter 15

Something in Sonya's voice tightened the cold knot in Rush's stomach. Her power over Clara gave her power over him. The woman was aware of this, and Rush knew that she would use it to her advantage. This time she'd caught him off guard. But he couldn't afford to let her get the upper hand.

"Just so you won't have to ask, Clara is fine," he said. "She's been having a good time here."

"I'm glad." Rush sensed an edge in Sonya's reply. "I know you had no choice except to take her."

"I was happy to take her," Rush said. "In fact, I'm counting on keeping her through Christmas. I didn't realize you'd be back so soon."

"Neither did I." Her humorless chuckle sounded forced.

"Actually, it's fine if you keep her through Christmas and maybe longer. I'd rather not have her here until I've hired a new nanny." Her tongue made a clicking sound. "It was so thoughtless of Annie and Cecil, leaving like they did. At least they could have given notice."

Rush could have pointed out that Annie and Cecil had a family emergency. But that would have been a waste of words.

"I'll keep her for as long as you'll let me," he said. "But meanwhile, what do I tell Clara? When will you and Andre be taking her home?"

There was silence on the phone.

"Sonya?" Maybe they'd lost the connection.

At last she sighed and spoke. "All right. It's like this. Andre isn't in the picture anymore. The bastard's been cheating all along. I finally caught him when we were on the ship—with a woman in a third-class cabin, mind you. I'm seeing my lawyer tomorrow to file for divorce."

Rush's first thought was that now Clara could take her kitten home. But there were more serious complications. What would this mean for Clara? Would Andre demand joint custody? And where, Rush wondered, would *he* stand with Clara when the dust settled?

"I'm sorry," he said, meaning it. "I know we had our problems, but I wouldn't have wished this for you."

"You were always a decent guy, Rush," she said. "I was a fool to end our marriage the way I did. That's why I'm calling now. I've thought about this long and hard, and I want to give our marriage another chance."

"What?" Rush almost dropped the phone.

"Hear me out," she said. "Andre doesn't want

Clara. In exchange for my waiving child support, he's willing to give up his parental rights. You could come back, Rush. You could have it all—me, the house, the clinic you left, and Clara. You could adopt her. She'd be your legal daughter."

Rush switched on the bedside lamp, the sudden light a blinding flash. He could feel a headache coming on. This had to be some kind of crazy dream. Any minute now, he would wake up, sweating with relief.

"Think about Clara," Sonya said. "Think how happy she'd be to have her real family together again."

"We need to talk about this in the cold light of day," Rush said.

"Why? I know you loved me once. Is there a problem?"

"If that's what you want to call it. But now I'm in love with someone else. She's a wonderful woman. When the time's right, I plan to propose to her. But I very much want to be in Clara's life. If we could agree to some kind of split custody—"

"No!" Sonya's voice had taken on the tone of a demanding child. "I won't share my daughter, especially not with another woman. This is an all-or-nothing offer, Rush. Either you come back home to your family, where you belong, or you won't see Clara again until she's grown."

He had to be dreaming. Real life couldn't be this crazy.

"Sonya, there has to be some way we can work—"

"No. You've heard my offer. I'll give you until the day after Christmas to think it over. Then you can let me know whether you want to have Clara or that woman you're so keen on. You know my number."

The phone went silent as she ended the call.

Rush fell back onto the bed and lay there, staring up at the ceiling. He wouldn't tell Clara about this, of course. Not until a final decision had been made.

But what was there to decide? In the beginning, he'd been dazzled by Sonya's beauty and sophistication. But she'd turned out to be a cheating, self-centered manipulator. And people didn't change. All he felt for her now was an odd sort of pity. She was a spoiled child who could never decide what she wanted.

That aside, he loved Tracy to the depths of his soul—her warmth, her tenderness, her honesty . . . He could no longer imagine his life without her.

But what about Clara?

How could he tell his precious little girl that he was giving her up forever to be with Tracy? The hurt of rejection could scar her young life.

And what about Tracy? He'd be seeing her in the morning. There was no way he could keep this from her.

Somehow, there had to be a better option than the ultimatum Sonya had offered him—and it was up to him to find it.

With a groan, he turned over, punched his pillow, and willed himself to sleep. But why even try, when sleep was no escape from the nightmare that had begun with tonight's phone call?

* * *

By 7:30, when Rush pulled up in the Hummer, Tracy had a fire going in the living room and breakfast warming on the stove. She greeted him at the door with a brief but passionate kiss. Only when she stepped back afterward did she notice the shadows of weariness that framed his eyes.

"You look exhausted," she said. "Are you all right?"

"Fine." He sounded as weary as he looked. "Just didn't get much sleep."

"Is everything all right—did something happen with Clara?"

"Clara's okay, but Bucket's in trouble for ripping up her favorite toy."

"Oh, no! Snowflake? Poor Clara! I can just imagine how upset she must've been. Come on in the kitchen. You'll feel better after a good breakfast."

Rush held up his medical bag. "Let's take care of those vaccinations first. Rainbow's going to need her shots, too. When that's done, we can relax and talk."

Relax and talk. It sounded innocent enough. So why, as she followed him down the hall to the laundry room, did Tracy sense a dark premonition hanging over her? Something was wrong. It was written in every worried line of Rush's face.

She held Rainbow and the kittens, petting and soothing each one while Rush vaccinated them against rabies and distemper. He was good at his job. The work was done swiftly, with minimal discomfort to the furry patients.

"All done." He cleaned up the used gloves and needles and put his bag next to the door, almost as if he thought he might be leaving in a hurry. Tracy's worry deepened. Maybe she was only imagining things, but her instincts were shouting that something was seriously wrong.

Tracy seated him at the kitchen table, poured coffee, and dished up scrambled eggs, sausage, and hash browns before joining him. Rush made a show of eating, but mostly seemed to push the food around on his plate. After a few minutes of this, broken by awkward small talk, Tracy could stand it no longer.

"What's wrong, Rush?" she demanded. "I can tell something's bothering you. Please don't keep it from me."

He put down his fork, shook his head, and took a deep breath. Tracy could almost feel him struggling.

"It's all right," she said. "You can tell me anything."

His jaw tightened before he spoke. "I got a phone call last night from Sonya, my ex-wife. Evidently Andre was cheating on her. They're getting a divorce."

Tracy felt a surge of relief. "I'm sorry, of course. But won't that make things easier? With Andre gone, Clara can have her kitten. And surely, you'll be able to see her more often, won't you?"

Rush didn't answer. It was as if the shadows had deepened around his eyes.

"Won't you . . . ?" Tracy's voice trailed off as the realization hit her like a thunderclap. "You're going back to her, aren't you?"

He shook his head. "I didn't say that, Tracy."

"You didn't have to say it." Numb with disbelief, she forced the words that would make this real. "I know how much your family means to you. Now you'll have them back, with everything the way it was. You could even have more children, your own children."

"Listen to me, Tracy." He rose partway out of his chair, then sat down again. "Sonya has given me an ultimatum. Either I go back to her, or she won't let me see Clara again. But I can't just walk away from you. I love you."

Tracy fought back tears, knowing that there could be just one reply. She had to say and do the right thing.

"I know you love me, Rush. But you can't have this both ways. You can't choose me over Clara and break her heart. You can't choose me over your family. Just go. I'll be all right."

"Damn it, Tracy—" He rose to his feet.

"No, just go. Now, before things get ugly." The tears spilled over. She wiped them furiously with her hand. "Just go!"

He walked to the front door, picked up his medical bag, then paused in the open doorway. "I love you, Tracy," he said. "Give me a chance to work this out."

"Don't say another word. Just go."

Looking as if he'd just had the wind kicked out of him, Rush walked out the door and closed it behind him.

* * *

Even though it was Sunday, Rush had made a 9:00 appointment to check on the bull he'd cut loose from the barbed wire. He drove through town and took the road to the farm. It was early, but he needed something to keep him from going back to Tracy's house, breaking down the door, taking her in his arms, and forcing her to listen.

He should have known that she'd react the way she did. Tracy wasn't the kind of person who'd stand in the way of someone else's happiness. But there was one thing he'd failed to make her understand. No power on earth could make him go back to Sonya. That relationship was over. But he needed time to work out a plan—one that wouldn't hurt Clara.

Until he had that plan, trying to see Tracy again would only make the situation worse.

Maybe he should talk to a lawyer. But the lawyer he'd hired in Phoenix had been no help at all. *Damn!* This whole dilemma was tying his brain in knots. He only knew that he needed to find answers fast, before he lost the woman he loved.

Tracy opened the file drawer in her desk and took out her copy of the document she'd printed and given to Maggie. The text was a paraphrase of an Arizona law, written in answer to a question on a website about child custody. Line by line, she read it again.

A person who stands in loco parentis to a child may ask the court for custody or parenting time.

In loco parentis. That was the key phrase. It

meant "in place of a parent." Tracy continued reading.

To be in loco parentis, a person must have acted as a parent to the child and formed a meaningful relationship with that child for a substantial period of time.

That definition would certainly apply to Rush. He had acted as a parent to Clara for the first three years of her life. But there were restrictions in place—restrictions that would have made the law useless for Rush, until now.

Before such a request may be made to the court, one of the following conditions must exist. One of the child's parents must be deceased; the child's legal parents must be unmarried; or a case for divorce or legal separation between the legal parents must be pending (see section 25-415, Arizona Revised Statutes).

Tracy laid the document on her desk. She'd remembered it instantly when Rush had told her about Sonya's divorce. She could have given it to him right then. Maybe she *should* have given it to him. But offering him another option would only have put more pressure on him as he made his decision. If his choice was to go back to his former wife, that was that. Why show him a compromise that would satisfy the law but deny him his lost family?

There was also the matter of her own pride. Giving Rush the document could have been seen as trying to pull him in her direction. It would have seemed like begging. That was the last thing she wanted. Rush had chosen his ex-wife over her. End of story. She would accept that, deal with it, and move on.

She hadn't realized she was crying until she felt the wetness on her cheeks. Steeling her resolve, she dried her tears, got up, and went into the kitchen to clear away the uneaten remains of breakfast. Later today, people would be dropping by to pick up the kittens. She wanted to make the house, and herself, at least presentable.

She threw herself into a frenzy of cleaning. Starting with the kitchen, she loaded the dishwasher, scrubbed the stove and fridge, and mopped the floor. From there she moved to the bathroom, then on to the rest of the house, sweeping, vacuuming, dusting, and rearranging. Not that there was any great need for it. Tracy tended to keep her house tidy most of the time. But the furious cleaning gave her pain a release. She'd allowed herself to trust and love again, believing her heart was safe at last. But she should have known she was wrong.

The pine wreath still hung on the inside of the front door, spreading its fresh holiday scent through the house. Tracy had enjoyed it, but now the sight and smell of it only made her think of Rush. Fighting tears once more, she lifted the wreath off the door, carried it outside, and stuffed it in the trash.

When she came back inside, the fragrance lingered in the air. But every other trace of Christmas—and Rush—was gone.

As she sank into a chair, exhausted at last, the phone rang. It was Maureen, wanting to come and get Midnight.

Fifteen minutes later, she was at the front door. Tracy seated her while she went back to get the black kitten and the two cans of kitten food she'd planned to send home with each one.

"Oh, he's darling!" Maureen took Midnight from Tracy and cuddled him close. "My granddaughter is going to adore him!" She stood, glancing around the barren room. "But my goodness, Tracy, what happened to your Christmas spirit? I don't see so much as a candle or a sprig of greenery."

"I'm skipping Christmas this year," Tracy said. "You can just call me Scrooge."

"Well, here's wishing you a change of heart. I'll see you after the holidays." Maureen bustled outside with Midnight snuggled under her coat. Tracy closed the door and turned away. One kitten down and two more to go. And it looked as if Clara would get to keep Snowflake after all. At least that was a reason to be happy.

Since Francine was busy catering holiday parties, Tracy had arranged to drop off Ginger at the B and B tomorrow. But she was expecting Daniel to come and get Tiger today. He called at 1:30 to make sure she was home. "You're welcome to come now, Daniel," Tracy told him. "I'll have Tiger ready for you."

A few minutes later, Tracy looked out the front window and saw a small Toyota pull up to the curb. Daniel had mentioned that his father would be driving him. But she was surprised to see a young woman at the wheel. Tracy got a better look at her as the two of them came up the walk. She was slim and pretty in jeans, a pink sweater, and a flowered jacket. Her striking eyes were dark, her long hair tied back in a ponytail.

"Come on in and have a seat." Tracy ushered them into the living room. By then she'd realized there was something familiar about the young woman. Where had she seen her before?

"This is my sister, Megan," Daniel introduced her. "She lives in Nashville."

"I'm pleased to meet you," Megan said. "Daniel's been so excited about giving Katy this kitten. Thank you."

The voice triggered a flash of recognition. "Oh, my goodness!" Tracy exclaimed. "You sang with the band last night! You were terrific!"

"Thanks." Megan laughed. "That was the other me. This is the real me. And in case you're wondering about that coat, I bought it for fifty dollars at a thrift shop."

"So you live in Nashville," Tracy said. "Are you a singer there?"

"Only when I can get a gig," Megan said. "The rest of the time I have a day job. I teach kindergarten. Sam, the bass player with the Badger Hollow Boys, is the father of one of my students. When he heard that my family lived in Branding Iron, he invited me to come along and sing with the band."

"Will you be here long?" Tracy asked.

"I'd like to be. I've barely had time to spend with my parents and Daniel. But I'm singing at a club tomorrow night, so I need to leave soon, probably tonight."

Too bad, Tracy thought, remembering that Conner had been interested in the singer. But after what had happened with Rush, when would she get the chance to talk to Conner again? Those fun-filled days with friends at the ranch were over.

"I'll get the kitten." Tracy walked back to the laundry room and found Tiger. The little female tabby was a charmer. When Tracy placed her in Daniel's arms, she settled right down and began to purr.

Daniel grinned. "Katy will love her," he said.

Tracy took time to give Daniel some pointers on taking care of a cat, including a call to Dr. Rush-ford when she was old enough to be spayed. Then Megan and Daniel thanked her and carried Tiger, along with the canned food, out to the car.

Tracy stood at the window, watching them drive away. The sky was a dark, muddy gray, the dry wind blowing snowflakes as fine as dust. Rainbow jumped onto the windowsill and rubbed her head against Tracy's arm. Tracy stroked her silken fur. The Christmas holiday loomed ahead of her, as bleak as the weather outside.

But she'd survived worse, Tracy reminded her-self. A cheery fire, a good book or two, plenty of snacks, and a stack of DVDs from the library, and she would be fine. She'd be back on the bench in January before she knew it.

Wouldn't she?

The phone rang again. Her pulse leaped—but no, she knew better than to think it might be Rush. He wouldn't be calling her anytime soon.

She picked up the phone. The caller was Mag-gie.

"Hi, Tracy," she said. "I know you're busy, so I

won't keep you long. I was thinking of having a little dinner party at my place on Christmas Eve. Just
a few friends, including you and Rush, and Clara. I
hope you can make it. Nothing fancy, just—"

"Hold on," Tracy said. "Rush and Clara might
be glad to come. But I can't be there. Rush and I
just broke up."

Maggie gasped. "Oh, no! You two were perfect
for each other. What happened? Do you need to
talk about it?"

Tracy gulped back the lump in her throat.
"There's not much to talk about. His ex-wife's get-
ting a divorce. Rush is going back to her—for
Clara."

Maggie muttered something under her breath.
"I can't believe this. Did you show him the document you printed out?"

"There was no point in showing it to him. Why
complicate things? He's going back to Sonya. End
of story."

"And you didn't even try to change his mind?"

"He'll be getting his family back, Maggie. So will
Clara. How can I argue with that?" Tracy could feel
her emotions spilling over. "If I don't get off this
phone, I'm going to lose it," she said. "Enjoy your
dinner party."

Tracy ended the call, sank onto the couch, and
buried her face in her hands.

Rush had arrived home from checking the injured bull's barbed wire cuts to find that Clara was
still mad at him. Now it was midafternoon, and she

was still pouting, refusing to smile at him or let herself be hugged. Maybe the little princess took after her mother in that respect.

Rush knew he shouldn't be surprised. He deserved to be in the doghouse for letting Bucket chew up her beloved toy. But now another issue had arisen, one he didn't know how to handle.

"Why can't I go to Tracy's house?" she demanded for maybe the fourth time. "I want to play with the kittens. If I could hold Snowflake and pet him, I wouldn't be mad anymore."

"Tracy's busy today," he said. "This isn't a good time to visit her."

"But I wouldn't be in the way. All I want to do is play with Snowflake." Tears welled in her big brown eyes. The sight of those tears tore at Rush's heart. None of this mess was her fault.

Should he tell her that her mother was back from the cruise, and that Andre was out of the picture? Should he tell her that as long as her mother approved, she could take the kitten home with her?

No, that would be a mistake, Rush told himself. Until everything was settled, it would be cruel to get her childish hopes up—and right now, *nothing* was settled.

"After your nap, how would you like to go to the mall?" he asked her. "There's a store there where you can choose your own toy animal, get it stuffed, and even buy clothes for it. You could pick out any animal you want. How does that sound?"

She shook her head. "I don't want another animal. It wouldn't be the same."

After Clara went down for her nap, under a quilt on Rush's bed, he put on his jacket and walked out onto the porch. The ranch was quiet today, the cut trees all sold except for the few that were left at Hank's. The sleigh rides were on hold until after Christmas, when they'd start up again and continue as long as the snow and customers lasted. Today the partners were resting and cleaning up after the sale season.

The dark sky and sighing wind matched Rush's mood. He was at a crossroads in his life, with no good choices ahead. Somehow, there had to be another way to resolve this godawful mess.

Something warm and damp touched his hand. He reached down and scratched Bucket's head. "Looks like we're both in trouble, boy," he murmured. "Too bad you can't tell me what to do."

Just then Travis came out on the porch, holding his cell phone. "This call's for you," he said, thrusting the phone at Rush.

"On *your* phone?" Rush asked.

"Yeah. It's Maggie. She's on the warpath. You'd better take it."

What else could go wrong in his life? Rush took the phone. "Maggie? What is it?"

"I just spoke with Tracy." Maggie's voice fairly crackled with annoyance. "You and I need to talk."

"Here?" Rush was still stunned.

"No. Not at the ranch. Buckaroo's. Twenty minutes. Be there."

Rush handed Travis the phone. "That's one tough woman you've got there."

Travis grinned. "We'll keep an eye on Clara till you get back."

As he drove, Rush turned on the wipers to brush away the fine-grained snow. Maggie would probably take a piece out of his hide for hurting Tracy. Fine. Let her. He deserved it. And he had nothing to lose except what he might have already lost.

Maggie's old Lincoln was parked outside Buckaroo's when he arrived. He walked through the door to see her sitting in the corner booth with two cups of coffee in front of her. As he sat down, she scooted one in his direction.

"Maggie, there's been a misunderstanding," he started to say.

"Shut up, Rush." She shoved a sheet of white copy paper across the table. "Don't say another word until you've read this."

Rush picked up the paper, skimmed the short text. Then, as his heart climbed into his throat, he read it again, carefully. It was the answer he needed, the answer that could save him—if it was real.

He looked up at Maggie. "Where the hell did you get this?" he demanded.

"Tracy found it online a few weeks ago. She gave me this copy as a backup, to make sure someone would have it, in case—"

"In case what?"

"In case it might be needed later on, when she wasn't around. At the time, there was no reason to believe it would ever be useful. Now all that has changed."

Rush forced himself to stay seated and keep his voice calm. Maybe this was why Maggie had chosen to meet him in a public place. "And this is real? A real law?"

"It is. I double-checked it myself."

"So, if Tracy had this, why in blazes didn't she tell me about it this morning?"

"Maybe you should ask Tracy that question. You two should try talking to each other instead of just jumping to conclusions. I have a feeling you've both got some explaining to do." Maggie laid a bill on the table, stood, buttoned her jacket, and walked out.

Tracy was dozing on the couch when the door-bell rang—jangling repeatedly and insistently. She jerked fully awake and sat up, dislodging Rainbow, who jumped to the floor and fled down the hall.

"Let me in, Tracy!" Rush's voice cut through the door like a power saw. "I've got questions, and I need some answers."

He sounded angry. But Tracy wasn't feeling like Little Miss Sunshine herself. Bracing for a battle, she opened the door.

Rush's eyes blazed as he thrust a sheet of paper into her face. "Why did I have to get this from Maggie?" he demanded. "Why didn't you give it to me this morning?"

Tracy let him in and closed the door. Her reply met his fire with ice. "When you gave me your news this morning, I thought you'd already made up your mind. You certainly sounded that way."

"Damn it, I was drowning. I was asking for help and support, maybe some solution for resolving this crazy mess—a solution you had and didn't think to give me."

"I didn't think you'd want it. I know you, Rush. You'd do anything for Clara, even go back to her mother and try to make the marriage work. I knew you were making a sacrifice, but I told myself that you were making it for your family, and that you believed you were doing the right thing. Giving you an alternative—I was afraid that giving you that document would only make your decision harder."

The paper fluttered to the floor as his hands clasped her shoulders, almost hurting. "Tracy, I've been through hell, trying to find a way to be there for Clara without losing you. I love you. I would never walk away from the life we could have. I'd have told you that, but you threw me out before I could explain."

"I love you, too. And if you'd explained, I'd have given you the document." She looked up at him, her eyes brimming with tears.

"We're a couple of idiots," he said. "You know that, don't you?"

"Yes, I know it," she whispered. "But at least we're a pair."

Their kiss was long, deep, and full of promise—a promise of lifetimes together, building a future, raising a family bound with ties of love.

As he released her, Tracy glanced around the room. "I know what this place needs," she said. "A Christmas tree!"

Epilogue

Christmas, that same year

Rush and Clara came to Tracy's house to cele-brate Christmas morning. Under a gloriously lit tree, they sat on the floor and opened their pre-sents.

Clara gave each of them the Christmas cards she'd made, which would be saved on the refriger-ator and cherished always. When Rush unwrapped the photo of Clara, from the mall, he was visibly moved. Telling her it was his best gift ever, he gave her a big hug.

Tracy's and Rush's gifts for each other were practical, hastily bought items—warm hats, scarves, and gloves. Next year, they could buy something costlier and more meaningful. For this year these simple things would be enough. This was Clara's Christmas. The important gifts were for her.

Clara opened Tracy's gifts first. She loved the

snow globe and the books. But there was more to come.

The first gift from Rush came in a big box. She opened it to find a cowgirl hat and a pair of cowgirl boots. "This gift has a special meaning, Clara," he said. "It means that, yes, you'll have to go home to your mother. But every year, you can come back here at Christmas and in the summertime to be a cowgirl again."

Clara squealed with joy at the news, even though she was too young to understand the implications. Two days ago, Rush had called the private number of Sonya's lawyer, who'd agreed that Rush would have a good case for partial custody if he chose to take it to court. The lawyer had persuaded Sonya to avoid a costly trial and give Rush visitation rights twice a year. As for the question of Rush's going back to her, Sonya had already moved on. She was dating a man she'd met on the cruise.

"One more present." Rush handed Clara another box and helped her open it. Inside was a small, sturdy pet carrier.

"What's this for?" Clara asked.

"It's for your next present. Wait here." He disappeared down the hall and came back with a lidded box. Something was moving inside it. He set it on the floor. "Open it, Clara," he said.

She raised the lid with a little cry. Happy tears flowed down her cheeks as she picked up Snowflake and cuddled him close. "He's yours," Rush said. "You can take him home with you in the carrier. You can even bring him back if he turns out to be a good traveler."

Clara jumped up and hugged Rush. "I love you, Daddy," she said. "I knew that Santa couldn't bring my miracles, but I never gave up. I knew that you could do it."

While Clara played with her kitten, Tracy went into the kitchen to check the turkey she was roasting for Christmas dinner. Travis, Conner, and Maggie would be over later to share it with them.

As she closed the oven, Rush slipped his arms around her from behind and nuzzled the back of her neck. "I hope she doesn't expect miracles from me every Christmas. That's a pretty tall order."

Tracy laughed. "Shall we share the other surprise, that she's going to be the flower girl at our wedding this summer?"

Rush turned her around and kissed her. "That can wait," he said. "I think we've had enough surprises for one Christmas."

Please read on for an excerpt from HART'S HOLLOW FARM by Janet Dailey, available now!

For some folks in small-town Georgia, Hart's Hollow is a forsaken farm that has seen better days. But for the Hart family matriarch, it's a home worth fighting for . . .

From the moment Kristen Daniels arrives at Hart's Hollow, something about the place speaks to her soul. So when seventy-three-year-old Emmy Hart asks Kristen to help return the farm to its former glory, Kristen accepts—despite her fears about getting involved with Emmy—or the two kids in Emmy's care. Then there's the matter of Emmy's ruggedly handsome grandson, who stirs feelings Kristen believed were long gone . . .

When Mitch Hart left Hart's Hollow at age eighteen, he thought he'd kicked the red dust off his boots forever. But his heart bears the scars of his violent upbringing and his mind aches with the loss of the sister he couldn't save. Now he's determined to see his orphaned niece and nephew settled in a better life. Emmy's ideas about saving the farm for the family's sake only convince Mitch that his grandmother is as crazy as everyone in town suspects. Everyone except the blond beauty helping her sow the land. Something about Kristen's mix of spirit and vulnerability has Mitch sticking around. And soon enough he's working by Kristen's side, and wondering if he's gone a little crazy himself—crazy in love. Because suddenly he's hoping he might just find happiness in the very home he left behind . . .

Kristen Daniels stood at the mouth of a red dirt road. The long path in front of her sloped eastward, weaving its way through sprawling fields to meet dark, low-lying clouds on the horizon. Warm late-afternoon sunshine peeked between the gathering masses and dappled the flat landscape. The spring breeze, a gentle whisper for the past hour, intensified. It kicked up a cloud of dust that drifted across the road, sparkling briefly in the sunlight, before a massive cloud rolled in and covered the sun completely.

Stomach dipping, Kristen glanced over her shoulder at the isolated stretch of Georgia highway she'd been traveling for hours. The paved road was unlined, the white and yellow markings having faded long ago, and the worn edges were either buried beneath weedy overgrowth or cracked beyond repair. With no cell service, landmarks, or street signs, it was impossible to tell if she'd made it to the right place—if there even was such a thing.

At this point, one road would serve just as well as the other. So long as she kept moving in the opposite direction from the life she'd had three years ago when she was twenty-six and optimistic. When she'd been sure, without a modicum of doubt, that life had more to offer if she just believed and prayed and hoped. Even when the devastating truth had literally stared her in the face.

All the way up until the day she'd had to bury her five-year-old daughter.

The straight line of ragged pavement warped into the distance, making the earth feel as though it tilted beneath her feet. Her stance faltered, and she strained to hold on to the empty numbness she'd clung to for more miles than she'd ever be able to count.

"You break down?"

Kristen started, the shout and slow crunch of gravel beneath tires jerking her to alertness. A rusty truck idled nearby, the male driver leaning out the window, studying her.

The wind blew harder. It swirled her long hair around her neck and spit grit in her face, stinging her eyes.

"No." Teeth clenching, she blinked hard and dragged her forearm over her dry cheeks. "Just trying to figure out where I am is all." She gestured toward her beat-up Toyota parked at the edge of the dirt road. "Do you know the name of this road?"

The older man laughed and scrubbed the heel

of his hand over his stubble-lined jaw. "It ain't got a name. It's just one long driveway."

"To where?"

"Hart's Hollow." He shook his head, his salt-and-pepper hair falling over his creased brow. "Doubt that's the direction you wanna go. There's nothing out there."

Kristen fumbled in her jeans pocket and retrieved a crumpled piece of paper. She pressed it flat against her thigh, then smoothed the edges that flapped in the wind.

Wanted: Jane-of-all-trades. Hard work. Decent pay and board. Hart's Hollow Farm. 762 Hart Rd. Stellaville, Georgia. See Emmy Hart, owner.

"Hart's Hollow Farm?" she asked. "Could you please tell me if I can find Emmy Hart there?"

"Yep, that's the place." He cocked his head to the side, a slow grin appearing. "And Emmy's there all right."

Kristen nodded, stuffed the paper back in her pocket, then headed toward her car. "Thank you."

"Might want to make it a quick visit." Squeaky gears shifted, then the truck rolled forward as the man tipped his chin toward the overcast sky. "If those clouds open up, that clay's gonna turn to sludge and that low car of yours won't make it out. You don't want to be stuck in a storm with Emmy Hart."

Her steps slowed. "Why?"

"She's ornery enough to make a saint cuss. My

own mama—good Christian woman—says she's the damn devil." He laughed again and revved the engine. "Good luck to you."

The big truck moved swiftly down the center of the worn highway.

Kristen returned to her car and, after staring at the red path through the dusty windshield for a few minutes, decided a lot of nothing—even if it was owned and run by an ornery devil—was preferable to sleeping in the backseat and going hungry for the second day in a row. She didn't do charity and needed a job. The last farm where she'd worked for a year had gone belly-up due to drought and financial woes, and this position was the only promising one she'd come across that offered the silent, wide-open space she'd grown to crave.

It was, at the very least, worth checking out. Especially since she'd spent the last of her emergency stash on a full tank of gas to make the drive.

She cranked the engine and drove slowly down the driveway. The deep ruts in the dirt rattled the bottled water in the cup holder and bounced her around in the driver's seat. The bottom of the car thumped over a pothole, metal scraping the firm ground.

Wincing, she slowed the car even more and continued to creep along. A tall pole stood near a bend in the road. She leaned closer to the window, squinting up at the makeshift birdhouse. Several battered gourds hung from the top rack, but one dangled loosely at half-mast and the thick shell clanked against the pole with each gust of wind.

There were no purple martins perched on the rack, just two buzzards circling high above the stripped fields, swooping low in tandem with the air current.

Reaching the final leg of the circular driveway, she eased around a sharp curve, then stopped the car abruptly at the edge of lush grass. Large oaks towered toward the stormy sky, framing an aging two-story farmhouse with a wide front porch and large windows. Tall, red chimneys were aligned on each side of the white structure and Gothic trim along the porch roof added an elegant air.

Kristen whistled low as she climbed out of the car. "Nothing out here, huh?"

That wasn't altogether accurate. She strolled across the expansive lot, her tennis shoes squashing the soft grass and thunder rumbling overhead. The magnificent oaks swayed with the approaching storm, their leaves ruffling. Ducking beneath the lower branch of one, she reached up and trailed her palm across its rough bark as she passed.

Tall and sturdy. Broad, thick trunk. Long, sprawling branches.

"You've been around a while haven't you, beauty?" Kristen whispered.

She looked at the house, its details clearer from this vantage point. Time and the elements had chipped the white paint of the house and faded the deep red tones of the chimneys. The wooden front door had lost its luster and a hole was punched through the flimsy screen door covering it. An orange cat weaved in and out of the exquisite—but rotted—porch balusters.

Rather than strengthening with age like the old oaks, the structure presented a tired, resigned veneer. One at odds with the sweet aura of home beckoning from the wide, welcoming steps. One which clearly said the glory days of this house had passed.

Her fingertips jerked at her sides as she imagined breathing it back to life on canvas—a dab of yellow ochre here and there to recreate the shingles, long sweeps of ivory to define the walls, several pushes and drags of crimson to erect the chimneys. The structure was so reminiscent of the house she'd dreamed of as a child, when she'd lived in shelters and longed for a home—and family—of her own.

Kristen shook her head, a heavy ache pulling at her chest. Oh, but it'd be impossible for anyone to deny this place must have once been majestic.

"Emmy!"

The screen door slammed and a man stumbled out onto the porch, clutching a briefcase to his chest and fumbling his way backwards to the front steps. A second slam, then a wiry woman stomped out after him, leaning heavily on a cane.

Kristen eased back beneath the cover of the tree's branches, watching.

"Now, Emmy," the man sputtered as he reached the grassy lawn. "There's no need to get upset—"

"*Mrs. Hart.*" The woman—owner Emmy Hart, Kristen supposed—clomped down the stairs, her cane clacking along the way. "My sweet Joe, God rest his soul, may have died over thirty years ago but I'm still his wife, and if he were here right now, he'd toss you out on your butt for making such an insulting offer. Joe wouldn't stand for it. He gave his life to this place, raised it from ruin. This land was in his blood."

"I didn't come out here to cause trouble, Mrs. Hart. I came to help."

"No, you didn't. I agreed to humor you on account of thinking you were a decent man, but you suits are all the same." Emmy stopped on the bottom step, gripped the thin handrail, then sagged against it. Her chest lifted beneath her worn T-shirt on heavy breaths. "You came to take my land. To tear down my home." Blue eyes flashing, she stabbed a gnarled finger at him. "To steal from me."

The Suit held up a placating hand. "Now, that's not true at all. I'm offering you a more than fair price for this . . ." He waved careless fingers toward the second floor of the house. "Establishment." He grimaced. "Believe me when I say you won't find a better offer. No one else would be willing to pay what I am for this place, and if it weren't for Mitch, I wouldn't even be out here."

The man's cheeks reddened. He drew his head back and clamped his mouth shut.

"My Mitch?" Emmy's mouth opened then closed silently, the gusty wind blowing her short gray hair against her wrinkled cheeks. "What's he got to do with this?"

He sighed. "Mitch is a friend of mine. He's the one who asked me to come out here and make you an offer. I was surprised he wasn't here when I arrived. Said he was flying down today himself and wanted us all to sit down and talk it over. He knows it's just a matter of time before—"

"He wouldn't do that to me." A wounded light entered her eyes.

Kristen cringed and shrank back, feeling like an interloper. Sporadic raindrops smacked against the leaves overhead, shaking them.

"I'm sorry, Mrs. Hart," the man continued. "I know this is hard for you, but Mitch is just doing what any decent grandson would. He's trying to get you something to live on for a short time at least." He blinked and jerked his head as rain hit his face. "This place is done and you're the only one who won't admit it."

"No." Expression contorting, Emmy straightened and stepped toward him. "You're just like all them others. You came to steal from me. And you're lying about Mitch."

He hissed out a breath, mumbled something involving the word *ridiculous,* then frowned up at the black cluster of clouds. "This is my final offer. You'd do well to take it."

She poked her cane at his chest, shoving him back. "Get off my land."

"Please reconsider." His tone softened. "For Mitch's sake if not your own. He deserves the chance to put this place behind hi—"

"Go!" Her voice broke. "You don't know nothing about Mitch—or me. This is my home. My family still lives here. You probably never worked a day in your life. Don't have a clue what real work is." She continued stabbing her cane at him, backing him up until he fell into the gleaming bumper of a sedan. "You're a thief. And a liar. Nothing but a damned lying th—"

"This place is dead and buried." He slapped her cane away, voice curt. "Mitch is trying to help you, though hell if I know why he even bothers anymore. He won't tell you like it is, so I'll do it for him. Dead and buried, Mrs. Hart."

Emmy faced off with the man. Her chin trembled and the solid line of her shoulders, which had stood so proud before, slumped.

It was a look Kristen knew well. Her face heated, a familiar nausea roiling in her gut. She should walk away, get back in her car and keep driving. This wasn't her business or her fight, and the last thing she needed was to get tangled up in a stranger's troubles. But even so . . .

"Excuse me." Kristen sucked in a strong breath, the sharp scent of rain filling her nostrils, then ducked beneath the branches and stepped forward. Fat raindrops plopped onto her cheek and bare shoulder, cooling her skin. "I'm looking for Mrs. Emmy Hart."

They turned toward her. Stared.

She moved closer to Emmy. "Are you Mrs. Hart? Owner of Hart's Hollow Farm?"

Emmy nodded. The haunted look in her eyes deepened. Her focus strayed beyond Kristen to the darkening sky above, her whispered words barely discernable. "What'd you bring, girl?"

Kristen hesitated as she searched Emmy's expression. "I'm sorry, I'm not sure what you mean?"

Emmy remained silent.

Kristen glanced at the man, who shook his head and looked down. "I-I'm looking for work. I brought two overnight bags," she continued, gesturing behind her. "And I parked my car over there behind the trees."

Emmy blinked, then refocused on Kristen.

Thunder boomed again, shaking the windows of the farmhouse and the ground beneath Kristen's feet. She flinched then tugged the wrinkled ad from her pocket. "I'd like to speak to you about a job, if I might?"

"That my ad you got there?" Emmy asked.

"Yes. The one with decent pay and board. I was interested in—"

"There won't be any board, ma'am." The Suit shoved off the car to a standing position and straightened his tie. "At least not for long. In six months, the county will give the green light to pave a bypass on this land." He pointed behind her. "Across those fields and right over this house. Something Mrs. Hart's grandson thinks is important she understand."

"Forgive me," Kristen said softly, "but I wasn't speaking to you. I was speaking to the owner, who's already asked you to leave."

He frowned, his measuring gaze raking over her from head to toe. "And you are . . . ?"

A has-been artist. Rootless stranger. Alone. Kristen swallowed the thick lump in her throat and squared her shoulders. "No one. Just a hard worker looking for a job and place to stay."

More from Bestselling Author
JANET DAILEY

Calder Storm	0-8217-7543-X	$7.99US/$10.99CAN
Close to You	1-4201-1714-9	$5.99US/$6.99CAN
Crazy in Love	1-4201-0303-2	$4.99US/$5.99CAN
Dance With Me	1-4201-2213-4	$5.99US/$6.99CAN
Everything	1-4201-2214-2	$5.99US/$6.99CAN
Forever	1-4201-2215-0	$5.99US/$6.99CAN
Green Calder Grass	0-8217-7222-8	$7.99US/$10.99CAN
Heiress	1-4201-0002-5	$6.99US/$7.99CAN
Lone Calder Star	0-8217-7542-1	$7.99US/$10.99CAN
Lover Man	1-4201-0666-X	$4.99US/$5.99CAN
Masquerade	1-4201-0005-X	$6.99US/$8.99CAN
Mistletoe and Molly	1-4201-0041-6	$6.99US/$9.99CAN
Rivals	1-4201-0003-3	$6.99US/$7.99CAN
Santa in a Stetson	1-4201-0664-3	$6.99US/$9.99CAN
Santa in Montana	1-4201-1474-3	$7.99US/$9.99CAN
Searching for Santa	1-4201-0306-7	$6.99US/$9.99CAN
Something More	0-8217-7544-8	$7.99US/$9.99CAN
Stealing Kisses	1-4201-0304-0	$4.99US/$5.99CAN
Tangled Vines	1-4201-0004-1	$6.99US/$8.99CAN
Texas Kiss	1-4201-0665-1	$4.99US/$5.99CAN
That Loving Feeling	1-4201-1713-0	$5.99US/$6.99CAN
To Santa With Love	1-4201-2073-5	$6.99US/$7.99CAN
When You Kiss Me	1-4201-0667-8	$4.99US/$5.99CAN
Yes, I Do	1-4201-0305-9	$4.99US/$5.99CAN

Available Wherever Books Are Sold!

Check out our website at **www.kensingtonbooks.com**.